SECRETS OF THE LOST LEDGERS

THE GLASS LIBRARY, BOOK #5

C.J. ARCHER

WWW.CJARCHER.COM

ABOUT SECRETS OF THE LOST LEDGERS

An invisible message from a dead man resurrects a decades-old mystery.

With her sharpened magical senses, Sylvia recognizes invisible writing while cataloging an obscure book for the library. She's shocked to discover the message, written many years earlier, pleaded for help. She's even more shocked to discover the author of the message was married to a paper magician. Could there be a connection to Sylvia's father?

With a magical mystery on her hands, Sylvia engages the help of Gabe Glass, and together they follow the clues to the location of two hidden ledgers that implicate a very dangerous individual in an illegal bookmaking scheme. Although not named, Gabe is convinced he knows who the bookmaker is, and sets out to prove it.

The investigation draws them into the shady underbelly of the horse racing industry and uncovers a link to Gabe's parents that takes everyone by surprise. As they unravel the mystery's tangled threads, unexpected twists and turns lead them to the truth.

But the greatest twist of all is the danger no one saw coming.

CHAPTER 1

LONDON, SUMMER 1920

I'd spent a lifetime studying the faces of men I passed in the street, looking for any resemblance to my own. Although I had my mother's gray eyes and small stature, my fair coloring must have come from my father. I'd pay close attention to the noses, hoping to find a matching pattern of freckles to mine.

I employed the same scrutiny as I studied the photograph of the late Mr. Peterson, Walter and Evaline's father. I saw no similarities to myself. The photograph had been taken when he was middle-aged, his two teenaged children standing either side of him. He was short and boxy like Walter, with brown hair, and not a freckle in sight. That particular paper magician was most likely not my father.

A few weeks ago, after learning that I'd just discovered my paper magic, a long-time employee of the Petersons' paper factory accused me of making it all up. He suspected I was going to pass myself off as the half-sister of Walter and Evaline to gain a portion of their inheritance. He watched me now from the doorway to Walter's office, as if he was worried I'd steal the valuables.

"You look nothing like him," he said.

I returned the photograph to the table by the window, where it was flanked by two more—one of Walter's wife and children, and another of Walter and Evaline on the front steps of the factory's administrative building in which I now stood, waiting for them.

The employee glanced over his shoulder before taking a step into the office. "Mr. Peterson might seem foolish, but he's smarter than he looks. And Miss Peterson is as sharp as a tack. Neither will fall for any tricks."

I looked past him to my escape route. I almost took a step in that direction. I wanted to. But I dug in, settled my feet apart, and remained put.

Once upon a time, I would have fled from such an antagonistic man, but I'd gained confidence in the last few months. Nothing would happen to me here. This man was no threat, merely protective of his employers. Even so, it took effort to hide my apprehension.

"I have no tricks, sir." There was more I could have said, more I *wanted* to say, but it was none of his business.

Evaline's arrival put an end to our conversation. He acknowledged her politely, if a little curtly, handed her the report he'd come to deliver, and went on his way.

She placed it on the desk and gave me her full attention. "This is a pleasant surprise, Sylvia. Are you here to speak to Walter or me?"

"Both. Either." I laughed nervously.

Evaline's employee was right when he called her sharp as a tack. She missed nothing. She picked up the photograph I'd been studying and handed it to me. "Take a closer look. I want you to be sure, one way or another."

She knew. We'd never discussed the possibility that her father and mine were the same man, but it had clearly crossed her mind.

"I'm not after anything," I said on a rush of breath. "I don't want any part of this." I indicated the office. "But...tell me honestly. You and Walter knew him best...do you see a resemblance?"

She shook her head without hesitation. "I'm sorry."

"Don't be." I glanced over the photograph of the late Mr. Peterson one last time before returning it to her.

She studied it, too, then with a sigh, placed it back on the table. It must pain her to know that her father had kept mistresses. It must be even more painful knowing that everyone else knew, too. No matter how much she may have adored him, his memory would always be tarnished.

Evaline invited me to sit at the desk, then poured tea from the fine silver teapot the assistant must have brought in shortly before my arrival. She'd just finished filling both cups when Walter walked in.

He greeted me heartily, a genuine smile making his cheeks as round and red as ripe apples. "Don't get up," he said to his sister, who'd taken the chair behind the desk. He sat in a guest chair alongside me. "You look well, Sylvia. Clearly the heat doesn't affect you as much as it does me." He removed a folded handkerchief from his pocket and patted his sweating forehead. "I don't know how you ladies always manage to look so cool and composed."

"We can't give away all our secrets to you men," Evaline teased. "Tea?"

"Please." Walter pocketed the handkerchief. "Have you been practicing your spell, Sylvia?"

Walter had taught me the paper-strengthening spell, the only one he and his sister knew. The magic from the spell gave the paper they manufactured a superior quality, and it was this quality that had made their father wealthy. They didn't speak the spell into every batch of paper—it had to be specially ordered— but even their ordinary paper was better than the paper made by an artless manufacturer.

The magic didn't last, of course. No magician's magic lasted forever, although my friend Gabe's mother could extend the magic of another magician, as I'd recently learned. My magic, however, had so far lasted for the three weeks since I'd first used the spell.

I removed two pieces of paper from my bag. "I have, every day. I'm conducting an experiment, as it happens. One that will help me discover how strong my magic is. These pages came from the same notebook. This one has my magic, and this one doesn't."

Walter accepted the pages from me. "Oh, yes, I can feel it." He waved the one that held my magic. "Very strong indeed, Sylvia! Did you place the spell only this morning?" He handed the page to Evaline, swapping it for a cup of tea.

Evaline tried to tear the page but couldn't. "It's still very warm."

I was so thrilled that I couldn't contain my excitement any longer. "I placed the magic in that page three weeks ago."

Walter choked on his tea, then began to cough.

Evaline tried to tear the paper again. When she couldn't, she handed it back to me. "That *is* impressive."

"Is it?" I asked. "I thought your paper didn't tear for months after you placed a spell on it."

"That's true, but ours doesn't feel this warm after three weeks. If your magic still feels like this, then it's strong. *You* are strong, Sylvia."

"Stronger than either of us." Walter sounded proud.

"Oh," I murmured, not quite sure what to say. It was overwhelming, yet so satisfying. So much about casting the spell felt satisfying. Now that I'd discovered magic and actively used it, it was like finding a missing piece of myself.

There were more pieces to find, however. One of them being the identity of my father.

I placed the papers back in my bag and closed the clasp. "This isn't why I came. I wanted to ask you both about invisible writing."

"A curious and rather fun thing," Walter said, smiling.

"I'm helping an ink magician with a new business venture where he creates secret messages for clients using his invisible ink on paper infused with my spell."

Walter looked intrigued by the idea. I suspect the childish wonder in him was piqued.

His sister, however, had a less whimsical view of the world. "Does he know he'll have to write *and* read the secret messages? Unless the recipient is an ink magician or can find one, he or she will only see a blank page. It's inefficient and I suspect it's why invisible writing never became a viable method of passing secrets."

"Or did it?" Walter teased.

"Coded messages would work better. It requires no magician or any particular skill."

"My ink magician friend is aware of the drawbacks," I said.

"Then how can we help?" Walter asked.

"We hoped you knew how long invisible writing lasted, and whether it's dependent on the strength of the paper magic, ink magic, or both."

Walter and Evaline exchanged glances. Walter shrugged. "I don't know. It's not an area we're familiar with."

"I suspect the strength of both types of magic matters," Evaline added.

"Didn't a graphite magician decipher an old invisible message for you?" Walter asked.

I nodded. "It was decades old, but, so far, my friend and I haven't managed to make his invisible ink last more than two weeks. He suggested the magic may not be strong enough."

"*His* magic," Walter pointed out. "Yours is certainly strong."

Evaline frowned in thought. "Perhaps there's a word or two missing from his spell."

"Why not ask the graphite magician who helped you decipher that message?" Walter said. "He or she may know more about it."

I would have gone to Petra Conway, if Huon Barratt hadn't

forbidden me from speaking to her about his new venture. The traditional rivalry of ink versus graphite meant they were naturally disinclined to get along, but I suspected their antagonism towards each other went deeper. I wouldn't be surprised to find that long-suppressed desire coupled with stubbornness fueled their fiery encounters.

I thanked the Petersons and accepted Walter's invitation to join them for dinner the following week. I'd met his wife and children and found them to be delightful company. It would be easier to enjoy myself now that I was sure I wasn't the illicit offspring of one of the late Mr. Peterson's transgressions. While a part of me would have liked to belong to the kind-hearted Peterson family, there would always have been that shadow between us. This way, we could be friends and fellow paper magicians without the awkwardness.

* * *

THANKS to its narrowness and the tall buildings on either side, Crooked Lane was shady for all but a brief window in the middle of the day. On a hot day in summer, the shade should have provided some relief, however the small entrance and lack of a breeze trapped the heat inside. Despite my loose-fitting dress, I was sweating in unmentionable places by the time I opened the library door. I regretted not taking a parasol with me. My friend Daisy had told me that fashionable women were dispensing with the accessory this summer, but I still sometimes used one on sunny days. Today, I'd left home without it.

I found Professor Nash chatting with a patron, seated on the brown leather sofa in the ground floor reading nook. A brass fan on the side table whirred noisily and did little to cool the air. Both men greeted me amiably before resuming their discussion about magic in ancient South American tribes.

I ate a wedge of egg and bacon pie my landlady, Mrs. Parry, had packed for me that morning. It was rare for there to be any leftovers, but one of the other lodgers hadn't dined with us the previous night, so Mrs. Parry had graciously given me her portion this morning. I suspected I was her favorite lodger, although I was under no illusion that I was her favorite because she liked me best. I was her favorite because I'd introduced her to Gabe and Gabe's cook, Mrs. Ling. The two women had struck up a friendship that involved swapping recipes and exchanging ideas and sample dishes. I didn't care why I was the favorite, as long as I received the benefits in the form of delicious leftovers.

I ate as I worked at the front desk, cataloging a stack of books we planned to add to the library shelves. The books had been stored in the attic for years. One of my main tasks since starting work here in March had been to create a list of uncatalogued titles for the professor. Sometimes, that had meant translating the titles and subject matter from the original language into English. Other times, I merely had to peruse the contents. More than once, I'd found myself reading the entire text, simply because it intrigued me.

I still had more than half of the attic's contents to go through, but the professor wanted to begin cataloging those I'd already listed. Together we determined which ones to add to the shelves, and which to set aside for repair or further study. It was now my job to create card files and assign unique codes according to the professor's system.

The task would be dull for most, or so Daisy and Willie had blithely informed me on separate occasions. But I liked it. It wasn't just the magician in me that liked handling paper; the knowledge contained within the pages appealed to me, too. It was a heady feeling, knowing I was among the first to read the texts in years and rediscover knowledge that had been thought lost. Besides, many were quite fascinating.

Yet it wasn't the text of the thin volume titled *The Dung Beetle in Ancient Egyptian Culture as a Representation of the Concept of Transformation and Rebirth* that made me take a closer look at the book's blank first page. It was the lack of it. There was nothing written or typed there, just a small brown stain at the edge, yet I could feel magic on the page. Paper magic, but something else, too.

I must have first handled the book before I became aware that I was a magician. Back then, I didn't know what a page infused with a spell felt like. I did now, and I could definitely feel the paper magic on the blank page, but more than that, I could feel the sensation of paper magic combined with another kind. I'd felt the linked spells before, when I'd discovered invisible writing.

I contained my enthusiasm until the patron left and Professor Nash was alone, then I joined him in the reading nook. He sat on the sofa, head bent over a book that rested on a portable writing desk on his lap. The light from the floor lamp shone unflatteringly on the bare patch on the top of his head, but he needed it even during the day as the smaller of the library's two reading nooks received little natural light. Not that he cared about his own appearance. He wore a brown tie to work each day, the same thick-rimmed spectacles, and often forgot to comb the strands of hair that still clung to his head.

He was also kind and agreeable. I'd never heard him raise his voice or begin an argument, although his calm, factual responses sometimes ended them. Despite his thoroughly agreeable nature, he had few friends. His entire life centered around the library.

Most would say that was just his way, and how he preferred it, but I wasn't so sure. Now that I'd got to know him better, I detected a deep sadness within him. He hid it well, and it was possible he didn't even know it existed himself, but it was there in his quiet stillness, his distant gazes. Sometimes, he seemed far away, and perhaps in another time, too. A time when he and his friend Oscar Barratt traveled the world retrieving many of the books the library now housed. He sometimes recounted their adventures to me. It was clear that the professor missed Oscar, that his death had affected him immensely. There was a part of me that suspected Professor Nash had loved Oscar, but he showed no sign of being inclined towards men, so I assumed his love was more brotherly, platonic. On the other hand, he showed no sign of being interested in women, either, so perhaps I was wrong.

"Professor, do you recall where you acquired this book?"

He studied the title page, frowning. "It's not familiar, so we didn't obtain it on one of our overseas adventures. It was most likely donated to the library and placed in the attic. I don't recall putting it there, but it might have arrived here while I was away." He closed the book and read the spine. "Does ancient Egyptian mythology interest you?"

"Not especially. It's the very first page that interests me. I think I feel invisible writing on it."

His brows shot up his forehead. "Indeed?" He reopened the book and inspected the blank page under the light of the lamp. "How intriguing. I wonder what it says."

"Probably nothing exciting, but I'll take it to Petra Conway to see if she can read it for me."

I waited until the end of the working day, then walked to Petra's stationery shop, once again regretting the exertion in stifling weather. I found her preparing to close. The smile she gave me was as wilted as I felt.

"Long day?" I asked.

"Immeasurably. This heat is unbearable." She picked up a hand fan painted with a scene of blossoming trees and flapped it at her face. "When will this heat end?"

"You should get an electric desk fan and train it on yourself. It helps a little."

She arched her finely shaped brows at me then swept the fan in an arc to indicate the shop's contents. "With all this loose paper? It'll wreak more havoc than a cyclone."

I couldn't help smiling at my silly mistake. "Have you at least taken a break today?"

"My mother relieved me for a little while and I sat in the shade at Hanover Square with my eyes closed. There's no need for us both to be in lately. Business has been so quiet, which is to be expected at this time of year. Many of our clients have gone on holiday to the seaside, or the country. Getting out of the city in summer seems to be a national pastime for most."

"Lucky devils."

Her pretty dark eyes flashed with mischief. "I'd wager Gabe Glass has a lovely family estate somewhere nice, perhaps with a lake for swimming, or a stream." She leaned an elbow on the counter and her chin on her fist and gave me a suggestive smile.

"His family does have an estate, as it happens, but I don't know if it has a lake or stream." I spoke with as much blandness as I could, feigning disinterest in all things Gabriel Glass.

Petra was too clever to fall for my pretense. Her smile widened. "If he invites you, I volunteer to be chaperone."

"And who will chaperone you?"

"Willie."

We both laughed.

"So…" she said, straightening. "How are things between you and Gabe?"

"The same." I didn't want to talk about Gabe, nor my feelings for him. I liked him a great deal, but his feelings for me were less clear. While sometimes I was quite sure he liked me, too, he'd just ended a serious relationship that had been forged in the powerful, intense days of wartime. He was still untangling his own emotions from its ending, as well as coming to terms with his magic and its role in his miraculous wartime survival.

Or so I told myself. As time went on, I was no longer sure if anything would build between Gabe and me beyond friendship.

I didn't want to discuss any of that with Petra, or with anybody. It was easier to focus on the matter at hand. I showed her the book, opening it to the blank page with the invisible writing. "Can you read that?"

She looked at the page, looked at me, then looked at the page again. "Read what? There's nothing there."

"But I can feel the magic from the paper. It contains a paper spell and something else. It isn't invisible writing?"

"Not from graphite magic." She handed the book back. "It could be ink."

"But ink magicians don't know how to create invisible writing."

"That's what Huon said, but perhaps he's wrong. He's not the keeper of all ink magician knowledge. In fact, I guarantee he's wrong. He is an idiot, after all."

I chuckled. "He isn't, and you know it. He's merely..." I tried to think of the right word to describe the man with more facets to him than a diamond.

Petra offered several possibilities. "Foolhardy. Arrogant. Lazy. Rude. Crude. Slovenly."

"I have to stop you there. He's no longer slovenly. Last time I saw him, he'd shaved and cut his hair. He even wore shoes and a clean shirt with all its buttons." I tucked the book back into my bag. "I'll take this to him now."

"May I come with you? I'd like to see this miraculous change for myself."

* * *

HUON BARRATT PRESENTED QUITE the handsome figure as he greeted us in the drawing room of his Marylebone house. Gone was the unkempt and unwashed hair, the bags under bloodshot eyes, and the housecoat opened to the waist. The tattoo on his chest was covered by a crisp white shirt with the sleeves rolled to his elbows, and a light gray waistcoat with silver buttons monogrammed with his initials.

The son of a successful magician who manufactured fine quality ink, he'd lived in his father's townhouse since before the war. According to Professor Nash, Huon clashed terribly with his father, but had idolized his uncle, Oscar. Losing him when war broke out, then heading off to the Front to fight shortly afterwards had changed him from a carefree youth to a deeply scarred man drowning in his own vices. The professor gave him leeway for his transgressions on account of his profound losses, but his own father wasn't so understanding. Isaac Barratt continued to allow his son to live in the house, but the two rarely spoke and when they did it was only to argue.

Perhaps it was time for Isaac to see Huon in person again. He would be relieved to see the change in his son. It remained to be seen if the change was in appearance only, or whether it extended to Huon's attitude.

Before she sat on the sofa beside me, Petra made a show of studying him. "Congratulations on looking like a human again. Sylvia tried to tell me, but I didn't believe her. I'm glad to see you remember how buttons work."

Huon asked his butler to bring in refreshments, then smiled at Petra. It was as lopsided and mischievous as ever. "Glad, eh? Glad enough to go to Rector's with me tonight?"

"Don't be absurd. I wouldn't be caught dancing with you even if you were the only man in the club."

"Don't get on your high horse. I was only asking you out of pity. You obviously don't have too many offers or you wouldn't be here flirting with me."

"If this is your idea of flirting then it's no wonder you're still single despite the scarcity of young men. Is that what brought about this change in your appearance? A desperate attempt to appeal to women who care more about the way a man looks than his character?"

Huon gave her a smug smile. "Find me handsome, do you? I thought so."

For once, Petra didn't have an answer. Her only response was to blush.

Huon settled further into the chair, not sprawled as he used to, but there was still an air of arrogance about the way he sat, as if he was comfortable with this version of himself. "Women adore me no matter my appearance. The suit is because I now have clients."

Petra sparked up again. "Yes, it does help one's business when the owner looks professional and not as though he just crawled out of bed after a night drinking and womanizing."

I thought it best to intervene before their banter escalated and one or both said something they regretted. I removed the small book from my bag and handed it to Huon. "I came across this in the library. I can feel what I think is invisible writing on the first page. Petra says she can't see it, so it isn't written with pencil. Can you see it?"

He opened the book and his lips parted with a gasp.

I sat forward. "You *can*. What does it say?"

"It's addressed to my uncle."

"Oscar? Who is it from?"

"A relative of mine, named Daniel Barratt. I never met him, but I've heard the name." He flipped the page and studied the reverse side. "Bloody hell," he murmured.

"Stop with the dramatics, and just tell us," Petra snapped. "What does it say?"

"The message to Uncle Oscar is begging him for help. Daniel got entangled in a scheme and at the time he wrote this, he was afraid for his life." Huon flipped the page to the reverse again. "On this side is a diagram, or map as Daniel refers to it, with some sort of code written alongside it." He looked at me, and a chill slithered down my spine. I'd never seen Huon look so grave. "Daniel writes that if Oscar receives this book, then it was sent after his death."

CHAPTER 2

The butler brought in martinis on a tray while Petra and I waited for Huon to finish speaking to his father over the telephone. When Huon had asked for refreshments, I'd thought he'd meant tea. It would seem he hadn't changed all that much after all.

Petra must have been thinking the same thing. "I don't know why I expected anything else." She sniffed the contents of the glass and shrugged. "I suppose it is cocktail hour." She sipped, wrinkled her nose, then sipped again.

I glanced at the door as I sipped, too. I could hear Huon's voice, but not his words. The wait shredded my nerves, and I found my cocktail glass half empty by the time he returned a few minutes later.

"Well?" Petra prompted.

Huon handed me the book. "Daniel Barratt is—was—a distant cousin. He died years ago, in 1891. His wife and children went missing around the same time and haven't been seen or heard from since."

"How tragic," I murmured.

Huon indicated the book I clutched in both hands. "In light of that, I'm no longer sure he died of natural causes."

Before telephoning his father, he'd read the invisible message to us, or as much of it as he could see. Some of it had faded away, the magic having run out. Daniel wrote to tell Oscar that he was afraid, hence the secrecy. He'd been coerced into working for a bookmaker of dubious character. He'd become nervous, however, and wanted to stop. He sent his wife and children into hiding, and hid some evidence, then planned to inform the police about the illegal transactions. However, if Oscar received the book with the invisible message and accompanying map, it meant something had gone wrong and he—Daniel—had been killed. Some of the next sentence was faded, but it was easy enough to understand the gist. Daniel's will would state his wish for Oscar to be sent the book, as he was the only one with the bravery and contacts to bring his killer, the bookmaker, to justice using the evidence that could be found following the map. The villain's name was unfortunately no longer readable, but Daniel stated that he, in turn, was an associate of Lord Coyle.

That was a name I knew.

"Uncle Oscar must never have seen the message," Huon went on. "He would have investigated if he'd known."

I traced my finger over the book's title. Perhaps if Daniel had chosen a more unique book on a more interesting subject, it may have gained some attention. The small, slim volume on dung beetles in ancient Egyptian mythology was somewhat uninspiring.

"Did the police look for Daniel's wife and children?" Petra asked.

"They conducted a search, but they were never found," Huon said. "My father says they've all wondered what happened to Daniel's family ever since. They could still be alive."

And still in hiding.

My heart thudded, a heavy weight pressing down on my chest. I swallowed, my mouth suddenly dry. "The two children... How old were they when their father died?"

"The boy was aged four and the little girl was one or two."

An older boy with a younger sister, hidden away to keep them safe. Their mother must have been scared after learning of her husband's death. Scared and alone, with a killer looking for her and her children. A mother would stay hidden forever if she suspected there was still a danger. She would move cities to throw him off the scent. She would teach her children to protect themselves.

It was all sounding dreadfully familiar.

But not everything added up. I was born in '94 so I wasn't two years old until 1896, and Daniel Barratt had died in 1891. Also, my father was a paper magician, not an ink magician. Being a Barratt, Daniel's talent was ink, too. But he needed to *work* with a paper magician to write invisible messages, including this one in the book.

"That's a good point," Petra said when I mentioned it. "Magicians were in hiding then, but some were aware of the existence of others, so it's conceivable Daniel purchased spell-infused paper for his work for the bookmaker and asked the same magician to place their spell on the page in this book."

Huon shook his head. "He didn't need to purchase magic paper. His wife was a paper magician. That's why she was in danger, too. She knew her husband was writing secret messages for the bookmaker on her paper. She must have also placed her spell in the book before her disappearance."

My fingers began to ache, and I realized I'd been clutching the book tightly. I released it and smoothed my hand over the innocuous cover. If the children's *mother* was the paper magician, then she couldn't be my mother. I knew for certain that my mother was Marianne Folgate, a silver magician.

"Daniel's wife's maiden name was Hendry," Huon said.

It was another name that rang a bell. I must have read it in the list of magicians collated by Gabe's parents.

"What of the map and its code?" Petra asked. "Can you read it?"

"Most of it's clear," Huon said. "There's an address in

Whitechapel written at the top of the page. The map is really a diagram that depicts an interesting pattern. I'm not sure why Daniel refers to it as a map. Beside it is a code consisting of a series of letters and numbers. We should go to the address and see if we can make any sense of it."

"I think the police should do that." I checked the time on the mantelpiece clock. "We could call on Gabe and ask him to look into it, given he's a consultant for Scotland Yard on magical crimes."

"Or we could go directly to Alex's father and if they assign Gabe to the case then so be it," Huon suggested.

Beside me, Petra gave a surreptitious shake of her head, or tried to. I saw it and knew what she was trying to convey.

Huon caught on, too. "Ohhhh, of course. Sylvia wants to see Gabe."

Petra groaned. "You're a blundering oaf."

Huon plucked his cocktail glass off the table and drained it in a single gulp. "Come on then, Sylvia, let's go."

Petra finished her cocktail, too, and stood. "I should telephone my mother first and let her know I'll be home late."

"There's no need for you to come along." Huon stepped aside and indicated the door.

"I suppose you're right, and I should get home. Mother has invited guests to dinner."

"And you wouldn't dare do the wrong thing. Missing dinner and upsetting your mother would be far too rebellious for someone who likes to follow the rules."

"No, it would be rude. Besides, one of her guests is young and apparently rather handsome." She tossed him a smile over her shoulder as she left. The butler, who'd been hovering, followed her.

Once she was out of earshot, Huon muttered, "She's as prickly as ever." He turned to me. "You didn't ask her how long invisible writing lasts, did you?"

"No. I called on the Petersons. They didn't know, but suspect it depends on either the strength of the two magics or a word in the spell itself." I didn't mention that if it was the former, then his magic was rather weak.

"I need to find out. I've got a client, but I can't sell him my services until I've perfected the process. I don't want the message fading too soon."

"What's the nature of the message?"

He tilted his head to the side. "I can't tell you that, Sylvia. It's highly sensitive."

"If you'll heed some advice, Huon, then I suggest you tread carefully. You don't want to attract the wrong type of client or…" I waggled the book in his face, before tucking it back into my bag.

His only response was a flattening of his lips, which could have meant anything.

* * *

I TELEPHONED Gabe from Huon's house before leaving, but instead of heading directly to Park Street, we returned to the library first. We both wanted to speak to the professor about the message and the book it had been written in.

He wasn't able to shed any more light on it, however. "Oscar never mentioned invisible ink to me, so I assume he'd never heard of it."

Huon indicated the page in the book containing Daniel's message. "He would have been able to read this. I can."

The professor sighed. "I suppose he never opened the book after receiving it, and simply donated it to the library. It must have been one of the first books added to our collection. What was the name of the cousin who wrote the message?"

"Daniel."

The professor shook his head. "It doesn't sound familiar."

"My father says they weren't close. I suspect Daniel wrote to Uncle Oscar because of his connection to Lord and Lady Rycroft and their connection to magic and the police. He probably thought Lady Rycroft could help."

"Poor fellow. He must have been desperate to organize for the book to be sent after his death. When did he die?"

"1891."

"A complicated year. Which month?"

"April."

"That's not a month I'll forget easily," Professor Nash said darkly. "It's likely this book fell through the cracks during a very chaotic time."

"We're going to call on Gabe now to ask him to bring it to the attention of Scotland Yard," I said.

"Why not call on Cyclops? I'm sure he'd welcome your visit, as would Catherine."

"Oh, I, uh..."

Huon winked at the professor. "Don't deny her the pleasure of seeing Gabe Glass."

Professor Nash smiled. "I wouldn't dare."

I snatched the book out of Huon's hands. "Actually, I wanted to ask Gabe about a paper magician named Hendry."

"Hendry! Why him?"

"Him? You know the name?"

"Oh, yes, I remember him. What does he have to do with this?"

"Daniel Barratt's wife was a Hendry. I think I've seen or heard the name before." I didn't want to mention Lord and Lady Rycroft's list of magicians in front of Huon. Its existence wasn't common knowledge.

"Willie or Cyclops may have mentioned him." From the professor's tone, I suspected there was a story behind the name. I think I knew what he was alluding to, but I refrained from making assumptions until I'd heard more.

I slipped the book into my bag. "Will you come with us, Professor?"

"I have a bit to do here…" He looked around his flat. It was as neat as a pin.

I took his hand and squeezed. "Come with us. I'm sure they'll be pleased to see you."

He gave me a wan smile. "And I'd like to see them."

* * *

I HAD SEEN Gabe several times in the weeks since wrapping up the investigation into the decades-old disappearance of a youth we thought may have been my father. The young man proved to be someone else entirely, but I didn't regret the time we spent on the case. Not only did we bring closure to his family, but it brought me closer to Gabe. Being with him, even just as his friend, was deeply satisfying. Like using my spell, it felt right, as if we should be precisely *there* at that moment, enjoying one another's company. Yet I was very aware of a wall between us. I could jump over the wall and be intimate with him, but only if he wanted me on his side.

Yet he never invited me, never so much as nudged the wall with his toe. He seemed content to simply be friends. If he felt the tug of desire and longing, he never showed it. Well, almost never. Once or twice, when we brushed up against each other, I saw the flare of heat in his eyes, felt the unexpected caress of his fingers as he reached for me. Then there was the time he'd moved so that, instead of kissing his cheek, I'd kissed the corner of his mouth. I was almost, very nearly, quite sure that he'd moved on purpose.

He visited the library often of late, not for any particular reason, simply to chat when he wasn't working. His two constant companions were always present, however. Alex and Willie hadn't let Gabe out of their sight since the stabbing at Rosebank Gardens Hospital. Gabe seemed to be fully recovered now, although I suspected there was still a significant scar. The patient who'd stabbed him had been arrested at the scene, but hadn't said a word since except to mutter that God made him do it. The shell-shocked former soldier was incapable of coherent conversation, but we all suspected he'd acted under the instructions of another. Nobody was sure of that figure's identity. Out of the several possibilities, the most likely seemed to be the same person who was behind the earlier abduction attempts. The patient could have killed Gabe if he'd wanted to, but he'd merely wounded him.

Whatever the reason for the stabbing, nothing like that had happened since. But Gabe's friend and cousin weren't going to allow him to leave the house without them.

We found Gabe, Willie and Alex in the drawing room. Gabe looked as relaxed as always when at home, albeit this time he wore no waistcoat over his shirt, given the heat. He and Alex had also dispensed with ties. Willie wore men's trousers and a shirt with a crimson-and-black-striped waistcoat. She'd started adding a little color to her wardrobe these past few weeks as she attempted to impress Nurse Tilda Wallbank.

Despite her more stylish appearance, she was less than enthusiastic about the change in Huon. She stood with hands on hips as she cast a critical eye over him, finishing her study with a heavy sigh and shake of her head. "You're a disappointment."

"Why?" he asked.

"I had high hopes for you. These two ain't no fun no more." She jerked her thumb at Gabe and Alex. "But you had promise. You threw wild parties. You drank until you passed out. You didn't care that everyone thought you were a no-good wastrel. Now look at you. I feel like I should be asking you to balance my books."

"You don't have books to balance," Gabe said with a wry grin.

Huon clasped Willie's shoulder. "Don't worry. I'm still fun. This is just for the clients."

Willie grunted. "So, it ain't because of a woman?"

"Most women adore me no matter what I wear or how

unkempt I look. If they don't, then they're too prim and proper for me, and I'm not interested in them, no matter how pretty and clever they are."

Willie frowned. "You talking about anyone in partic'lar?"

"No." Huon cleared his throat and turned to Gabe. "I don't suppose your butler was about to serve drinks."

Gabe asked Bristow to make cocktails and the elderly butler shuffled out. "Tell me more about the invisible message. It sounds intriguing."

I produced the book from my bag and handed it to Huon.

He read aloud the words written by Daniel Barratt, then told them about the so-called map on the reverse of the page. "The diagram has various shapes—diamonds, triangles, flowers, all bordered with a rope design. There's a series of letters and numbers written on the side."

"If Daniel calls it a map, then perhaps those are coordinates," Gabe suggested.

"I think they're a code."

"Can you copy them for us?" Gabe removed a sheet of paper and a pencil from a drawer in one of the side tables.

As Huon wrote, Willie watched him with a pensive expression. "I can't believe Coyle is making an appearance again, after all this time. He just won't die, will he?"

"He is most definitely dead," Gabe said.

The professor pushed his glasses up his nose. "Oh yes. He died around the same time as Daniel, in fact."

"Perhaps his operation didn't die with him," Alex said. "The bookmaker that Daniel mentions may have continued it. If the evidence is still *in situ* when we get there, we can bring him to justice."

We all made noises of agreement, except for Gabe. Before he could explain why, Alex shook his head. "No, Gabe. It's not him."

"Him who?" I asked.

"Gabe," Alex warned. "It's highly unlikely. He was young when that was written."

I suddenly realized who they were discussing. "You think *Thurlow* is the man Daniel refers to?"

Thurlow was a thoroughly nasty fellow we'd met at Epsom Downs Racecourse while investigating the origins of a collection of untitled books. Gabe had posed as an American trying to circumvent prohibition laws, but when his story unraveled, Thurlow had retaliated by having his men drive us off the road, destroying Gabe's motorcar. If it hadn't been for Gabe's magic slowing down time, allowing him to save us, I doubted we would have survived the crash.

"I doubt Thurlow is the man Daniel mentions in the message to Oscar," Alex said. "You're jumping to conclusions."

"He was old enough," Gabe said.

"There's no evidence whatsoever that it's Thurlow. There must have been dozens of corrupt bookmakers back then."

"As there are now," Willie muttered.

"The bookmaker Daniel refers to was ruthless," Gabe pointed out. "That puts him at a rare level. Thurlow is at that level, and he had to start somewhere."

Alex's frown deepened.

Willie peered over Huon's shoulder. "You done yet?"

"Almost," he said.

She drummed her fingers on the table where he was working. As if infected by her impatience, Gabe started tapping his thumb on his thigh. Neither was aware of their habit.

"It has to be Thurlow," Gabe said again.

Alex looked worried, although I wasn't quite sure why. Gabe was right that we ought to consider Thurlow, but Alex was most likely also right in that Thurlow was rather young at the time and corrupt bookmakers in London were common. The chances of it being him were slim.

"There's more." The professor eyed Willie warily, as if she

were a firecracker near a flame. "Daniel Barratt was apparently married to a paper magician whose maiden name was Hendry."

Willie's head snapped up. "What did you say?"

"She was a Hendry before she married Daniel Barratt. I see from your reaction you remember the name."

She answered him with a series of curse words that had me blushing. Based on her reaction, my first instinct must have been correct. Hendry was the name of the paper magician who knew a spell to direct paper to fly. With their sharp edges, the papers became weapons, which he'd used to attack Willie and Gabe's mother years ago.

"Could *he* be the bookmaker Daniel refers to?" Alex asked. "We know Hendry was an associate of Coyle's. If he's a close relative of Daniel Barratt's wife, then he might have discussed invisible writing with Daniel and be the one who coerced him to write secret messages for him."

Willie didn't think it likely. "He wasn't a bookmaker at the time. Doesn't mean he didn't become one, I s'pose. If he was desperate, he might have needed to survive any way he could while he was in hiding."

"Thurlow is definitely the type, though," Gabe muttered.

Alex sighed.

"What happened to Hendry?" I asked.

Willie shrugged. "He disappeared and hasn't been heard of since. Hopefully he's dead."

Another disappearance. They seemed to be plaguing us of late.

"Why didn't Oscar tell us he recognized the name Hendry back then?" Willie asked. "He should have said a Hendry was married to a relative of his when the paper magician attacked us."

"He probably didn't know," Huon said as he checked his copy against the original. "Daniel was merely a distant cousin. Uncle Oscar probably didn't even go to their wedding." He held the paper out to Gabe, but Willie snatched it off him.

24

"It doesn't make sense." She passed it to Gabe. "It's just random letters and numbers."

Gabe disagreed. "It *is* a code. The letters L, R, U and D appear several times."

"But what do they mean? This is going to be impossible to crack without a cipher like the one we used for the Medici Manuscript."

"L is probably left, and R is right," Gabe said. "Which means U is up and D is down."

Willie crossed her arms. "And the numbers, Mr. Know-it-all?"

"The number of steps to move either left, right, up or down."

"Not steps," Huon said from where he was studying the seemingly blank page in the book. "Spaces, or whatever these shapes on the diagram refer to. They form a pretty pattern. That's why Daniel called it a map—when used with the codes, it takes you to a particular position on the diagram. If you knew where to start and traced a path by following the number of spaces up, down, left or right according to this list of instructions, then the final destination could be where the evidence is hidden."

"Draw the diagram for us," Willie ordered.

"I'm no artist and it's too complicated. There's an address on here in Whitechapel, which is presumably relevant. If we take this map and the codes there, it might become clear what this is referring to."

"Unless it's gone," Alex pointed out.

"We won't know until we see it in person." Huon passed the book back to me. "Is it too late to go after dinner? What's your cook preparing, Glass?"

Gabe invited us to stay for dinner, but insisted on waiting until the morning before trying to find the pattern depicted by the diagram. "Whitechapel isn't a place we should be walking through at night."

Willie looked like she'd protest until Gabe shot her a flinty glare. After a moment, it seemed to occur to her that I was the reason for his caution. "Sylvia doesn't have to come. She can stay here with the Prof. Anyway, she doesn't want to come. Do you, Sylv?"

"Actually, I do."

She grunted and slumped into the chair. "You're all going soft."

"I would have gone with you tonight," Huon told her. "You have your gun and I have my fists and my wits. Nobody in Whitechapel would dare touch us."

"No one is going to Whitechapel without us," Gabe growled.

Willie slumped further into the chair, only to suddenly brighten a little. "Want to go to the Buttonhole or Rector's tonight, Huon?"

He thought for a moment then shook his head. "I don't want a late night."

She jabbed her finger at him. "I knew it! You have changed, and it ain't just the fact you've taken a bath and had a haircut."

"I'm still the same old me, just in a tidier package." Huon self-consciously smoothed a palm over his neatly combed hair. It was the first time I'd seen him self-conscious about anything.

"You've become *responsible*." Willie spat out the word as if it tasted bitter.

* * *

DINNER WAS A CASUAL AFFAIR, in keeping with Gabe's relaxed character. Even his footman, Murray, joined in with our conversation, much to Bristow's disapproval. The butler's expression didn't change overmuch, yet he somehow managed to exude annoyance at his underling crossing class boundaries.

Despite the easy banter tossed around the table, I couldn't enjoy myself entirely. I was desperate to ask Willie a question in private, but she was all the way at the other end.

I could tell by the way he shot surreptitious glances my way throughout the main course that Gabe sensed my disquiet. He waited until the pudding was served before leaning closer and asking. "You hardly ate a thing. Will I ask Mrs. Ling not to serve kedgeree next time?"

"I'm sorry. It's not the food or the company. Both are excellent."

"Ah. It's as I thought. You think he's your father, don't you? This Hendry fellow?"

His bold statement momentarily took my breath away. "Are you sure your magical power isn't reading minds?"

He smirked. "I'm glad it's not. I don't want to know what's on everyone's mind. Willie's thoughts, for example, would make me blush." He glanced at his father's cousin as she told Huon that he used to remind her of her second husband, but now that he'd become more responsible, he reminded her of her first.

Huon choked on his mouthful of pudding, but recovered quickly. "I am not marrying you, Willie. I have other plans."

Gabe turned back to me. "I want to tell you that Hendry probably isn't your father."

"But you can't, because there's a good chance that he is," I finished for him. "My father was a paper magician, and Hendry was a paper magician. My mother was running from someone dangerous, most likely from the man she refused to talk about—my father. Hendry was dangerous." I nodded in Willie's direction. "I'll see if she has any insights for me."

"Don't rely on Willie's account. She's prone to exaggeration."

She was the only one in the room who'd met him. Not even the professor had. "I'll keep it in mind."

"Whatever happens, don't worry." His hand closed over mine, resting on my lap under the table. "If Hendry is your father, it won't affect what anyone thinks of you."

I wished I could agree. I suspected Willie would like me even less.

Gabe followed my gaze. "Ignore her."

"She's impossible to ignore, especially if you and I—" I cut myself off, before I revealed raw feelings. I didn't want to add another vulnerability to my mounting list.

He leaned in even closer, expectant. "Especially if you and I...what? Tell me, Sylvia."

"Nothing."

"No, go ahead. I want to hear it." His thumb massaged mine. The intimate gesture, coupled with the flare of intensity in his gaze warmed me all over. I found myself inadvertently leaning closer to him, too.

"You two!" Willie shouted down the table. "What are you talking about?"

I jerked away from Gabe. "Nothing!"

Huon snickered.

Willie's gaze narrowed. "Are you talking about me?"

Alex rolled his eyes. "Not everything's about you, Willie."

"It often is."

Before she could dig any further, Gabe suggested we return to the drawing room for coffee and liqueurs. Gone were the days when men and women went their separate ways after dinner. Even if the formality was still observed, I couldn't imagine Willie wanting to be stuck alone with me while the men enjoyed cigars and billiards. I would find it incredibly trying, too.

While we filed out of the dining room, Gabe placed a hand to my lower back. "I'm going to check my parents' catalog of magicians for more information about Hendry. I won't be long." He spoke quietly, confirming my earlier suspicion that Huon didn't know about the catalog.

He made his excuses to the party then headed up the stairs, while we returned to the drawing room. I was considering how to get Willie alone when Alex drew me aside.

"I'm worried about Gabe," he said. "He's becoming obsessed."

"Obsessed?" I asked weakly.

"Thurlow is a dangerous individual, but I don't think he warrants the sort of attention Gabe's been giving him lately."

"Ohhh, he's obsessed with *Thurlow*."

"Perhaps obsessed isn't the right word, but he certainly was quick to attribute Daniel Barratt's message to him. It's not the first time Thurlow's name has come up since our last encounter."

"He was worried about Francis Stray becoming entangled with him." Gabe's mathematician friend worked for Military Intelligence, but when Thurlow had discovered he was extraordinarily intelligent, he wanted Francis to work for him. We'd managed to convince him that Francis wouldn't be a good employee for someone whose activities required secrecy.

Alex watched me closely. "I don't think that's why. It's more...personal."

"What do you mean?"

He suddenly looked away. "I think the professor wants to talk to me."

I glanced at the professor, chatting to Huon by the window. Alex joined them before I could make further enquiries into Gabe's obsession with Thurlow. I decided to talk to Willie instead, since she was on her own.

Murray entered carrying a tray of sherry glasses. I plucked up two and handed one to Willie. I watched as she took a sip.

"May I ask you a question, Willie? I'm afraid it might conjure up painful memories for you, but I need to know."

"If it's about murdering my husbands, nothing was ever proved. Anyway, I liked my husbands. Why would I want to kill them?"

"Actually, it's about Hendry."

A shadow passed over her face. "That low-down pigswill. I wish I'd killed him when I had the chance. Hopefully he's dead now and I never have to see his face again."

"His face is actually what I wanted to talk to you about. What did he look like?"

She wrinkled her nose. "Ugly. Real mean looking."

I wasn't sure if she was remembering correctly or if her memory was colored by her opinion of him. "Was he fair?"

She gave another shrug. "I think he had blond hair."

"Did he have freckles?"

"I don't know! I was too busy trying not to get sliced to death to notice why he was so ugly."

I gave up. Gabe was right. She was prone to exaggeration, and I needed a levelheaded opinion. I'd ask Cyclops the next time I saw him.

Gabe returned to the drawing room and gave a slight shake of his head. Later, when he managed to speak to me alone, he said, "The information about Hendry doesn't say much. He disappeared in 1891. He has no known family or offspring, and he's presumed dead."

"I asked Willie what he looked like."

"And?"

"She says he was blond. My hair is fair."

He tilted his head to the side, waiting for more, but I had nothing else to offer. We both left it at that.

CHAPTER 3

*T*he Whitechapel address was an old building in a dead-end court off a market street where a range of cheap clothing and homewares could be purchased. The entire world seemed to be encapsulated in the bustling market, with the diversity of accents forming a tapestry as varied as the goods for sale. We jostled with women carrying baskets over their arms, small children on their hips or clutching their mother's skirts. Stallholders tried to drown out each other when they spied us approaching, advertising their products with pride. I would have walked away with a pretty pair of black patent leather shoes if it hadn't been for Willie ushering me along the cobblestone street. I made a mental note to return another day to browse.

The Cockney accent of the woman who answered our knock made a change from the Irish and European ones of the market. She studied us with the indifference of a woman with a lifetime of hardship behind her and a bleak future to look forward to.

Gabe began by asking her if she knew a man named Daniel Barratt.

"No. Why?"

"He may have lived here in the early Nineties. Were you here then?"

She thrust a hand on her hip. "I'm twenty-five, Mister." She was younger than she looked.

Gabe removed his hat and held it to his chest. "I apologize. Do you know who lived in this house back then?"

"No. Folk come and go around here." She turned to look over her shoulder as a child began to cry. Another squeezed past her to sit on the stoop near her feet. She blinked at me with big eyes not yet touched by the hopelessness that shadowed her mother's.

"Do you mind if we come in for a few minutes and look around?" Gabe asked.

The woman crossed her arms. "Why?"

"We have a diagram—"

Willie nudged him. "Give her something to make it worth her while."

Gabe removed some coins from his pocket. "We'll be as unobtrusive as possible."

The money disappeared into the women's skirt pocket before he'd finished speaking. She tapped the little girl on the top of the head and ordered her to move aside.

We filed past them and into the house. It took a moment for my eyes to adjust to the dimness, but when they did, it became painfully obvious how poorly the family lived. Broken windows had been boarded up, internal doors were missing altogether, and some of the floorboards, too. In one section of the kitchen, I could see through to the cellar below. The table had been positioned over the hole. Fortunately, the hole wasn't big enough for a child to fit through, but they could cut themselves on the jagged, broken boards.

Alex scooped up the crying toddler and tickled him until the boy began to giggle. "You should fix the floor before one of them has an accident," he said to the children's mother as he handed the toddler to her.

She made a great show of pressing a hand to her cheek in mock horror. "Oh, thank you, kind sir! I never thought of that. I'll telephone the landlord straight away so he can fix it before my husband gets home." She arched her brows at Alex, challenging.

He merely grunted. "Barratt, anything in here?"

Huon had been looking around at the walls and floor, but shook his head. He headed into the adjoining room with Gabe, Alex and Willie in tow, but I hung back in the kitchen. The woman sat at the table, the toddler on her lap, and pulled a stack of flattened boxes towards her. The stamp on the topmost one read *A. & F. Pears Transparent Glycerine Soap.* Her movements as she folded the flaps to create soap boxes were so quick, they were difficult to follow even though I watched carefully.

She nodded in the direction the others had gone. "You paid for the tour, so take it."

I joined the others in the bedroom, pushing past Willie standing in the doorway with her hands on her hips.

"This is hopeless," she whined. "There ain't no way a painting will still be here after all these years. What was Barratt even doing here anyway? Your family's rich."

Huon looked up from the book, open to the page displaying the invisible map and its code. "Daniel's branch of the family wasn't well-off. They didn't manufacture ink like mine." He shook his head. "I can't see anything here that uses the same pattern."

The downstairs consisted of the kitchen and bedroom, which I suspected was once a sitting room in the house's former days. We headed upstairs, where another family rented rooms. They spoke little English and didn't understand what we wanted, but they took Gabe's money and allowed us to look in each room.

Again, Huon shook his head, and again, Willie called the expedition hopeless.

I was about to agree when Gabe told us to follow him. We returned downstairs to the kitchen where the pieceworker had amassed a pile of folded soap boxes. She had another stack of flattened boxes still to go.

Gabe indicated the hole in the floor under the table. "May I look?"

She narrowed her gaze at him. "Why?"

He simply gave her more money.

She squirreled it away then closed her hand over her now bulging pocket as if reassuring herself that it was all still there. "The bloke who rents the cellar is at work. Just don't touch anything and he won't know."

"If we do, we'll put it back."

She pointed to the adjoining pantry where I could see several crates stacked with more flattened boxes. It would take her all day to get through them, then the assembled boxes would be collected and returned to the factory where the soaps would be slipped inside, and the boxes sealed. Within days, they'd be distributed to pharmacies, perfumers, and shops around the country.

Gabe opened the trapdoor in the pantry floor. He peered down, then asked Alex to hand him the oil lamp hanging from a hook on the wall. Alex opened the tin enclosure and Willie used her own matches to light it. On his knees, Gabe lowered the lantern inside and peered through the trapdoor.

"This is it," he said, handing the lantern to Alex. "This is the room."

"There's a painting in the *cellar*?" Huon asked.

Gabe climbed through the trapdoor. When he was part way down the steps, he held out his hand and Alex passed him the lantern.

Willie darted in front of Huon to go down next. Huon followed and Alex indicated I should go ahead of him. When Gabe realized I was following, he put out his hand to assist me the final few steps, even though there was a railing down one side of the staircase.

He smiled at me. I smiled back.

"We found it!" Huon's voice echoed around the near-empty room. "It's not a picture or rug we're looking for. It's the floor tiles."

Gabe held the lantern high although it didn't illuminate the entire cellar, which seemed to occupy the same footprint as the kitchen above. The shard of light piercing through the hole beneath the pieceworker's table fell across the stained mattress. Willie pushed it aside with the toe of her boot to reveal more of the mosaic tiled floor.

She covered her mouth and nose with her hand. "It stinks down here. Someone needs to speak to the tenant about hygiene." She pushed a bundle of rags and a few belongings aside, too, but left the bedpan alone.

"This must have been laid in ancient Roman times," I said. "This floor is far older than the house."

Despite its age, the mosaic was in near perfect condition. All the small tesserae were in place, although the colors had probably been more vibrant when it was laid centuries ago. It would have been the spectacular floor of a wealthy Roman's private villa or other important building, designed to impress guests. The builders of the nineteenth century house had kept the original floor instead of laying flagstones over it. Due to its depth below the modern-day street level, they'd turned it into a cellar that would have been used by the household to store provisions. The families who lived in the tenement now had no spare provisions to store. They needed to sublease as many rooms as possible to people even more destitute themselves. Going by the bible written in Polish—a language I recognized from my recent translation efforts at the library—the cellar's tenant was most likely a newly arrived migrant.

"The floor pattern matches the diagram?" Alex asked Huon.

Huon tapped his finger in a line across the page, silently counting, then counted the triangular shapes at the mosaic's top edge. "It does."

"What's the first instruction?" Gabe asked.

"U-four."

Willie stood in the middle of the floor, hands on hips. "Up four tiles. But the tiles are tiny. Do we have to count each one? There are hundreds here. Thousands! Where do we start?"

I indicated the steps from the kitchen. "It's the only way into the cellar." I stood on the bottom step and began to count tesserae.

Huon stopped me. "I don't think it's the number of little tiles."

"Tesserae. I learned about them one summer when I found a book on ancient Roman Britain. It was fascinating."

Willie snorted. "Yawn."

"I think you should count the diamond shapes," Huon went on.

The diamonds appeared in a line running from the base of the steps all the way around the entire mosaic as well as across the middle in four rows, dividing the entire pattern into segments of equal sized squares.

Huon pointed to the page that only he could read. "Up four."

I moved forward four diamonds, each one the size of my palm. The black diamond shapes surrounded several flowers made of red and white tiles, with green ones depicting leaves. The entire repetitive pattern was bordered by intertwining strands and Solomon's knots in black, red and white tesserae. It was an elegant, timeless pattern.

"R three," Huon told me.

I turned to my right and stepped across three diamonds. It was like a child's game of hopscotch, only I could use both feet. Huon continued reading the instructions out loud and I followed them until I ended up two diamonds from the back corner.

He lowered the book. "What now?"

I moved off the diamond. "Unfortunately, we have to destroy it."

Gabe crouched to get a better look. "We can remove each tessera carefully then replace them when we're finished."

"Why bother?" Willie asked. "It's old and I reckon the folk who live here won't care."

"It's been here for a very long time, and I won't be the one to damage it." He signaled to Alex. "Have you got a knife on you?"

"Why would he carry a blade?" Huon asked.

"Kidnappings," Alex said as he handed Gabe his automatic knife.

There was no grout between the tesserae that made up that particular diamond although it appeared to be used elsewhere on the mosaic. Gabe was able to pick out each tessera individually and place them off to the side, recreating the same diamond pattern. Once all were up, he brushed aside the sand to reveal the lid of a metal box. From my reading, I knew mosaic floors were laid on a base of concrete. At some point, the concrete beneath that section had been removed, a hole dug out of the earth, and the metal box placed inside, its lid providing a nice hard surface for the tesserae to be relaid on top.

Willie rubbed her hands together. "I've always wanted to find a treasure. What do you reckon's inside? Gold? Silver?"

Gabe opened the box's lid. "Two books."

I gasped and dropped to my knees. "How exciting!"

Willie made a scoffing sound.

We crowded around Gabe as he opened one. It was a ledger, not a book, the sort used for accounting purposes with ruled lines and columns. The pages were blank, although they showed signs of use with some stains that could have been put there by dropped crumbs or spilled tea. The second ledger was the same.

Gabe handed them to me, and I immediately felt the magic warmth of the paper, blended with another magic. I glanced at Huon, leaning over my shoulder. "Can you see anything?"

"There's a list of entries for money coming in and going out," he said. "Some of the magic has faded so I can't read every line."

"Are there any names?" Gabe asked.

"It looks like each entry has a name associated with it, but I can't find one to indicate who the mastermind is."

"Wise," Alex muttered.

"Daniel Barratt knew there was enough evidence in that ledger to prove a crime had been committed," Gabe said. "He wrote the name of the man behind the operation in his message to Oscar, but not in the ledgers."

"Oscar never saw the message," Alex continued with a heavy dose of disappointment in his voice. "And the name has now faded away."

Willie was more philosophical than the two men. "It was a long time ago. The villain has probably been caught in the meantime or died."

"Or he could still be at large," Gabe said. "If the police haven't had enough evidence to convict him in the past, these might provide the evidence they need."

"How? They don't mention the bookmaker's name."

"We can use these to investigate."

"Why bother? I got better things to do than chase ghosts."

"No one is asking you to be involved."

"You should be looking for whoever's behind this." She lightly poked him in the shoulder where he'd been stabbed. "The sooner we find out who wants to kidnap you, the sooner we can stop babysitting you."

"I'm not asking you to follow me around. Besides, I know who's behind it and there's nothing we can do to stop him. He's above the law."

"Then we deal with him without involving the law." She poked him again. "You're as bad as your father, but even he would agree that when it comes to protecting kin, sometimes you got to take the law into your own hands."

They were referring to Mr. Jakes, the Military Intelligence operative who'd made inquiries into Gabe's background, and asked questions about his miraculous wartime survival. Jakes seemed to suspect that mutated magic was behind it. He'd even asked to see books from the Glass Library on the topic. If it was him, Gabe was right. He *was* above the law. It was most likely he had full government permission to perform tests on Gabe with a view to learning the secret to his survival.

In that case, Willie was also right, and Jakes would need to be stopped another way.

Huon tucked the ledgers under his arm. "I'll get to work transcribing these after we settle on a fee."

"You expect us to pay you?" Willie snapped.

"I have expensive vices. My father has cut me off and I have no plans to marry an heiress. Until my business venture is successful, this is all I have."

Gabe offered him a figure and Huon accepted.

Willie shook her head. "It ain't worth it, Gabe. You ain't going to earn a penny from this."

"If it puts Thurlow behind bars, it's worth it."

Alex's gaze met mine.

Gabe returned the empty box to the hole in the ground and smoothed the sand over the top. I crouched down to help him place the tesserae into position to recreate the pattern within the larger mosaic. Once we finished, it looked just as it had when we entered the cellar.

We headed back up the stairs, thanked the pieceworker still seated at the table making boxes, and exited the building. I squinted into the bright morning sunshine. I thought I saw a woman's face at one of the second-floor windows, watching us, but it may have been a trick of the light.

We parted ways with Huon, but instead of returning to the Park Street house or the library, Gabe suggested we call on Cyclops to let him know about our investigation. I readily agreed, as I wanted to speak to him for other reasons.

We found Cyclops in his office at Scotland Yard, tugging on his lower lip in deep thought as he studied a map of London pinned on the wall. He signaled us to approach and look at the map with him. "What do you think of the Westminster Borough?"

"It's full of toffs," Willie said.

"It encompasses my home," Gabe told her.

She lifted a shoulder in an innocent shrug.

"But is it the dullest precinct in the city?" Cyclops asked.

"It might be," Alex told his father. "You could ask for some statistics from the Met. Why do you need to know if it's dull?"

Cyclops did a dreadful job of feigning disinterest. "No matter. It's not important. What are you all doing here?"

I told him about the discovery of the book with the invisible message and map and taking it to Huon to read, which then led us to the Whitechapel residence this morning. "We found what could be evidence to convict someone of criminal activity, although Huon couldn't see who. He'll transcribe the ledgers so we can study them ourselves. If no culprit is named, Gabe and Alex want to investigate and try to tie the evidence to someone."

"Not me," Willie chimed in. "Tell them, Cyclops. It ain't worth anyone's time."

The big man leaned back in his chair, his one-eyed gaze drilling into Gabe and Alex. If I didn't know he was a gentle giant, I'd have expected him to growl his displeasure at having his time wasted. "Why do you think it's worth investigating? The crimes were committed years ago, and the perpetrator is most likely already behind bars or deceased."

"It could be Thurlow," Gabe said simply.

Alex shifted his weight from one foot to the other, but made no comment.

"That's a slim chance, at best," Cyclops said. "But it is a chance, I suppose." He took a pen from the stand and dipped it into the inkpot. "I'll give approval for you to investigate and access to our resources as required." He scribbled a note on a piece of Scotland Yard letterhead as he spoke. "Where will you begin?"

"With Hope," Gabe said.

Cyclops stopped writing without lifting the pen from the page. "What does Lady Coyle have to do with it?"

"Her husband was mentioned in the original letter from Daniel Barratt to Oscar. She may know nothing, or she may have some insights."

Ink bloomed on the paper from the pen nib. Cyclops stared at it a moment, then slowly nodded. "It's worth speaking to her, but I doubt she'll know anything. She knew nothing about her husband's affairs years ago and I'm sure this is no different."

"She *claims* she knew nothing," Willie said. "But I never trusted her. I reckon she knew more than she let on. Matt just never investigated her properly because she was his cousin. He decided to let her live in peace, as long as she never bothered him again."

Alex's gaze slid to Gabe. "Sometimes it's better to leave things alone."

Gabe's jaw firmed, but he didn't look at his friend.

Cyclops returned the pen to the stand. "You should also call on any known associates of Daniel Barratt. Neighbors, friends, family... His wife might still be missing after all these years, but perhaps *her* family can identify his associates from the time."

Willie sucked air between her teeth and let it out in a hiss. "You ain't going to believe it, Cyclops, but she's a Hendry."

Cyclops sat back heavily. His gaze turned distant as he rubbed his jaw. "I suppose that's where Barratt got the magic paper for his invisible ink."

Willie slapped her palms down on the desk and leaned forward. "That's all you got to say?"

"Just because she's a Hendry doesn't mean she's closely related to the Hendry we knew. It doesn't mean she was like him in any way. Don't jump to conclusions, Willie."

"I ain't!" She stabbed a finger into the desk. "But you got to see there could be a link. Daniel said in the book that the fellow who forced him to write invisible messages was an associate of Coyle's. Hendry worked for Coyle. Maybe *he's* the bookmaker."

"He didn't seem the type."

"That's what I thought at first, but then I got to thinking. Maybe he changed. Folk do, especially if they're desperate. I reckon even you'd agree that Hendry became a desperate man at the end."

Cyclops conceded the point with a nod.

"Imagine if this investigation leads us to Hendry," Willie went on. "We could put him behind bars, and close that chapter for Matt and India while they're away."

"Close it for you, you mean. You're the one with a deep hatred of the fellow, decades later."

"He tried to turn me into sliced bacon!"

Cyclops rolled his eye. "Whether the criminal Daniel Barratt refers to in his message is Hendry, Thurlow or someone else, it's worth looking into. Let me know if you need any resources and I'll see what I can do."

Gabe's fingers brushed against mine to get my attention. He nodded at Cyclops. He then ushered Willie and Alex out of the office and closed the door behind them. I heard Willie question him before their footsteps receded.

I cleared my throat. "I wanted to ask you something about Hendry. I've already asked Willie, but I think her answer was somewhat tainted by her experience."

Cyclops huffed a humorless laugh. "Willie does tend to exaggerate, but in this instance, her account was probably accurate. What did you want to know about him?"

"What did he look like?"

"Ah." He rubbed the scar dripping from beneath his eye patch. "You want to know if he looks anything like you?"

"He could be my father."

Cyclops gave no indication whether he agreed or not. Like a policeman giving evidence in court, he simply stated the facts. "He was blond with fair skin and light eyes. He had a slim build."

"Freckles?"

"I can't recall. Sylvia..." He expelled a measured breath. "Your parents don't define who you are. You're in your twenties. You have a career tied to your magic, friends who like and respect you, and a bright future ahead. If your father turns out to be Hendry, it doesn't change any of that, and it shouldn't change how you see yourself."

Despite my best efforts, my lower lip began to tremble. I wanted to thank him for his kindness but didn't trust my voice. He stood and rounded the desk to envelop me in a warm hug.

When I rejoined the others in the busy foyer, it was obvious from Willie's unhappy face that Gabe hadn't given her an explanation as to why I needed to speak to Cyclops. She pressed me as we exited the building.

I decided to admit the truth. "I wanted to ask his opinion on Hendry's appearance."

"I already told you what he looked like. Ugly."

"I wanted to know whether he could be my father."

She stopped in the middle of the pavement to stare at me. "Your father!"

I nodded.

She looked me over from head to toe, assessing me anew. "You're too pretty to be his daughter."

Gabe held open the door to the Unic taxi at the front of the queue of waiting cabs. "Stop flirting with Sylvia and get in. We'll call on Hope now."

"I ain't flirting with Sylvia. She ain't my type."

"Pretty women aren't your type? Don't let Tilda hear you say that, or you might hurt her feelings."

I blinked at Gabe. He thought I was pretty? My mood instantly lifted.

Cyclops was right. The identity of my parents was irrelevant. If it didn't bother my friends, then it wouldn't bother me if my father was Hendry.

But from the way Willie eyed me, with deep distrust, I could see that it rattled her. She wouldn't want me associating with her family out of fear that I would attract Hendry to their door again after all this time.

My mood deflated as quickly as it had risen. When it came to Gabe's safety, Willie and I were on the same page.

CHAPTER 4

$\mathcal{L}$ ast time I'd seen Lady Coyle, her grown son Valentine had not been present. This time, we could hear him through the walls of their flat before we knocked. We could hear them both, shouting at one another. It wasn't clear what the argument was about, but she called him stupid, and he called her a rather crude word that had Willie snickering.

She nudged me with her elbow. "And you thought your family had problems, Sylvia. I reckon you and your brother never called your mother *that*."

Gabe knocked loudly and the shouts instantly ceased.

The lanky redheaded man in his twenties who answered the door must be Valentine. According to Willie, he was most likely the son of Hope's driver, not the late Lord Coyle, although he'd inherited the title upon his birth. She'd also told me he had a list of vices that put Huon to shame, including shirking conscription by claiming an exemption for medical conditions that didn't exist. I preferred to make up my own mind about his character, but the sallow-faced man smelling of alcohol and cigarettes who regarded us with a sneer didn't do himself any favors. When his gaze fell on Alex, standing at Gabe's shoulder, his sneer turned to outright disgust. I decided then and there that Willie hadn't been strong enough in her condemnation.

"Well, well. It's been a while. What brings my favorite cousin to our humble abode?" He had one of those accents that only boys who attended the most exclusive schools seemed to have, all nasally vowels with disdain dripping from every syllable. Gabe hadn't acquired it, even though he must have attended such a school. I suspected the humble nature of his upbringing had something to do with that. There was nothing humble about Valentine.

"Good morning, Val. How have you been?" Gabe's tone wasn't amiable, but at least it was polite.

"Life's just a peach, dear Cousin. I simply adore living with my mother in this quaint little abode. And now you're here, too, so my life is complete."

Gabe simply patted Valentine on the shoulder as he pushed past him. "Glad to hear it. Is your mother in?"

Valentine looked disappointed that Gabe hadn't risen to his sarcasm. "She's not home."

Willie pushed past him, too. "We just heard her. You really are an idiot, Val."

"It's 'my lord' to you."

"You really are an idiot, my lord."

He sniffed. "I remember you. Willie, isn't it? Short for William?"

"Close enough."

His top lip curled even further. "My mother's not receiving callers."

"We're not callers. We're family."

Valentine pointed his cigarette at her. His hand shook. "*You* are not family." He drew on the cigarette then blew smoke into Alex's face as he passed.

Alex stopped. "Be careful where you do that. Do it inside a club and some men might think you're insulting them, and you wouldn't want your evening to end prematurely."

"Why would it?"

Alex looked Valentine over from head to toe, smiled, and walked away.

The glare Valentine gave Alex's back made me shiver. As the last person to enter, I tried to slip past him as unobtrusively as possible. My efforts failed.

He leaned against the doorframe, the hand holding the cigarette near the corner of his mouth as if he were about to plug it back in. His slippery gaze slid over me. "Aren't you a pretty little thing."

I shivered again, wishing I had an offhanded quip to toss back at him, but I couldn't think of a thing to say. I was about to hurry after Gabe when Valentine caught my arm.

He leaned down to whisper in my ear. "Don't get too attached. He's not finished with the last one yet."

"The last one?" I echoed.

"The Hobson girl. Her mother was here recently."

"Why?"

He straightened and shrugged, before taking another drag on his cigarette. "Let me know when he tires of you. I'll show you things that'll loosen that tightly bound hair of yours."

I kept my hands at my sides, but it took effort not to touch my hair, arranged into a bun with my hat perched above it.

Instead of following us into the parlor, Valentine plucked his straw boater off the hallstand and left the flat, slamming the door behind him.

His mother winced but otherwise pretended her son hadn't just insulted all of us, including her. "He's very busy, as I'm sure you understand, Gabriel. An earl has many demands."

I wasn't sure how many demands an earl without an estate had, but I suppose there must be some. Last time, she'd made a point of telling us about his investments, in particular his latest one, an American-based venture that went by the name of its founder, Ponzi. If it was going as well as she'd claimed, then their fortunes were about to turn around.

Hope was clearly not ready for callers, just as Valentine had mentioned. She pretended not to care that we were seeing her without her wig and wearing a dressing gown and slippers, but the self-conscious touching of her short gray hair said otherwise.

Willie couldn't resist checking her wristwatch. "It's almost midday and still in your nightgown."

Hope thrust out her chin, her pride coming to the fore. "I had a late night at the opera with one of my sisters."

"The opera with a sister? Was it Charity? It must be, because Patience doesn't speak to you anymore, so I heard." Willie pulled a face. "Glad to see your life hasn't changed much after you lost everything, despite outward appearances." She indicated the parlor with its threadbare armchairs and simple, inexpensive decorations. The only thing of worth in the room was most likely the portrait of Hope, hanging above the fireplace. The contrast between the young beauty and the frumpy, sad-eyed dowager seated on the faded sofa was stark.

Hope saw me looking at the painting. "I had it commissioned shortly after my husband's death. He'd never got around to it after we married, so I decided to do it myself. How carefree I look, don't you think?"

Gabe cleared his throat. "We came to ask for your help. Lord Coyle's name appeared in a document that was recently discovered in the Glass Library."

Her lips pinched. "I had nothing to do with his business affairs."

Willie plopped down onto a chair without being invited. "Don't pretend with us. We know you ain't as idiotic as your son."

"I beg your pardon!"

Willie waved a hand in dismissal. "We heard you call him an idiot yourself a few minutes ago."

Hope folded her hands on her lap and turned to Gabe. "I always have time for you, Gabriel, but I won't tolerate her insults in my own home."

Gabe didn't have to say anything. Willie simply got up and walked out.

After she heard the front door close, Hope smiled at me. "How lovely to see you again. Miss Ashe, isn't it?"

"Please call me Sylvia."

When she didn't greet Alex, Gabe reintroduced him. "You remember my good friend Alex, Cyclops's son."

"I remember." She turned to Gabe. "I really don't know anything about my late husband's business. He kept that side of things close to his chest."

Alex seemed unconcerned by her snub. He probably expected it, based on their previous encounters. He stood by the door and crossed his arms and let Gabe deal with his father's cousin.

"Does the name Daniel Barratt mean anything to you?" Gabe asked her.

"Wasn't he the journalist who traveled overseas to collect magic books?"

"That's Oscar Barratt. Daniel is a distant cousin of his. He knew a man who was an associate of Lord Coyle. We're trying to discover the identity of that man."

"If he was an associate of my husband's, then this Daniel fellow knew him a long time ago."

Gabe waited.

"I didn't keep my late husband's records or papers after he died. I am sorry."

"Have you heard of a man named Thurlow?"

Hope shook her head. "I'm afraid not."

"Hendry?"

She hesitated before shaking her head.

"Your husband owned a house in Wimbledon that he rented to a young couple who went by the name of Cooper."

"I must stop you there, Gabriel. All of my husband's assets were sold off some time ago, and I don't know any Coopers."

"They vacated the property quickly, perhaps because they were fleeing your husband."

Her gaze lifted to the portrait above the fireplace. The mysterious smile that touched the middle-aged woman's lips matched the younger version of herself. "Then his death would have been a blessing for them."

Gabe thanked her and indicated that I should leave ahead of him. I hesitated, however. Valentine's words still rang in my ears. I had to ask Hope about it, for Gabe's sake. She would probably tell me to mind my own business, but so be it.

"Just now, Valentine—"

"Lord Coyle," she reminded me.

"Lord Coyle mentioned that Mrs. Hobson called on you. How pleasant that you two are friends."

"If you want to know why she was here, just ask, Sylvia. Don't beat about the bush." Hope turned to Gabe who was staring at me. "Mrs. Hobson did visit, as it happens. She wanted to speak to me about you."

"I'm not interested in what she had to say," he said.

"Sylvia clearly is. For her sake, I'll tell you that Mrs. Hobson asked me about the two of you, and whether you were...more than friends."

"I assume you either told her it was none of her business, or you said you don't know, because of course you don't."

"Ah, there's that Steele spirit you inherited from your mother. You're correct on both counts. I found the woman to be rather grasping, actually, with airs above her station. She tried to tell me that her daughter is a better match for you, since she's a magician *and* from a wealthy family, but that's the problem, isn't it?"

Gabe took my elbow to steer me from the room, but I wanted to hear what Hope had to say. I knew, deep down, that I might regret lingering, but I felt compelled to.

"A girl like Ivy Hobson doesn't need rescuing, but you're just like your father. So noble and heroic. You both need someone who needs you."

Alex lowered his arms to his sides, but Gabe quickly shook his head at him, urging him not to rise to her bait. With a grunt, Alex strode out of the parlor.

I, however, couldn't help smiling at Hope. When she finally noticed, she bristled.

"Did I say something amusing?"

"Your honesty is very welcome, Lady Coyle." I looped my arm with Gabe's. "Thank you."

I was glad I'd lingered. Hope may have wanted to remind me that I was not worthy of Gabe, but she'd inadvertently dispelled my concerns that a man as perfect as him must prefer a polished and perfect woman like Ivy. By all accounts, Gabe *was* like his father, and he'd chosen a woman who was nothing like Ivy. What Hope thought of as Lord Rycroft rescuing a woman that society thought was beneath him, was in fact nothing of the sort. It was love. I may not know his father, but I did know Gabe, and I knew he had no interesting in being thought of as a hero. He, too, would choose a companion out of love. Hope, and others like her, would never understand that.

On the landing outside the flat, Willie and Alex stood with their arms crossed, twin scowls on their faces.

"I wouldn't put it past *her* to be the one Daniel referred to in his letter," Willie said as she led the way down the stairs.

"Barratt's letter speaks about a *man* associated with Coyle, not a woman," Alex pointed out. "Besides, I thought your money was on Hendry."

"Maybe they're working together. It wouldn't surprise me." She tossed me a glare over her shoulder when she mentioned Hendry, leaving me in no doubt she now strongly suspected he was my father.

"I don't think Hope's involved," Gabe said. "If she continued her late husband's legacy after he died, she'd be well-off, like he was. She wouldn't be living here, trying to keep up appearances."

"You're forgetting that she has an idiot for a son. I reckon he's capable of squandering her fortune just as easily as he lost his inheritance."

With no clear path forward until we knew what Daniel Barratt had written in the ledgers, we decided to return to the Glass Library. I thought Gabe intended to leave me there and continue home, but he walked me along Crooked Lane and came inside. His two bodyguards followed.

Willie picked up a newspaper from the front desk and fanned herself with it. "We should have gone for ice cream. There's a new shop in Kensington that's owned by a confectionary magician. It's expensive, but their flavors are worth it." She clapped Gabe on the back. "Besides, you owe me and Alex for protecting you."

Gabe gave her a lopsided smile. "I'll buy you an ice cream when we leave here. Sylvia, you should come."

"I should work," I countered.

Willie agreed. "The professor needs her."

Gabe opened his mouth to say something, but the professor strolled in from the main part of the library. "Hello, everyone. Did I hear my name?"

"I was just saying you need Sylvia in the library, ain't that right, Prof? Some folk seem to forget she works here."

He pushed his glasses up his nose. "The heat has kept most of the patrons away, so there's just some cataloging of old books to do. They've waited years, and can wait a little longer." He smiled at me. "How is the investigation into Oscar's cousin's message coming along?"

"We found some evidence that points to the illegal activity he was involved in," I said. "But we won't know more until Huon transcribes the invisible writing for us."

"I'm so pleased you've given Huon this opportunity. He needed something to do, something worthwhile and engaging. It was a shame to see him wasting away in that house, miserable and alone. Perhaps this will give him a purpose, something to build a new foundation upon."

Willie snorted. "There ain't nothing wrong with having no purpose. I've made it my lifelong ambition."

The professor patted her shoulder. "And you've done a thoroughly excellent job of it, Willie."

She beamed.

"Oh, I almost forgot," Professor Nash went on. "Lady Stanhope came here looking for you, Gabriel. She asked me to tell you to call on her at your earliest convenience, as long as your earliest convenience is today."

Gabe thanked him and asked to use the telephone to call her to see if she was home.

Willie blocked his path to the desk. "We ain't going to see her. I've had enough of snobby old ladies for one day."

"Lady Coyle and Lady Stanhope are the same age as you."

"Age is an attitude."

Alex chuckled. "So that would make you a fourteen-year-old brat."

She crossed her arms over her chest. "I ain't calling on Lady Stanhope today. I want ice cream."

"You don't have to do anything," Gabe told her. "I'm capable of taking care of myself." This last part he said for Alex's benefit, too. "Why don't you both go home while I take Sylvia out for ice cream."

He might as well have asked them to shoot him. Their protests were loud and long. Gabe, however, didn't give up that easily. Instead, he compromised. "You can walk a few paces behind. Near enough in case someone should try to harm me, far enough for privacy."

"All right," Alex said at the same time Willie said, "No!" with such vehemence that we all stared at her.

"Why?" Gabe asked.

I suspected her reason had more to do with not wanting

Gabe to be alone with me than his safety, but she didn't get a chance to answer. My friend Daisy arrived, a stack of magazines in her arms. She opened her mouth to greet us, but the moment her gaze fell on Alex, she closed it again. She blushed.

He smiled at her. "Hello, Daisy."

She tucked a strand of hair behind her ear. "Hello. Everyone," she added as an afterthought. "You all look *so* well."

"As do you. Very, *very* well."

The last time I'd seen Alex and Daisy together had been at the Buttonhole club a few nights ago. They'd hardly spoken, but had stolen glances at each other across the dance floor. Their usual frostiness had melted away after the Bailey family picnic, where he'd given her his paper boat to race on the lake. Despite their obvious interest in each other, neither had taken the first step. Although they were both accomplished flirts and good conversationalists, I'd begun to suspect they didn't know how to move forward with someone they wanted a relationship with. Their previous entanglements had been casual. This one had potential to be more.

"Did you ride your bicycle here?" Alex finally asked. "It's too hot to be exercising."

"I caught an omnibus, which wasn't much better. The man next to me perspired like a leaking tap."

The old Alex would have pointed out that taps didn't perspire, but the new Alex sympathized with her.

"We were all about to head out for ice cream," Gabe said. "Do you want to come?"

Daisy brightened. "That would be lovely."

"Are those all *Les Modes*?" I asked her.

She looked down at the stack of French fashion magazines in her arm. "I'm studying these for my new career venture. I'm going to be England's answer to Coco Chanel."

"Who?" Willie asked.

"Coco Chanel, the French *couturière* who's gaining quite a

reputation for her clothes and hats. Her outfits are the bee's knees. I thought I'd try my hand at designing, too."

"Are you skilled at sewing?"

"Not particularly. Do you think I need to be?"

"Probably."

Daisy's face fell.

"You're very fashionable," Alex said quickly. "You've got an excellent eye for fabrics and colors, and your taste is modern. That outfit, for example, is very fetching on you. I doubt Coco Chanel could look as stylish."

She stood a little straighter and self-consciously touched the tangerine toque on her head. It was a bold color that few women would be brave enough to wear, but it contrasted nicely with the narrow cerulean blue skirt and matching blouse. A belt in the same tangerine as the hat showed off Daisy's slim waist.

Alex smiled at her, pleased by the effect his words had on her. I'd never seen him smile as much as he had these last few weeks when he was in Daisy's company. If anyone needed confirmation that these two were right for one another, they just had to look at the change in him. The somber man I'd met in March rarely made an appearance anymore.

The telephone rang and, feeling guilty for not working much lately, I picked up the receiver before the professor could reach it. I heard the click as the operator connected me to the caller. It was Huon.

"Have you transcribed the ledgers already?" I asked.

"I've hardly begun, but I wanted to tell you about an idea I had. You see, my father didn't know much about Daniel's life, and knew almost nothing about his wife except that she was a Hendry. She and the children could have reappeared for all he knew. He refused to follow up with relatives," Huon added bitterly. "So, I took it upon myself to telephone gossipy aunts. I discovered that she *hasn't* reappeared. I also learned where Daniel Barratt lived at the time of his death."

"Was it the Whitechapel house?"

"The Smithfield area." He rattled off an address that I committed to memory. "That's not all I discovered." The usually nonchalant, indolent man sounded excited. "I learned that his neighbors were his wife's family, and they still live there."

I sat heavily on the chair behind the desk. My gaze sought out Gabe, who was watching me with a concerned frown.

Huon's voice boomed down the line. "Sylvia? Are you still there?"

"I am."

"You should visit them and find out what they know about Daniel's wife and children."

"Yes," I murmured. "Yes, I should."

He gave me the address for Daniel's two sisters-in-law.

"What did he say?" Gabe asked after I hung up the receiver.

"He found out that Daniel used to live in Smithfield. Apparently, his wife's sisters lived next door."

"The other Hendry—Melville—also used to live in Smithfield before his disappearance. Perhaps he was closely related to these Hendrys, after all."

"Huon suggested we speak to them."

Gabe sat on the edge of the desk near me. His green eyes softened. "Is that what *you* want to do?"

I gave an emphatic nod. I wanted to meet them. I wanted to see for myself if there was any physical resemblance to me. I wanted to know once and for all whether they were closely related to my father.

My family.

CHAPTER 5

*A*ccording to Gabe's parents' notes on Melville Hendry, when they first met him, he lived alone above his stationery shop in Smithfield. He made paper using traditional methods in the adjoining workshop. It was there that he secretly used the strengthening spell on some batches for special clients, and that's probably how he became entangled with Lord Coyle. Coyle was known to exploit magicians by threatening to expose them if they didn't do as he commanded. Gabe assumed Coyle demanded Hendry work for him and use his flying paper as a weapon.

I wasn't convinced. A circus performer could throw a knife with accuracy and death would be instant, and of course guns were easy to come by. Why did Coyle need a paper magician to wield paper? It was an inaccurate, slow and cumbersome method to kill or control someone.

We passed Hendry's former shop but did not go in. It was occupied by a tobacconist and newsagent now. Willie slowed down. I thought she was reading the newspaper headlines on display outside the shop, but her thoughts turned out to be on the pipes and boxed cigars in the window. "I need to smoke something," she said with a deep sigh.

"You can't relapse," Gabe told her. "If you do then I might, too."

"Why have we given up anyway? It ain't causing anyone harm."

"You know why."

She grunted. "Because India doesn't like the smell and we live in her house. Maybe I'll move out again."

"Hallelujah," Alex said. "How quickly can this miracle occur?"

She shot him a withering glare.

The address Huon had given us for Daniel Barratt was a few blocks from the market. Positioned near the middle of the long street of row houses, it was typical of the area. Whereas Whitechapel's residents lived a more desperate existence, finding work where they could, Smithfield was a more eclectic area, made up a large market, a hospital and a great many shops. Residents were shopkeepers and clerks. Their homes were still modest but larger than those in poorer parts of the city. They didn't have to rent out spare rooms unless they found themselves in reduced circumstances.

We didn't knock on the door where Daniel Barratt had once lived. Instead, we knocked on the neighbors'.

I was surprised when a man answered, given it was a weekday and most men were out working. He was aged in his sixties, and his prominent nose was made more hawkish by his bald head and otherwise plain features. It wasn't until Gabe put out his hand for the man to shake that I noticed his right hand was missing and he shook with his left. Perhaps that was why he couldn't work.

"My name is Gabriel Glass," Gabe said. "These are my friends, Miss Sylvia Ashe, Alex Bailey and Willie Johnson. Are you married to one of the Hendry sisters?"

"That's right. Fred Laidlow. I'm married to the eldest, Myrtle. Are you acquainted with my wife, or Naomi?" At Gabe's blank look, he added, "Myrtle's younger sister. She lives with us."

"Our business is with both of them. May we come in? It's about their other sister."

Fred's eyes widened. "Please do. The girls are in the kitchen."

'The girls', as he called them, were also aged in their sixties. Both stood at the central kitchen table, preparing dinner in silence. One shelled peas while the other peeled potatoes. A large pot sat on the stove. The heat from the stove made the room stifling.

Both looked up upon our entry and gave us welcoming but questioning smiles.

Fred made the introductions, having no difficulty remembering our names. "They want to talk to you about Rosina."

The one shelling peas gasped, while the other dropped the peeler. It clattered onto the edge of the table then fell to the floor.

"Your shock is understandable," Gabe said. "Hearing her name after all this time must be difficult."

"Have you found her?" asked the one who'd been shelling peas.

If I had to guess, I'd say she was the elder of the two, although both women looked well for their age, with trim figures and only a few lines fanning their eyes and shallow ones scoring their foreheads. Their fair hair blended naturally with the light gray, which both had arranged in loose pompadour styles popular a decade ago. Both had light freckles dusting their noses.

I couldn't stop staring at them. Fortunately, neither noticed. They were both intent on Gabe.

"I'm afraid not," he said. "I gather from your reactions that she and her children never returned?" They shook their heads. "We work for Scotland Yard as consultants and have some questions for you about Rosina and Daniel. Is there somewhere we can talk?"

"The sitting room," Fred said, leading the way.

The two sisters glanced at one another then followed us. The sitting room was crowded, but we all managed to find somewhere to sit, although the two women and Fred had to squash together on the sofa. Beside them, on the table, was a collection of photographs. I itched to take a closer look.

They introduced themselves, and the one shelling peas did turn out to be the eldest, Myrtle, married to Fred. When the one peeling potatoes introduced herself as Naomi Hendry, I realized she was a spinster.

It was Myrtle who peppered us with questions. "I don't understand. What's changed? Why are you asking questions about Rosina now?"

Gabe invited me to explain.

Both women looked properly at me for the first time. If they saw a resemblance to their younger selves, they gave no indication. "I'm a librarian at the Glass Library. Do you know it?"

"Of course," Myrtle said.

"I came across a book with invisible writing in it."

Fred scoffed. "Invisible writing?"

"It can be created when either a graphite or ink magician merges their magic with a paper magician's. In the case of this book, it was ink magic."

Fred looked to his wife, seated beside him. She stared stoically back at me. None of them confirmed or denied whether they knew an ink or paper magician. These days, there was no reason for secrecy. At least, there shouldn't be.

I cleared my throat. "It so happened that the ink magician who read the writing for me was related to the intended recipient of the invisible message, Oscar Barratt. The message was written by Daniel, his distant cousin. Oscar never saw it and has since died."

"Why did our brother-in-law write a message in invisible ink?" Naomi asked.

"Daniel was asking Oscar to help him. Daniel states that he was working for a man who was involved in criminal activity. The man threatened Daniel, so he hid his wife and children to keep them safe."

Naomi pressed a hand to her throat and her face paled.

Myrtle showed no surprise. "I always knew their disappearance was his fault."

"Seems he tried to protect them," Fred pointed out.

"Perhaps he couldn't save them after all."

"He wouldn't have intentionally put them in harm's way. He was a doting husband and father."

"He was a fool. Good riddance."

"Myrtle!" Naomi cried.

Some of the stiffness left Myrtle's shoulders. "Sorry." To us, she said, "It was a difficult time, and you coming here today has brought it all back. If you don't have any news about our sister's whereabouts, then why did you come?"

I hesitated. Her hostility unnerved me.

Gabe took over, his voice smooth and reassuring. "A few reasons, but firstly, we wanted you to know that the message from Daniel suggests he didn't die from natural causes. He may have been murdered."

Naomi gave another gasp.

"Good lord," Fred murmured. "Who by?"

"We don't know. The invisible ink magic has faded, and the name isn't legible."

"To think he was meeting someone dangerous right next door, under our noses," Fred said. "I never suspected. Did either of you?"

Both women shook their heads. "Rosina never mentioned what Daniel was up to," Naomi said. "What they were both up to. *She* was most likely the paper magician who helped Daniel create the invisible writing. Did you know she was a paper magician?"

"Of course they did," Myrtle told her. "Anyway, that doesn't mean Rosina was involved. Daniel could have got hold of her paper without her knowledge."

"Whether she knew or did not know is irrelevant now," Fred said. "But all of this talk about criminal activity does explain where the money came from in those months before Daniel died." At our blank looks, he added, "Daniel was quite flush. More than a clerk ought to have been."

"He didn't follow a trade closely associated with his ink magic?" I asked.

"Clerks use ink," Willie offered.

"Who did he work for?" Alex asked.

"Harrods, in the finance department," Fred said. "Up until nine or ten months before his death."

"Why did he leave?" Gabe asked.

"He wouldn't say," Myrtle said tightly. "Which probably means he was dismissed. Typical. He was a pathetic man, quite hopeless. I knew he was no good for Rosina. Our parents should never have let her marry him, but the silly girl insisted. She said she fell in love." Myrtle rolled her eyes.

Naomi placed a hand over her sister's, quietening her.

Fred looked a little embarrassed at his wife's outburst. He apologized on her behalf, but Myrtle's jaw firmed. She looked like she wanted to scold him, but she remained silent. Her sister's knuckles turned white as she held onto Myrtle's hand.

Naomi's soft voice was in stark contrast to her older sister's. "What else did the invisible message from Daniel say?"

It would have been the right time to tell them it led us to the house in Whitechapel, but Gabe hadn't wanted anyone to mention it until we knew what the contents of the ledgers contained.

"Daniel said the man he worked for was an associate of Lord Coyle." I watched them carefully for any signs of recognition. There were none.

"Did it mention something he'd hidden?" Fred asked.

"No," Gabe lied. "Why?"

The two sisters exchanged glances, but it was Fred who answered. "Someone went through their house on the night Daniel died. We found their belongings strewn all over the place the next day, drawers emptied, floorboards pulled up...it was a mess. It seemed as though the intruder was searching for something. We don't know if they found it, or whether it's still missing."

The intruder must have been looking for the ledgers, but Gabe still did not tell them we had them in our possession. "Tell us about Rosina's disappearance and the time leading up to it," he said.

Naomi's fingers curled into her apron at her lap. "It's all a blur now."

Fred rubbed the stump where his hand ought to be and looked to his wife.

Only Myrtle met Gabe's gaze. "They were happy for a while after Daniel lost his position at Harrods. As Fred said, Daniel was quite flush with money. He showered Rosina with gifts— clothing, jewelry. She thought he was wonderful. Then everything changed suddenly around February '91. They became reclusive. They stayed indoors and kept the children home. We hardly saw our sister. She stopped calling on us every day like she used to. Daniel told us she'd gone on a holiday with the children. We didn't believe him. She'd never leave without telling us."

"I assumed she'd left him," Fred added.

"She would have told us," Naomi said, her tone gently chiding.

"Did you challenge Daniel?" Gabe asked.

Myrtle sighed. "I tried. He closed the door in my face."

Gabe fell silent. Although he didn't look at me, I got the distinct impression he wanted me to ask them about Melville Hendry. I suddenly felt restless. I could no longer sit still. I stood and picked up a framed photograph from the collection on the side table. It showed three smiling young women in their late teens. While none looked exactly like me, I could see small resemblances in each—the straight nose, the freckles, and shape of the mouth.

"That's Rosina in the middle," Naomi said wistfully. "She was always in the middle, with Myrtle first and me third."

"Did you two inherit paper magic, too?" I asked.

"No. Only the others did."

I almost dropped the photograph. "You have more siblings? A brother, perhaps?"

Naomi bit her lower lip.

It was Myrtle who responded. "She meant to say that Rosina was the only one of the three of us who inherited magic from our father."

It didn't quite answer my question. "Is the name Melville Hendry familiar to you?"

"What does he have to do with Rosina's disappearance?"

"Perhaps nothing, but—"

"Then why bring him up?"

Her renewed hostility unnerved me. I fell silent.

Gabe answered for me. "He was a known associate of Coyle's and is still wanted by the police. He also went missing in 1891, the same year Daniel died."

Both Fred and Naomi looked to Myrtle. She was clearly the leader of the trio, and certainly the stronger of the two sisters. She gave nothing away, however. Her face remained closed, unreadable.

"If you've got no more questions about Daniel and Rosina, then it's time for you to leave," she said. "We're very busy."

Willie snorted. "No, you ain't. Now see here. You're probably ashamed of him. I would be, too, and I'm related to a lot of outlaws. But the thing is, we know he lived and worked not far from here. We know he was a strong paper magician, like Rosina. He even looked like both of you."

Naomi glanced at her sister.

"So there ain't no point denying it. Tell us how he's related to you." When all three kept their mouths shut, Willie said, "Do you know he tried to kill me?"

Naomi covered her mouth with her hand.

Myrtle glared back at Willie. "You're not with Scotland Yard, are you?"

Willie bristled. "I'm a consultant, too."

"The Yard only employs women as WPCs, not detectives or consultants. They're not that enlightened."

If there's one way to Willie's heart, it's to agree with her that women ought to be given the same employment opportunities as men. Her rising temper instantly dampened, and she gave a grunt in response. It was the closest thing to admiration she was capable of giving.

Myrtle stood. "Fred will see you out. Come along, Naomi. We have to get the stew on the stove."

I worried that Willie would tell them we suspected I might be Melville's daughter, but she kept quiet. Perhaps she realized it would do us no favors in our investigation, when they were so determined to cut him off from the family tree. Telling them I could be the daughter of the black sheep of the family could make them even less inclined to help us.

Besides, we weren't sure. I needed to be absolutely positive before I admitted it to anyone. He wasn't someone I wanted in my family tree either.

I returned the photograph to the table and thanked the sisters for their time. As I followed Fred out of the sitting room, a long-stemmed pink rose in a vase on the hall table caught my eye. I felt compelled to stroke its soft petals, and that's when I realized it was made of thick paper, folded into the complex shape of a blooming rose, complete with green leaves and a stem, all made with paper.

Myrtle snatched it away. "Don't touch that. It's delicate."

It wasn't. It was tougher than it looked, because it held paper magic. *Strong* magic that made the petal warm to touch. I didn't tell her that I could feel it, but she seemed to suspect, going by the way she watched me closely.

"It's origami," Naomi said, a note of pride in her voice. "It's a Japanese art form."

"Your sister, Rosina, made it?" Alex asked.

"We don't remember where we got it," Myrtle said. "We've had it for years."

The two women returned to the kitchen while Fred saw us out. He stepped outside and closed the front door behind him. "I hope my wife didn't upset you," he said to Willie.

"It takes a lot to upset me."

Alex smiled to himself, but didn't point out that she could be as unpredictable as a volcano.

Fred glanced behind him at the closed door. None of us moved or spoke. Sometimes, the best way to get someone to talk is to say nothing. Most people loathed silence and felt the need to fill it. Fred was no exception.

"Melville was their brother."

Willie swore softly.

"Why didn't they just tell us?" Alex asked.

"They're good girls, with good hearts. They're very charitable, always cooking and baking for the poor. Melville's actions upset them deeply. They were never close to him, but after he was accused of murder and being involved with Coyle, they distanced themselves even further from him. His disappearance was a blessing, even though it happened around the same time their sister left, and Daniel died. It meant they could pretend he never existed."

"So you do know of Lord Coyle?" Gabe asked.

Fred realized his mistake. "Ah, yes. Sorry. We're all trying to forget those days, so nobody wanted to admit it. I've heard the name only in connection to Melville. A lord, was he? I wonder why he chose Melville to do his dirty work."

"He was a strong paper magician," Willie pointed out.

"Well, yes. Very strong, as it happens. The girls were so frustrated that he inherited their father's strength, while the two of them got nothing. Only Rosina was a magician, but her magic was quite weak."

If her magic was weak, then she couldn't have made that

paper rose decades ago before her disappearance. The magic wouldn't have lasted all this time. So, who had made it? And why?

"Myrtle was so frustrated with Melville, even before the business that led to his disappearance," Fred went on.

"Frustrated?" Gabe asked.

"He had so much talent, so much magical strength, yet he squandered it. He never bothered to expand his business beyond his little workshop and handful of clients. She thought it was a waste."

"Magicians were persecuted back then. He might have drawn unwanted attention to himself if he'd manufactured paper on a larger scale."

"Not if he was careful. Others did it. The Petersons, for example. Melville could have been rich by now. If Myrtle was the magician, she would have found a way to have her cake and eat it too, even then." He sounded as frustrated by what he saw as an injustice of birth as Myrtle. "The three girls never really got along with their brother, even as children. He was always different."

"You mean evil," Willie spat.

Fred scratched his bald head. "I don't know about that." He removed a pocket watch from his waistcoat and flipped the case open with his thumb. "If you'll excuse me, I have to get to a meeting." He opened the door and slipped back inside.

As our motorcar pulled away from the curb, we saw him leave the house with a newspaper under his arm.

"Blimey," Willie said, sounding more British than American. "What do you make of all that?"

"I understand why the sisters lied about Melville being their brother," Alex said as he checked over his shoulder before merging the Vauxhall Prince Henry into traffic. "They're ashamed of his criminal past."

Willie turned to Gabe and me, seated in the back. "Do you reckon that's all they lied about? Do you reckon they knew more about Daniel and Rosina's criminal activity than they let on?"

Gabe shrugged. "I'm not sure." He gave me a flat smile. "It's a shame they were so hostile about Melville. It was probably wise not to say anything about your magic or a possible connection to him."

Willie sucked air between her teeth as she glared at me.

Gabe cleared his throat and she glanced at him before facing the front again.

"They lied," I told them. "That paper rose was very warm. If it was made a long time ago, as they claimed, then it must have been made by a powerful magician for the magic to last. Fred said Rosina's magic was weak."

"Melville?" Gabe suggested.

"Why keep a piece of art from a brother they didn't like?"

"Or the magic was put in more recently," Alex suggested from the driver's seat. "That would explain why it still felt warm to you."

"They're hiding something. Is it the fact they are actually paper magicians themselves? If so, why lie?"

CHAPTER 6

*W*illie stood in front of the electric fan in the library's ground floor reading nook, her waistcoat open and neckerchief dangling from her fingers. She leaned in so close that I worried the loose strands of her hair might get caught in the spinning blades. "Anyone else feel like they have a furnace inside them?"

When the professor arrived carrying a jug of lemonade and glasses half-filled with ice, she pounced on him. She picked up one of the glasses before he'd had a chance to put down the tray and scooped out chunks of ice. She pressed them to the back of her neck with a contented sigh.

"I've missed this," she said. "We haven't had ice for days. Mrs. Ling didn't order enough this week."

"Ha!" Alex barked. "It would have been enough, but *you* used it all up within three days of delivery. Now everything in the icebox is going off."

"She should know I need it and order more."

"Didn't you come from a hot climate in America?" Professor Nash asked. "Aren't you used to it?"

"Years ago," Alex said. "Many, *many* years ago. She's more used to the English weather now."

Willie made a face at him. "No, I ain't! This place is still foreign to me."

The professor pushed his glasses up his nose. "Haven't you lived here longer than you've lived there?"

"That ain't the point. America is in my blood."

"But England is under your skin," Alex added.

Willie scooped out more ice from the glass and threw it at him. He ducked and it clinked against the bookshelves. Fortunately, Willie wasn't going to waste a single piece of ice and retrieved them all before they melted.

Gabe rolled his eyes. "I wish I could say this isn't my circus, but I seem to have inherited it."

I laughed. "Imagine how dull life would be if she'd returned to America with your parents."

"You mean peaceful. And I imagine it every day." To prove he was merely joking, he flashed me one of his charming smiles, the sort that melted my insides and heated my cheeks. "Come with me upstairs to—"

A block of ice hit him on the side of the face. Willie didn't even bother trying to pretend she hadn't thrown it. "Now that I got your attention, tell us what you think about the investigation so far."

"I think Thurlow is the man Daniel Barratt refers to in his message to Oscar," Gabe said.

Alex disagreed. "There isn't anything implicating Thurlow."

"It implicates Hendry," Willie said. "Or Hope. Or both."

"It doesn't implicate anyone yet," Alex pointed out. "We don't have the evidence and won't until Huon finishes transcribing the ledgers."

Willie narrowed her gaze at me. "It'll be Hendry. I'll bet everything I own on it."

Alex picked up the melting block of ice from the floor and tossed it back at her. She tugged the front of her shirt away from her body and caught the ice in it. She looked pleased with herself.

"Speaking of betting," Gabe said. "We should visit Thurlow at the races tomorrow."

"Not until we have evidence," Alex said. "You know we can't confront him yet, Gabe."

Gabe crossed his arms over his chest and glared at his friend.

"Alex is right," I said. "We can't confront Thurlow until we have something solid to pin on him."

Gabe's thumb started to tap on his bicep. I placed my hand over it to still it. His muscle twitched before relaxing. He lowered his arms, but caught my hand as he did so. He gave me a small, reassuring smile and a nod.

Willie scooped out more ice from her glass.

Gabe quickly released me. "Don't throw that," he growled at her.

She returned the ice to the glass and poured lemonade into it.

From the reading nook, we could hear the front door open and close but not see who entered. Professor Nash started in the direction of the foyer to greet the patron, only to stop as Lady Stanhope appeared. She paused at the entrance to the library proper. I suspected she was pausing for dramatic effect, not to gauge our mood before entering. The columns flanking the entrance framed her like a piece of art. She was more of a gothic statue than a classic one in her black dress made from stiff satin that clung to her luscious curves. She must be hot, but she showed no sign of it as she swanned towards us, a smile on her lips.

The smile was unnaturally stiff, but that was quite normal for Lady Stanhope. I doubted smiles came easily to her. I'd only ever seen her bestow them on Gabe, and this time was no exception.

She held out her hands to him. "My dear boy."

Obliged to take them, he leaned down for her to kiss his cheek. "Lady Stanhope. What a pleasure to see you."

Willie made a scoffing sound.

The professor greeted her ladyship, and she gave a nod in return, which she then bestowed on me and finally on Alex and Willie. It was one of the few times she'd acknowledged them.

"To what do we owe this surprise?" Gabe asked, releasing himself from her grip.

She sat on the sofa and plucked off her lace gloves by the fingertips. "Is that lemonade and ice?"

Professor Nash hurriedly poured her a glass then gave his excuses and left.

Lady Stanhope sipped then lowered the glass to her lap. "I've heard rumors about you, Gabriel."

"And you want to know if they're true?" he suggested.

"I know they're true. I've come to warn you. Mrs. Hobson is calling on various members of society, asking questions about you."

Her attempt at drama fell flat. Nobody showed surprise. We were already aware of Ivy's mother's visit to Hope, Lady Coyle.

"She has been asking questions about your relationship with Sylvia Ashe." Lady Stanhope didn't look at me when she said it. If I didn't know better, I'd have thought she'd forgotten I was the Sylvia Ashe in question.

A light blush touched Gabe's cheeks. "I, uh…"

"There is nothing between Gabe and me," I told her. "We're friends."

The last thing I wanted was for her, and others, to think that Gabe ended his relationship with Ivy because of me. He'd told me he'd ended it because they weren't right for each other, that he should never have rushed into it in the first place. I believed him. It would be a gross injustice to label him a philanderer.

Willie sat forward, intent. "Are folk saying they're more than friends?"

"Nobody knew the reason Gabriel and Ivy's relationship ended, and since Sylvia was unknown in society, her name wasn't bandied about as the cause."

I never thought I'd feel relieved to be of no consequence.

"Until now, that is. Before Mrs. Hobson's visits, Sylvia was nobody. Now, everyone is talking about her, linking her name to yours, Gabriel."

"So?" Gabe prompted.

She looked at him as though he were mad. "You need to stop it, of course."

"Let them think what they want. I don't care. You shouldn't either."

"My dear boy, consider what it means. Because of Mrs. Hobson's meddling, everyone now thinks *you* ended your relationship with Ivy, not the other way around, and for another woman, too. It puts you in a bad light."

"I don't care."

"You should. Nobody likes a gentleman who ends a relationship with a perfectly acceptable heiress to take up with...another girl." Still Lady Stanhope didn't look at me. "Particularly a girl whose origins are...unclear."

Gabe shot to his feet. "You should leave."

"I'm simply stating a fact and facts aren't insults." She swept her hand across her lap as if to flick dust off her skirt. "From what my friends have told me, Mrs. Hobson is telling everyone that Sylvia is not from anywhere in particular and the identities of her parents are shrouded in mystery."

"My mother was Alice Ashe," I said stiffly.

"There is no record of her birth, and your father could have been the local butcher for all anyone knows."

"That's enough," Gabe growled. "This is no one's business but Sylvia's."

Lady Stanhope stood. "Don't get upset with *me*. I'm simply the messenger. I'll do what I can to quell the rumors, of course, but you must be sure not to fan them either."

"Meaning?" Gabe bit off.

"You ought to stay away from the library."

Willie's grunt was one of agreement this time.

Lady Stanhope grasped Gabe's forearm. "You upset Mrs. Hobson when you broke off your engagement to Ivy, and you angered her when you wouldn't defend the family against the allegations of magical negligence made in the newspapers." Her thumb caressed his sleeve. "I'm concerned for you, dear boy."

Gabe didn't extricate himself from her grip, but instead clamped his hand over hers, trapping it. He then steered her towards the exit. "Don't worry about me. Apparently, I'm invincible."

"Don't be flippant. This is serious. Mrs. Hobson isn't someone you want to continue to anger."

"What could she possibly do to harm me? She has no power over me."

They disappeared from view as Gabe saw her to the front door. I sat down on the sofa and tried not to let her visit upset me. But it had. Gabe's reputation was being sullied because of me. He might not care what others thought of him, but some people did.

One who cared most sat beside me. Willie studied her finger-nails. "Is that Daisy's voice I hear?"

Falling for her diversionary tactic, Alex strode towards the foyer.

Willie leaned back into the corner of the sofa and rested her elbows on the sofa arm behind her. Her gaze settled on me. "You heard what she said, Sylvia."

"I did. And I know what you're going to say."

"Is that so?"

"You're going to tell me to stay away from him. That if I cared for him, I'd put some distance between us."

"So, will you?"

"Gabe says he doesn't care about his reputation."

"He doesn't. Nor do his parents. But Matt and India don't yet know that you could be the daughter of Melville Hendry, a man who tried to kill her. Matt's protective of his wife. He doesn't want that man anywhere near her again. But if Hendry's still alive, and he finds out his daughter is in London, he might come looking for you. And if he sees you with Gabe…"

"He may not be my father."

My weak response fell on deaf ears. "Hasn't Gabe got enough on his plate with the stabbing and the kidnappings? Do you really want to add more danger to his life? Ain't he been through enough these past years?"

Despite the heat, I suddenly felt very cold.

"You can step away from Gabe now before either of you develops deep feelings. Do it before it gets too hard, and no one will be hurt." She glanced at the entry to the foyer where Gabe and Alex could be heard having a discussion. She leaned towards me and lowered her voice. "It's for the best, Sylvia. I can see in your eyes that you know it."

The men reemerged from the foyer. "There's nothing between Gabe and me," I whispered.

"Keep it that way."

If only it were as easy as she made it sound.

* * *

DAISY CONVINCED me that dancing at the Buttonhole club would take my mind off the events of the past few days. It did not. Gabe was there with Alex and Willie. Either Daisy had assumed Alex would be there or Alex had told her. Either way, she didn't look surprised to see them. Gabe was surprised to see us, however. He looked pleased. Willie just looked cross.

For much of the evening, she stuck to Gabe's side. When we danced to the ragtime band's music, she joined us, even though she loathed dancing. When he ordered drinks, she insisted he buy her one, too. While his back was turned, she pulled me aside.

"You promised you and he weren't..." She made a rude hand gesture that left nothing to the imagination.

"We aren't," I hissed. "And I made no such promise. As I recall, you insisted."

"I don't like doing this, but it's necessary. You know it,

Sylvia. We both want him to be safe, so you have to stay away to keep Hendry away."

Gabe returned with a drink in each hand. He peered over our heads, frowning. "Willie, did you know Nurse Tilda is here?"

Willie whipped around, searching the sea of faces. "Where? I can't see her."

"That's because you're too short. She's near the door. She must be looking for you."

"She told me she doesn't like dance clubs. Too noisy."

"Then she must *really* want to see you tonight."

Willie took her drink then forged a path through the crowd towards the door.

Gabe grabbed my hand and led me in the opposite direction to the back of the club. We took the place of a couple who vacated a booth to dance, both of us occupying the same bench seat. We sat close, mere inches separating us.

"Is Nurse Tilda even here?" I asked.

He flashed a grin. "It was the only thing guaranteed to draw Willie away."

"She must like Tilda very much."

"She does." His smile faded. "I know she's worried about your possible connection to Hendry, but the point is moot. He has probably fled the country or passed away. If he *is* alive, then he can't know about you yet."

The key word in that sentence was 'yet', but I nodded. He was right. Whether or not Hendry was my father, it was most likely he'd died or moved away, considering no one in Gabe's circle had heard of him for a long time.

And yet... Willie was right, too. If Hendry was alive and if he found me, what would he do? If there was a slim chance that he would cause Gabe trouble, I didn't want to be the catalyst. I would never forgive myself.

And yet...staying away from Gabe would be one of the most difficult things I'd ever had to do. Especially when he looked at me as he did now, like I was the only thing in the world that mattered. The frenzied music and throbbing crowd on the dance floor may as well have not been there. It was just us. Just those sea-green eyes of his, the soft lips that invited me to kiss them, and my erratically pounding heart.

In the end, I didn't have to make a decision. *He* kissed *me*.

I kissed him back. I couldn't help it. All of my doubts were drowned out by the beat in my head, drumming out the same message, over and over: *This man, this man, this man.*

There was nothing tentative in our kiss, no hesitation, no testing of feelings. It was full of absolute certainty, from both of us.

Until Gabe tore himself away.

It took me a moment of wading through the fog of my desire to realize *he* hadn't ended the kiss. Willie had grabbed the back of his jacket and forced us apart.

He shot to his feet, towering over her, his fists clenched at his sides, and for one dreadful moment I wasn't sure what he'd do. Then he shook his head at her. He said something I couldn't hear over the music.

She swallowed heavily but did not back down. She crossed her arms and turned her glare onto me.

Alex appeared behind her. He spoke and Willie answered. His gaze shifted from Gabe to me. I saw the same worry in it that I'd seen in Willie's, although his wasn't accompanied by anger. He shrugged, part apology, part appeal to me to do what Gabe wouldn't.

Finally, my own thoughts broke through the clearing fog. I slid across the seat and stood. As I passed Gabe, he caught my hand. I shook my head at him. I couldn't trust my voice to speak.

I almost changed my mind when his face fell. But I summoned as much courage as I could and slipped my hand free. The confusion in his gaze turned to vulnerability.

"No," he said, in a throaty voice unlike his own. "Don't, Sylvia."

Despite the bone-deep ache in my chest, I walked away.

CHAPTER 7

D aisy must have been worried about me because she arrived at the library at the same time as me the following morning. I saw her riding her bicycle along Crooked Lane as I unlocked the door. She dismounted and embraced me in a warm hug.

"You poor thing," she murmured in my ear. "I've been thinking about you all night."

"I'm all right. It's for the best. Really." I'd been awake all night, too, telling myself that.

"You're so strong, Sylvia. I don't know what I'd do if I was forbidden to see Alex."

I didn't bother to tell her that I'd walked away of my own accord, not because I was forbidden. The less I discussed Gabe, the better. Not talking about him or thinking about him was the only way I'd be able to get out of bed each day. To that end, I needed to be busy. The combination of work and Daisy fit the bill nicely.

I pushed open the door and called out to let the professor know it was me. "Speaking of Alex, you seemed very cozy together last night."

She bit her lip then turned away to lean her bicycle against the wall. "Let's not discuss men today."

"Don't be silly. You can talk all you want about Alex. I don't mind. In fact, it'll be a welcome distraction."

"If you're sure…"

"I am."

Her smile broke free, but Professor Nash arrived in the foyer before she could launch into how wonderful her evening had been before she'd had to leave the Buttonhole with me.

"Good morning, ladies. I wasn't expecting you in today, Sylvia. I thought you'd be out investigating."

"Nothing can be done until Huon finishes transcribing the invisible writing." I didn't tell him that my part in the investigation had come to an end. I didn't want to go into it with anyone. I didn't want to talk about it at all.

"Hopefully he'll have news today. I must say, I am so pleased he's taken this on. Very pleased indeed. Oscar would be proud, and very grateful that you trust Huon." His gaze turned soft, wistful.

I attempted a smile of comfort, but it fell flat. I felt more inclined to wallow in misery with the professor rather than rally his spirits.

"I'll make us all a pot of coffee. Come upstairs where it's more comfortable and we'll have a nice chat. I want to hear all about your new career, Daisy."

"Oh good, because I wanted to show my designs to Sylvia. And you, too, Professor." She removed a sketchbook from the bicycle's basket. "I need opinions."

"I'm not sure I'll be much help unless it involves tweed."

Daisy hooked her arm through his. "All opinions are welcome."

I didn't think it a good sign that she needed opinions, but perhaps it was just nerves causing her to doubt herself. Despite outward appearances, Daisy was insecure. It had almost stopped her from becoming romantically linked to Alex, but fortunately he seemed to have convinced her that her lack of education and experience didn't matter to him.

Daisy showed us her sketches as we sipped coffees. They were quite good, particularly the color combinations, but all had a feature that didn't work. The pockets on one of the skirts were positioned too low to be of use, but when I pointed it out, Daisy said it would destroy the slim-hipped look she was trying to create if she made them higher.

"What if you remove the pleats?" the professor suggested.

"The pleats are the main feature," she whined.

"Change the fabric?" I asked.

She turned the page. "What about this dress? It's for the evening, dancing and parties, that sort of thing."

"It's lovely," I said.

"Very fetching and modern," the professor agreed.

Daisy glowed at our praise. "I'm particularly pleased with it, I must say. Sleek dresses are going to be popular, mark my words."

She looked so happy; I didn't want to dampen her spirits. But I had to. "Uh, Daisy, I'm quite sure this dress was in the April issue of *Les Modes*."

She studied the dress anew. "Are you sure?"

"Quite sure, because I wished I could afford it. You must have liked it, too, and inadvertently absorbed the design."

"I didn't mean to copy it." She sighed as she closed the sketchbook. "Perhaps this isn't the career for me, after all. I do so want it to work. Alex is going to think I'm flighty for changing my mind yet again."

I took her hand in mine. "That was just your first try. It'll take time and more attempts to find the perfect design to launch your career, but it'll be worth it." As she sighed again, I added, "If being a fashion designer is what you truly want."

"You're right. I shouldn't give up so easily. I'll go home and sketch some more. Perhaps a visit to the drapery will give me some inspiration. I do love to *feel* fabrics. It helps me envision my designs."

With Daisy's spirits lifted, I didn't feel quite so glum. I saw her off on her bicycle then settled in the ground floor reading nook with a book from the stack that hadn't been cataloged yet. I chose one that required further study before I could decide where to shelve it. That way I was applying myself to a library task while doing one of my favorite things—reading.

The early eighteenth-century book about the imperial magicians of China's Ming Dynasty was fascinating, but even so, I must have nodded off because I awoke to Willie's grating voice saying that I was asleep.

The sound of Gabe's whispered voice telling her to be quiet had me opening my eyes and leaping to my feet. I quickly checked the corners of my mouth for drool. I would have touched my hair to ensure it was still in place, but I was too embarrassed.

Gabe bent to pick up the book that had dropped to the floor as I stood. He handed it to me with a crooked half-smile. "There's been a change of plans."

I glanced behind him at his two bodyguards. Alex gave me a sheepish smile while Willie looked as angry as she had last night. I suspected Gabe had convinced one, but not both, to agree to the change of plans. Willie had been outvoted.

I found it difficult to look at Gabe while he was studying me so intently, so instead I stared down at the book's gold-edged crimson cover. "I don't think that's wise. We should leave things as they are."

"Ha!" Willie barked. "Good decision, Sylv." She pushed past Gabe and threw her arm around my shoulders. "It ain't personal. You know that."

"I do."

"Willie," Gabe warned. "You promised to let me speak."

She held up her hands in surrender and moved behind him again to stand beside Alex.

Gabe's shoulders lost some of their tension. "I ask the same of you, Sylvia, to listen without interrupting."

I nodded rather more eagerly than I should have, given I was determined that the plan made last night should *not* be changed.

He cleared his throat. "We should continue with this investigation together. It's as much yours as ours. In fact, it's probably more your investigation, since the book with Daniel's message was found by you, here, and it involves a Hendry who could be your relative. At the very least, it could rule *out* the fact that you're a Hendry. So, you shouldn't be pushed aside. You should take the reins. But without the support of Scotland Yard consultants, you'll find it almost impossible to do it alone."

"I don't want to take the reins alone," I said.

He glanced over his shoulder at Willie, who adjusted her stance and looked away. I suspected this was an argument they'd had beforehand, and she'd just lost.

"That's point number one," he went on. "The second reason we should continue together is that following the threads of this investigation might lead us to finding out what happened to Melville Hendry. He might not be your father." This was clearly said for Willie's benefit. "Finding him, or finding out what happened to him, will help *everyone* move forward, not just give you answers. It could help bring some long-needed peace to Willie, too, if we discover he's no longer a threat."

"He means if we discover he's dead," Willie chimed in.

"A little more empathy wouldn't go astray," Gabe muttered.

She screwed up her face, confused, then shouted. "He means if we discover he's dead!"

Alex rolled his eyes. "Empathy not emphasis."

Gabe touched my hand to get my attention.

"No touching!" Willie snapped. "That's one of the rules."

"As you just heard, Willie has rules if we're going to move ahead with my plan," Gabe said. "But first, I want your agreement. So, Sylvia, will you work with me?"

For some reason, I wanted to laugh. Gabe had managed to

turn a serious discussion about a topic that had made me miserable, into something lighthearted, almost fun. There was a reason I wanted to be with him all the time, and this moment encapsulated it. He made me happy without even trying.

He'd also managed to change my mind. I nodded. "I will."

He drew in a deep breath. "Good."

Willie snapped her fingers to get my attention. "Now the rules. Be professional at all times. That means no touching, no longing gazes, and at no time will you two be alone together. Understood?"

"Yes," I said on a rush of breath. I almost saluted, too, but I suspected she wouldn't find it amusing and I was already on thin ice.

"The final rule is this: if we find Hendry alive, you don't tell him straight away that you could be his daughter. Not until he's in custody. Do you agree?"

"I do."

Gabe moved to block my line of sight. He smiled at me then winked.

I had to press my lips together firmly to stop myself smiling back. I really shouldn't be so happy, but I couldn't help it. Gabe had not only found a way for us to be in each other's company, but he'd also made it clear we were going to find Hendry. If Hendry did turn out to be alive, and also my father, it was likely we'd be able to capture him and hand him over to the police, ending any threat he posed once and for all.

I didn't want to think about how I'd feel about that. I didn't want to ruin my good mood.

"Now that we're all in agreement, put on your head scarf," Gabe said. "We're going for a drive."

"But we can't do anything until we hear from Huon. We've hit a dead end."

"There is something we can do. We can go to the shops."

* * *

WILLIE WEDGED herself between Gabe and me as we walked along Crooked Lane. She ordered him to sit in the front of the motorcar while Alex drove, then once we reached Harrods, she ushered me through the revolving door alongside her, giving me no opportunity to be near Gabe. She didn't seem to realize that I would have maintained a safe distance anyway.

We walked single file between the glass display cabinets of the perfume department, the bright light from the low-hanging chandeliers glinting off bottles that came in all shapes, sizes and colors. It was my favorite department at Harrods, not just because it was like walking through a box of flowers, but because it was free to test the scents.

The white-gloved sales assistants asked me if I wanted to try a sample, but I politely declined this time. When Alex and Gabe passed, the women asked them if they wanted to purchase a special bottle for their sweethearts.

"Why don't they ask me if I want to buy something?" Willie whined.

"Because they know from the smell of you that you don't bother with perfume," Alex said.

She turned around to shoot him a glare. Not watching where she was going, she bumped into one of the sales assistants. The girl lost her balance and stumbled towards the four-tiered display of glass bottles on the counter. She couldn't stop herself. All she could do was widen her eyes in horror and emit a gasp as she fell.

The gasp died on her lips as she stared up into the green eyes of Gabe, holding her. She clutched his arms as he steadied her, and didn't immediately let go when she realized the prospect of disaster was over. His reflexes had been so fast that I began to doubt seeing him move and wondered if he'd slowed time with his magic.

"Are you all right?" he asked her.

She nodded quickly and released him, although she continued to stare at his back as he strode off. Her look of surprise changed to adoration. Sometimes I wondered if Gabe's heroics would be seen with the same sense of romance by the public if he wasn't so good-looking.

"Who was that?" she murmured.

"No one." Willie traipsed after Gabe who was now speaking to an officious looking shopwalker. "At least not everyone in this city knows who he is," she muttered to me.

The shopwalker directed us to the lift to take us to the administration offices. Gabe had telephoned before leaving the library to arrange a meeting with the store manager. We were lucky he could fit us into his schedule. Mentioning Scotland Yard probably helped.

"What did you do that for?" Willie hissed at him as we waited for the lift. "Anyone could have seen."

"I acted on instinct," Gabe said.

"I thought it only happened when your life was in danger, or the life of someone you care about. You've never met her before."

Gabe followed her gaze to the perfume department. "Willie—"

"Broken perfume bottles are not a disaster, Gabe. An inconvenience, yes, but not on the same scale as bullets coming at you. Looks like your sense of chivalry acts as a trigger, too, so stop it. Stop being chivalrous. This is 1920. Women don't want gentlemanly behavior, they want equality."

"Can't we have both?" I asked.

She poked Gabe in the chest. "You ain't a medieval knight. No more chivalry. Understood?"

"Willie," Gabe said with effort. "My magic didn't activate. When I said I acted on instinct, I meant my natural instinct, not magical."

"Oh."

The lift door opened and the operator asked us which department we wished to go to.

"Administration," Gabe told him.

Willie sulked in the corner of the lift, forgetting she was our self-appointed chaperone. Gabe took advantage and brushed his fingers against mine. I couldn't decide whether to do what my heart wanted and hold his hand or do what my head thought was best and move away. Paralyzed by indecision, I did nothing.

The store manager wasn't much help. He asked his assistant to fetch the employee file for Daniel Barratt, but she told us the older files were kept off-site in a storage facility. She had a better idea, however. She introduced us to the manager of the finance department, who'd worked with Daniel when he was dismissed from his position as junior accountant.

After we introduced ourselves as consultants for Scotland Yard specializing in magical investigations, Mr. Barrowman visibly relaxed. He must be artless and realized we didn't suspect he was involved in whatever had got Daniel dismissed.

That was the first question Gabe asked. "How well do you remember the day Daniel was fired?"

"Very well. It was June 1890." Mr. Barrowman reminded me of a bulldog, with a thick neck and heavy jowls that dragged the corners of his mouth downward into a frown. "It may have been a long time ago, but it's not every day the finance department witnesses someone being marched out of the manager's office in tears."

"Tears?" Gabe prompted. "Daniel was crying?"

Mr. Barrowman nodded. "It's unnerving seeing a grown man cry." He glanced between Gabe and Alex. "I doubt I need to tell ex-servicemen that."

"How do you know we served?" Alex asked. "We don't wear our kit. We could have been objectors." While some former officers still wore their uniforms in their daily lives, it was becoming an increasingly rare sight. Gabe and Alex hadn't worn theirs the entire time I'd known them, except at official gatherings.

"Two strapping lads like you...you must have served. It was your duty."

Gabe steered the conversation back to Daniel. "Do you know why he lost his job?"

"Not then. It was hushed up at the time. I found out when I became manager, years later. He embezzled money from the company by a process known as fictitious bad debt. He was responsible for debt collection, but sometimes customers fail to pay. When that happened, it was Daniel's task to record the debt as unpaid and the transaction is written off as a loss. If it wasn't for a very important customer complaining that she was being treated with disdain by the sales assistants in the women's clothing department, we would never have discovered that someone had informed them that she'd failed to pay off her shop credit. She insisted she'd paid, and the matter was brought to our manager. After conducting a secret internal investigation, he discovered that Daniel had pocketed her payment and recorded a bad debt against the transaction, writing it off as a loss. In fact, he'd done it several times, usually with different customers so as not to double up. If the customer in question hadn't been so horrified by her treatment on the sales floor, we may never have found out. As you can imagine, Daniel was dismissed immediately."

"Why weren't the police called?"

Mr. Barrowman settled back in the chair, resting his linked hands on his paunch. "Because of the tears, I suppose. I think management grew concerned that a criminal record might tip him over the edge and, well, desperate men can sometimes think there's no way of escaping their shame except to end things. Daniel had a wife and children. No one wanted to be the reason for him to do that."

"Did you know he died in April '91?"

"I went to his funeral. Tragic business." He shook his head sadly. "I doubt his dismissal had anything to do with it, though. As I said, there was no criminal investigation. It's more likely there was a rift between Daniel and his wife."

"Why do you say that?"

"She wasn't at his funeral. Nor were the children. Some men can't cope when their wives leave them." He shrugged. "Not that she was the only one missing. His brother-in-law didn't attend either, but he at least had a good excuse." At our raised brows, he added, "The accident that saw him lose a hand."

"Did you see Daniel after he was dismissed and before his death?"

"No."

Gabe had no more questions for Mr. Barrowman, but Alex had one. "Dismissal is upsetting, but not many men would cry over it. Do you know of any reason Daniel would take it particularly badly?"

Mr. Barrowman stroked his bushy beard and appeared to be warring with himself. Eventually, he decided to tell us. "This is purely speculation, you understand, but I think he may have been a gambler."

"Why do you say that?" Gabe asked.

"He kept a close eye on the racing results. Not just on Monday when the weekend's races are reported, but every day. He'd bury his nose in his newspaper at lunchtimes, circling a horse or two. I wondered if he lost more than he could afford, and the embezzlement was his attempt to pay off a gambling debt. It would explain his devastation at being dismissed." He continued to stroke his beard before he seemed to realize he was doing it and stopped. "It's just a guess. He didn't confide in me. We weren't that close."

"Close enough to attend his funeral," Alex said.

Mr. Barrowman's cheeks suddenly flushed. "Is that all? I'm very busy." He picked up some papers and shuffled them to prove just how busy.

We made to leave, but I paused before exiting. Something had bothered me ever since he told us the story of Daniel's embezzlement. "Who informed the sales assistants in womenswear?"

"Pardon?"

"You said the sales assistants treated the customer with disdain because they'd found out she hadn't paid her debts, or so they thought. Who told them?"

"I don't know."

"It had to be someone from this department. Someone with access to the ledger where the store credit transactions are recorded."

He pushed himself out of the chair and waddled towards us with a low bulldog's gait. He opened the door and indicated the array of desks in the large room beyond. Four women sat to one side, typing, while six men sat on the other side. They pored over large ledgers and entered figures into their adding machines. Between those machines and the typewriters, the *click-clack* of pressed keys produced a symphony unique to the office environment. "As you can see, we employ quite a few staff in the finance department. Most of those from the time Daniel worked here have left."

Not all, I could have pointed out. I kept my mouth shut, however. There was a chance he was the one who informed the sales assistants, knowing it would lead to the customer becoming upset and complaining, and ultimately lead to Daniel getting caught.

On the other hand, it was a long bow to draw.

We walked out of the manager's office, but Gabe had one final question. "Did you know Daniel was a magician?"

Mr. Barrowman's brows shot up his forehead. "What kind?"

"Ink."

"I had no idea. Not that ink magic would have helped him do his job better. It seems like a useless magic unless one is an ink manufacturer. Anyway, when Daniel worked here, magic was unknown to most of us."

"So, you aren't a magician?" Gabe asked.

Mr. Barrowman chuckled. "If I was, would I be working here?"

Willie resumed her role of chaperone as we left Harrods,

making sure she was always between Gabe and me. Not that either of us was thinking about the other. Gabe proved that, like me, his mind was on what we'd learned about Daniel Barratt.

"He must have met Thurlow at the racetrack," he said.

"Not Thurlow necessarily," Alex pointed out.

"Daniel must have become in debt to someone, which explains his embezzlement and why he was so distraught when he was dismissed. He knew he'd struggle to pay back what he owed to a very dangerous man."

"A man who then forced Daniel to participate in his illegal activities to pay off the debt," Alex finished. "Do you think the bookmaker knew Daniel's worth as an ink magician before that?"

"Impossible to say," Gabe said. "Perhaps Thurlow just wanted an accountant in his debt, then learned later that Daniel could write in invisible ink with his wife's help."

Alex's jaw firmed. "Gabe. Don't assume it's Thurlow."

Gabe's jaw set just as firmly as he opened the motorcar's door.

We returned to the library where the professor was waiting for us with a message from Huon. "He telephoned to say he has finished transcribing the ledgers. He wants you to meet him at Petra Conway's shop."

"Why there?" I asked.

The professor didn't have an answer.

Alex opened the door and we filed past him back into Crooked Lane. The last to exit, Gabe lengthened his strides to catch up to me. "You forgot your scarf." He whispered so that Willie couldn't hear.

I accepted it from him with a tentative smile.

He smiled back. "Not that you need to bother with the scarf. I like your hair a little ruffled from the wind."

I bit my lip and glanced at Willie up ahead.

"Don't worry," he said quietly. "*No flirting* wasn't one of her rules."

CHAPTER 8

*H*uon had arrived at Petra's shop before us. The ledgers we'd retrieved from the Whitechapel cellar lay open on the counter with some papers beside them, but neither he nor Petra were studying them. True to form, they were squabbling.

"Look at it!" Huon dipped a pen into one of the sample pots of ink Petra sold in her shop and drew some squiggles on a piece of paper. "It's watery, the color is weak. I wouldn't buy it."

"You don't have to," she shot back. "Your father supplies you with all the ink you need."

"Don't be so sure about that. He doesn't give me much."

She scoffed. "The use of the townhouse isn't much?"

"It comes with strict conditions."

"Which I doubt you're obeying. Does he know you laze about all day and party all night?"

"That's why he enforced conditions. Anyway, I'm more responsible now. I'm a businessman, like you."

"In case you haven't noticed, I'm a woman."

"Oh, I noticed," he purred.

Petra's eyes widened in alarm. She snatched the sample pot

off him, causing ink to splash onto her hand. "Now look what you've done."

He caught her wrist and took the inkpot from her. "Let me clean that up for you." He spoke a spell while keeping his gaze locked on Petra.

She stared back at him, mesmerized by his warm voice and the lyrical sounds of the strange words. She only tore her gaze away when the ink rose into the air from her skin. It lifted off her hand, drifted in the air like a ribbon on the breeze, then hovered a moment before pouring into the open ink bottle. He removed his handkerchief from his pocket and gently stroked her hand where the ink had dampened it.

Willie cleared her throat. "Should we leave you two alone and come back later?"

Petra jerked free. She touched her hair, her neck, and finally her wrist where Huon had held her. "Now is an excellent time. There are no customers and Huon is being particularly annoying. The sooner he leaves, the better."

He leaned an elbow on the counter and gave her a smug smile. "You didn't seem annoyed a moment ago when I cleaned your hand."

"It wouldn't have needed to be cleaned if you hadn't caused me to spill ink in the first place."

"You're right. Allow me to apologize. I'm sorry you were distracted by my handsome face and overwhelmed by my magnetism."

She made a sound of disgust and rolled her eyes. "You're impossible."

His smile widened. "You're all witnesses to the fact she didn't disagree with me about my handsomeness and magnetism."

Alex clapped him on the shoulder. "Give up before you make a fool of yourself."

"Too late," Petra muttered.

Huon shrugged then stepped aside to allow us closer to the

ledgers. "I wanted to meet you here because I thought I should check with Petra as to whether there is any invisible graphite writing on these. There isn't," he added before we could ask. "Apparently the writer thought invisible ink superior and didn't bother with pencil."

"It's no surprise considering the writer was an ink magician," Petra shot back.

Huon picked up the loose papers covered with his untidy scrawl. "I transcribed as much as I could, but a lot has faded. The magic has weakened considerably over the years." He fanned the pages on the counter, each ruled with vertical lines to form columns. Each page listed dozens of entries with amounts in the final column. Huon had left a number of gaps where he couldn't read the original. He pointed to three of the pages. "These are copied from the expenses ledger, showing money going out." He tapped his finger on the remaining pages. "And these are from the income ledger, showing money received."

Gabe picked up one of the pages while Alex picked up another. "There are several expenses with names beside them. Just surnames, not full names."

"At least we've got some now," Willie said. "Recognize any, Gabe?"

"Coyle appears regularly with the same amount. The bookmaker must have been paying him for some reason. It doesn't say why." He ran his finger down the column, pausing at one entry near the bottom. "I think I know this name. I need to check something at home before I can be sure." He meant his parents' list of magicians, but he didn't want to say it in front of Huon and Petra.

"Do any of the entries note what the expenses are for?" I asked.

"Shoes," Gabe read.

Willie frowned. "Shoes?"

"I think it's referring to horseshoes. Other entries just say

'Ride' beside the surname, along with what I think are horse names. 'Lightning Bolt', 'Tiger Eye', 'Queen's Revenge.'"

"Payments to jockeys?" Willie suggested.

"Names of horses appear beside several surname entries, but without the word 'Ride.' I wonder what service they rendered the bookmaker if it wasn't riding."

"There are a lot of people a bookmaker can bribe at a race-track," Huon said with a note of authority.

Alex, peering over Gabe's shoulder, pointed to another entry. "I know this one. He was arrested just before I left the force to enlist in '16. The government had started growing concerned about addiction among the army, so they prohibited the sale of cocaine and other substances under the Defense of the Realm Act. He was caught selling cocaine to troops."

"What does cocaine have to do with horses?" Petra asked.

"It's injected into them to make them run faster," Gabe said.

"How cruel."

"Is he still in prison?" Willie asked. "We can ask him which bookmakers he worked for."

"He died in incarceration. He wouldn't have given anyone up anyway."

Huon handed Gabe the transcribed pages for the second ledger. "These payments are from the other ledger, which is labeled 'Income'. Many names appear several times, alongside amounts and horse names. They must refer to bets placed with the bookmaker because odds are given, too."

The names weren't familiar to any of us.

"All entries in both ledgers are dated between early July 1890 and February '91," Huon said.

Gabe scooped up the documents. "From shortly after Daniel lost his job, up until his wife and children going into hiding, two months before his death."

"Entries from those two months could be in other books," Alex said. "He didn't need to hide all evidence, just enough to give Oscar something to give to the police if Daniel died."

Gabe tapped the documents. "What happened in February? Why did he become afraid at that point?" He shrugged, unable to think of an answer. "Send me the bill and I'll pay you for your time, Barratt."

Petra picked up one of the ledgers and squinted at the page. After a moment, she shook her head and closed it. "Why did Daniel work for this man?"

"It's likely he owed someone a lot of money," Gabe said. "Perhaps even the bookmaker himself. Daniel kept the books for him, using invisible ink to keep the transactions secret, since it seems the bookmaker was paying jockeys to throw races, as well as doping horses, and most likely using numerous other illegal methods to cheat. In an act of defiance or desperation, Daniel hid the evidence in Whitechapel, and sent a clue to the whereabouts of these ledgers to Oscar. We can only assume that he asked Oscar specifically because he could read the invisible ink and perhaps because he was friends with my parents."

"The link to Matt and India implies it's a crime that involves magicians," Alex clarified.

It was an interesting point, and not one I'd considered until now, although it was clear Alex and Gabe had. I'd thought the only magical connection was the invisible ink, but the close association between Oscar Barratt and Gabe's parents gave the investigation a new angle. A magical angle.

Petra placed a hand to her throat and swallowed heavily. "Did Daniel start working for the bookmaker when magicians were still being persecuted?"

Gabe nodded. " While at Harrods, he was forced to hide his ability like all magicians, although it wouldn't have led to his persecution even if it became known, since he wasn't manufacturing ink."

"It is a rather useless magic if—"

"Useless!" Huon picked up the sample pot of ink. "I'll spill this again to prove just how useless, shall I?"

"Don't you dare." Petra went to snatch the pot off him, but he moved out of her reach.

"Admit that ink magic has its uses, or I'll tip it out on the floor."

"You are such a child!"

He flipped open the lid and began to slowly tilt the bottle.

"All right! Ink magic is useful for cleaning up ink spills."

"And?" He nodded at the ledgers.

She blew out a breath. "And writing in invisible ink."

"And?"

She frowned. "And what?"

"And it's superior to graphite magic."

She thrust her hands on her hips. "I'm not saying that. It's not true. You can't sketch with ink."

"You can."

Gabe reached between them to retrieve the ledgers from the counter. It broke the standoff.

Huon returned the inkpot to the display alongside the others. "I'll bring you some samples from my father's factory."

Petra lifted her chin. "I don't want Barratt ink in my shop."

"You don't want to sell superior quality products?"

"I wish I didn't have to sell ink at all, but the customers expect it. So, I choose ink from a manufacturer I trust, whose son isn't a buffoon with an over-inflated sense of self."

"You forgot handsome and magnetic, but I'll forgive you since I know you're thinking it."

She rolled her eyes again.

A customer entered, our cue to leave the shop. Gabe offered to drive Huon home, but he declined, saying he had a potential client to meet. He cast a look through the shop window before sauntering off with a small smile on his face.

"They make a handsome couple," Willie said as Gabe retrieved the crank handle from the floor of the Vauxhall's front passenger seat.

Alex slid into the driver's seat. "They're chalk and cheese. They'd be terrible together."

"Sometimes the best relationships are between opposites. Look at me and my first husband." She turned to me as I settled into the back seat alongside her. "You should find someone like Huon, Sylvia. Someone who challenges you. Someone you can fix."

"I don't want to fix anyone," I said.

"Why not? You ain't *that* broken yourself." She placed her finger and thumb close together. "Just a little bit."

I didn't think I was broken at all, but her words had me wondering. My mother's controlling nature had ensured I led a sheltered life. I'd had few friends before arriving in London, no real home and no ancestral roots. I'd been afraid of men before meeting Gabe, and afraid of rocking the boat, although when pushed too far, I often couldn't contain an outburst.

I remained quiet for the rest of the journey to Gabe's Park Street house. It wasn't just me who fell silent, however. We all seemed lost in thought as we battled through the traffic.

When we reached our destination, Gabe opened the motorcar door for me, but Willie clambered over me to climb out first. She shooed Gabe out of the way before allowing me to emerge from the Vauxhall.

Bristow met us at the door, greeting us individually with his usual formality. When it came to me, he politely told me that Mrs. Bristow would be thrilled to know I'd called.

"Is she in the kitchen?" I asked. "I'll pop down and say hello."

I headed into the basement service area with the butler, while Gabe took the stairs to the office where his family kept the records of known magicians. I found Mrs. Ling in the kitchen, her hands dusted with flour. Murray the footman had been seated at the table in the adjoining room, polishing the silver. Hearing voices, he joined us at the same time that Sally, the maid, and Mrs. Bristow appeared. The only staff member missing was Dodson, the chauffeur, mechanic and general man-of-all-work.

We chatted for a while until Gabe arrived, Alex and Willie in tow. Although the kitchen was large, it felt crowded, and we were getting in Mrs. Ling's way. She flapped her apron to shoo us out, but not before giving me a recipe to pass on to Mrs. Parry.

We returned to the drawing room upstairs, followed by Murray and Bristow carrying trays laden with tea and cake. Bristow went to pour the tea, but his hand shook so much that Murray had to take over.

Gabe passed me a slice of lemon drizzle cake on a plate. "The name I recognized in the ledger—Ferryman—belongs to an iron magician who worked as a farrier."

Alex nodded, unsurprised. "That makes a lot of sense. The bookmaker must have been paying him to create stronger horseshoes."

"Or make the horses go faster," Willie said. "We once knew an iron magician who could make iron fly."

Gabe picked up his teacup, holding it by the cup, not the handle. Society matrons like Lady Stanhope would be horrified at the casual way he served and drank tea, but Gabe wasn't the sort to care about ceremony or tradition. I wondered if he'd behave differently in the presence of his parents.

"This investigation is more about magic than we originally thought," Alex said. "It doesn't just involve invisible ink, but potentially spell-infused horseshoes, and perhaps other magics, too."

"Like what?" Willie asked. "A magic leather saddle ain't going to help a horse win. And jockeys ain't magicians, but they were on the bookmaker's payroll."

"It appears he used a combination of magician and artless methods," Gabe said. "Either way, the farrier magician is another potential link between the bookmaker and Coyle."

"I don't understand," I said.

"According to the ledger, the bookmaker was making regular payments to Coyle. Coyle knew a lot of magicians, some of whom he was blackmailing in one form or another. My guess is that Coyle introduced the bookmaker to the farrier and Daniel, and the bookmaker had to compensate him for the introductions."

"Compensation that maybe continued after Coyle's death," Willie said. "I reckon Hope collected it."

"It's possible," Alex said. "The ledgers' entries stop when Daniel hid them in February, but the bookmaker's operation may not have ended then. It could have continued."

"I doubt Hope had anything to do with it," Gabe told them.

Willie clicked her tongue in disgust. "She ain't soft, Gabe. She's capable of running whatever schemes her husband started."

"If she did, she would be wealthier, but she and Valentine are barely scraping by."

"If he got a job, they wouldn't have to just scrape by," Willie said.

I tended to agree with Gabe and said so.

"Course you'd agree with him," Willie sneered. "But you don't know Hope like I do." She shoved a slice of cake into her mouth, inviting no further comment.

Alex took another slice of cake but instead of eating it, he pointed at it. "There are baking magicians, confectionary magicians, and probably other types of cooking magicians."

"Mrs. Ling often purchases goods from them," Gabe said, nodding.

Willie licked her fingers. "Like this cake. It's real good and the magic in it means you don't get fat."

Alex laughed. "Who told you that?"

"Your father."

"He was pulling your leg."

Willie pouted as she placed her empty plate on the table. "If anyone knows about getting fat, it's Cyclops. What's your point about baking magic, anyway?"

Alex indicated the slice of cake again. "The magic was put into this by the baker when he baked it, but his magic descended from flour magic, yes?"

"In a way," Gabe said. "Flour is made from grain, a natural substance, so a baker magician will have an ancestor who specialized in grain magic." He indicated me. "Sylvia's paper magic ancestor was actually a cotton magician, and my mother's watchmaking magic may have descended from a steel magician, since that's what a lot of timepiece parts are made from."

"Her maiden name wasn't Steele for no reason," Willie pointed out. "Speaking of steel magic, have you made up your mind about the Rolls-Royce, Gabe? And before you say anything, I want to remind you that just because you didn't agree to ask India to extend the head engineer's magic in exchange for a free motorcar, doesn't mean you can't still buy one."

"I told you, it was my father's motorcar that was destroyed, so it's up to him to buy a new one."

"They might not be back for an age!" She picked up another slice of cake. "Why all the questions about baking and flour, Alex? Do you reckon the bookmaker used a baking magician in his business?"

"Not baking. Cocaine."

Willie paused with the cake halfway to her mouth. "No. There ain't no such thing as a cocaine magician."

"Why not? Cocaine is derived from the leaves of the coca plant. Coca plants have been grown for centuries, just like wheat which gives us grain. The leaves of the coca plant go through a process to extract cocaine, just like grain goes through a process to turn it into flour." Alex sat back, looking pleased with himself.

Gabe rubbed his jaw. "There are no cocaine magicians on my parents' list."

"Perhaps it's rare," Alex said. "Perhaps it was one magic that remained hidden due to its controversial nature."

"You said yourself that it only became illegal to sell in 1916," I reminded him.

"True, but controversy has surrounded it for years, well before the law. It could be that cocaine magicians stayed in the shadows along with other magicians during the centuries of persecution, but when most emerged into the light in '91, cocaine magicians decided to remain hidden."

Gabe pointed at the pages transcribed by Huon. "Is the cocaine dealer you recognized in the ledger's entries definitely dead?"

"Yes, but there might be a sibling or child who inherited the same magic."

"And inherited his business," Willie added.

Alex rose. "I'll telephone my father and ask him to find an address in the Yard's old files."

"What would cocaine magic do?" I asked when he'd left the room. "Make it stronger, more powerful and addictive?"

"Or make the side-effects less and therefore easier to hide," Gabe offered.

It was a sobering thought. Magic had so many more branches than I'd realized. Of course, we shouldn't leap to conclusions without evidence; cocaine magic might not even exist.

Alex returned a few minutes later. "He's going to check the case file and will get back to me. But he gave me another idea, somewhere to go while we wait."

"The address of another, unrelated cocaine dealer to speak to?" Gabe asked.

Alex picked up the transcribed pages. "He suggested we return to the place where this cocaine dealer was arrested. Since I was involved in his arrest, I know it without having to look it up." He should look pleased with himself, but instead he watched Gabe warily.

"Where?" Gabe asked.

Alex put out a hand, as if placating an agitated horse.

It had the opposite effect. Gabe shot to his feet. "Where, Alex?"

"Epsom Downs Racecourse."

Gabe's nostrils flared. "Thurlow operates out of Epsom."

"It might just be a coincidence."

"I don't believe in coincidences."

CHAPTER 9

*O*ur acquaintance with Thurlow hadn't ended when his men tried to run our vehicle off the road. When his girl left him, he blamed us—quite rightly, as it turned out. He'd retaliated by attempting to hire Francis Stray, Gabe's very intelligent but naïve mathematician friend. We'd convinced him Francis would be useless to him. With that plan falling flat, Gabe expected Thurlow to strike again, hence his drive to capture him before he had the chance. It seemed to have turned into an obsession, however. It remained to be seen if the obsession was blinding Gabe to the truth.

It wasn't race day at Epsom, but there was still a lot of activity at the racecourse. Mentioning Scotland Yard got us past the security guard at the entrance, and we headed straight for the betting circle. It was empty, except for a lad in overalls picking up scraps of paper from the grass. Unhappy punters must have torn up their betting slips and left them there during the previous day's midweek race meeting.

Gabe rested his elbows on the barrier alongside the track and watched a horse being put through its paces. Two men also watched on. One called the jockey over after he crossed the finish line.

Alex leaned back against the fence beside Gabe, facing Willie and me. "There are a number of people we can question here today. We should get started."

Gabe gave no response, he simply stared directly ahead at the track.

Alex pushed off from the fence and strode past me. He stopped out of earshot of Gabe and signaled for Willie and me to join him. "This isn't like Gabe. I've never known him to become fixated like this. He's usually so affable." He cast a worried look in Gabe's direction, then suddenly turned to me. "Say something to him, Sylvia."

"Why me?"

Willie clamped her hands on her hips. "Yes, why her?"

"Because he listens to Sylvia more than either of us."

"He listens to me!"

"No, he doesn't."

She watched Gabe, his back to us, his head slightly bowed. After a moment, she blew out a breath. "All right. Speak to him, Sylv. But no touching. Understood?"

"Yes, ma'am."

"And don't make eyes at him."

"I don't even know what that means."

"Good. Keep it that way." She crossed her arms. "Speak up so we hear every word you say."

I didn't intend to follow her last rule. Some conversations were meant to be private.

I joined Gabe at the fence where he leaned his forearms on the rail, his hands loosely clasped. The thumb of one hand lightly tapped the knuckle of the other. With Willie watching on, I resisted the urge to cover his hand.

There were a number of ways to begin, but I suspected he'd appreciate the direct approach. "You know it's unlikely to be Thurlow. He would have been quite young then."

Gabe straightened and pressed his lips together. I thought I was about to receive the same silent treatment as Alex, but then he relaxed. He didn't look at me, however. Indeed, he looked everywhere *except* at me. "I know. But it *could* be him."

"It could be. But you seem to *want* it to be him."

The thumb tapping increased its tempo.

"Gabe...is it because he seems to be targeting you?"

The thumb tapping stopped. He finally looked at me, frowning. "It's not because he targeted me. It's because he's targeting *you*."

I blinked slowly. "Me?"

"Yes. He had no reason to approach you at the library, but he did. He flirted with you. And the way he looks at you...I don't like it." He dragged a hand over his hard jaw before turning away. "He's dangerous, and I want him out of our lives."

I dared to touch his arm. It was rigid with tension. "You can't let him get under your skin, Gabe, or you'll never rest."

"I'm trying not to..."

I took his hand in mine, risking Willie's ire. When I felt Gabe's tension ease, I was glad I'd risked it. "I hate seeing you like this."

He tilted his head to peer at me with eyes as fathomless as the ocean.

I removed my glove and took his hand. It made mine feel small, delicate. "Don't let Thurlow win."

He drew my hand to his chest. "I don't plan to."

"All right, you two, that's enough!" Willie marched towards us. "We need to get to work and question folk. Where do we start?"

Gabe nodded at the horse that had finished its run. The jockey dismounted and the two men watching on fell into a deep discussion. "With people who look old enough to have been here in the early nineties. Like them."

The jockey spoke to the two older men while one of them inspected the horse's left foreleg. He'd been carrying a large brown leather bag, so I assumed he was a veterinarian.

Gabe set off in their direction, but Alex called him back. "Look who's here."

We followed Alex's gaze to the man striding past the betting circle, his gaze cast down as he watched where he was stepping. He carried a newspaper under his arm and there was a stump where his hand should be.

What was Fred Laidlow doing here on a non-racing day?

Gabe called out and Fred stopped. He blinked in surprise. "Hello. What are you doing here?"

"Our investigation led us to Epsom," Gabe admitted. "And you?"

"I'm meeting a friend who works here. We're having a drink together when he finishes."

"Don't you have work?"

"Not since this." Fred rubbed the stump.

"What happened?"

"An accident in the factory where I worked. They employed me in the office afterwards, but I had no talent for numbers and reports. I spend a lot of time here, nowadays."

"You like to have a flutter on the horses?"

Fred glanced uneasily between Gabe and Alex. "I do, but I don't have a problem, if that's what you mean. I don't have debts."

Gabe put up his hands in surrender. "Sorry. Nosiness comes with our job. I don't mean to pry."

I was quite sure he did mean to, but his friendly manner put Fred at ease.

"Was Daniel a gambler?" Gabe asked.

Fred hesitated before nodding. "Don't tell the girls that I told you, but yes."

"We spoke to a former colleague of Daniel's, at Harrods. He said Daniel took his dismissal badly, perhaps because he was in debt. Do you know anything about that?"

"We weren't close. He didn't confide in me. If he was in debt then, his fortunes certainly reversed shortly afterwards. As I said, he seemed to have quite a bit of money at his disposal. The girls and I assumed he got a new job, but neither he nor Rosina mentioned it. Although the sisters were close, Daniel and the girls never got on. They made some unhelpful comments when he lost his position at Harrods—saying he was hopeless, that sort of thing—so when his fortunes turned around, he enjoyed lording it over them. He made a point of showing off a new piece of jewelry he'd bought Rosina, or a new toy for the children."

"But that all stopped before he died? You said they became reclusive right before Rosina disappeared."

"I don't know if the money stopped coming in, but they changed. They stopped calling on us altogether, then Rosina and the children suddenly left."

"You think she left him? Not that he hid them? That's not what you said yesterday."

He winced. "I didn't like to say it in front of the girls. Myrtle is adamant Rosina wouldn't have left without telling them."

"And Naomi? What does she think?"

"She thinks whatever Myrtle thinks. Myrtle has a strong will. She dominates her youngest sister."

I wondered if she dominated her husband, too.

Fred tugged the sleeve of his jacket, covering the stump. "May I ask how your investigation led you here?"

"We're looking for people who may have had links to Epsom when Daniel was still alive. Trainers, jockeys, officials."

"Farriers, stable hands," Alex added.

Fred shrugged, not seeming to notice that he didn't receive an answer to his question. "I'd say there were dozens. Can you be more specific? I might know them."

"Did Daniel mention anyone to you? Perhaps he gave you the name of a horse to bet on, a sure thing, or a trainer or jockey to watch."

Fred adjusted the newspaper under his arm. "It was a very long time ago. I'm not sure I can remember."

"Try. He was your brother-in-law, after all. We assume you want to find out who killed him."

"*If* he was killed. The coroner's report stated he died of natural causes."

Gabe simply waited.

Fred blew out a breath, then nodded at the two men still talking to the jockey and assessing the horse. "You can start with Charles Goreman."

Goreman! According to Daniel's ledger, he was one of the jockeys being paid by the mysterious bookmaker.

"He used to be a jockey in those days, and only became a trainer after a bad fall," Fred went on. "Daniel would sometimes tell me *not* to bet on one of Goreman's rides. I never asked why, but he was never wrong."

"Did you link Daniel's tip-offs to his newfound wealth?"

Fred shrugged a shoulder. "I never asked where the money came from."

It wasn't the same as not linking the two, but Gabe didn't point that out. "What about as a trainer? Does Goreman still cheat?"

"Cheat how?"

"Doping, perhaps."

Fred glanced towards the two men, deep in conversation. "Not that I'm aware."

"Do his horses win a lot?"

"He wins some, he loses some." Fred shrugged.

"Do you know a man named Ferryman?" Alex asked. "He was a farrier."

"No."

"What about bookmakers?" Gabe asked. "Are there any still working the totes here that Daniel may have known then?"

"No."

"Surely there's one or two."

"Maybe there is, but I'm afraid I don't know. Look, I have to go. My friend is waiting."

"Does the name Thurlow mean anything to you?"

"No." Fred touched the brim of his hat in farewell then went on his way.

Gabe grunted. "He's lying. Thurlow all but owns this betting circle. If Fred's a regular here, then he must know him."

"That ain't the only lie he told." Willie wasn't watching the retreating figure of Fred Laidlow. She was looking at Charles Goreman and the veterinarian. "Goreman is a *very* successful trainer. I've heard of him. There ain't no way a regular gambler would say 'he wins some, he loses some.'"

Gabe and Alex both nodded. "I've heard of him, too, and I rarely gamble," Gabe said.

"So, what's Fred covering up?" I asked. "His involvement in Daniel's death? Or just the fact he has a gambling problem and doesn't want his wife to know?"

"We should talk to Goreman," Willie went on. "All his success probably means he's up to no good. What's the name of that farrier magician, Gabe?"

"Reggie Ferryman."

"And the cocaine dealer, Alex?"

"Arthur Cody."

"Let's introduce ourselves to Mr. Goreman and his friend."

Gabe's gaze followed Fred Laidlow as he headed into the nearby bar. On race day, it was packed with rowdy drinkers, celebrating their wins or drowning their misery after losing, but today it looked innocuous. I thought Gabe might go after Fred, but instead he agreed with Willie.

"Follow my lead," he said, striding in the direction of the two men inspecting the horse.

Alex fell into step alongside him. "Not if you target Thurlow."

Gabe greeted Mr. Goreman amiably, shaking his hand and introducing himself, not as a Scotland Yard consultant, but as the son of India Glass.

Mr. Goreman knew the name. "Lady Rycroft? Remarkable woman. You must be the son who claims to be artless."

Only someone who knew Gabe well would have seen the tightening around his eyes. "I am artless. Don't believe everything you read in the newspapers." He smiled, oh-so charming. "I'm conducting some research for my mother, as it happens. She asked me to find out more about the emergence of magic in the early nineties, specifically relating to the racing industry in 1891."

"Ah, yes, such a strange time, very chaotic there for a while until things calmed down." Mr. Goreman was the same height as me, with ruddy cheeks and a bulbous nose. His bowler hat and smart pin-striped suit reminded me of the men who worked in the financial hub of the city. The hat brim wasn't large enough to keep the sun off his nose, and it glowed from exposure. "Why is Lady Rycroft interested in the racing industry? I'm not sure I see the connection to magic."

"We're trying to find out if there is one, and thought perhaps you could shed some light on what was occurring at Epsom Downs at the time."

Mr. Goreman still looked confused. "Why me?"

"A friend told us you were a jockey here in '91."

Mr. Goreman looked past us. "Who?"

Gabe cleared his throat and extended his hand to the second man, a much taller, thinner fellow with an energy about him. He shook Gabe's hand vigorously. As Gabe introduced us, he shook each of our hands with a firm grip. He introduced himself as Mr. Wellington, a veterinarian.

"Did you work at Epsom back then?" Gabe asked him.

His nod was as vigorous as the rest of his movements. "I'm here most race days. Mr. Goreman isn't my only client, but he is my favorite."

"He means I pay him the most, because I have the largest stable." The two men chuckled.

Gabe smiled, too. "Have either of you ever come across magicians working in the racing industry?"

"Magicians?" Mr. Wellington repeated. "Why would magicians be involved in racing? They manufacture things."

"Farriers, for example," Gabe said.

Mr. Wellington shook his head, but Mr. Goreman looked thoughtful. "There was a farrier, as it happens. He was employed by Epsom Downs before anyone knew magicians existed. Before we artless knew, that is. Reggie Ferryman, his name was."

"He no longer works here?" Gabe asked.

"Lord, no. They got rid of him when the race manager suspected he was using his magic in the horseshoes. Only for those trainers or owners who paid for the privilege, of course. There's no place for cheats like that in this industry." Mr. Goreman's speech became quite vociferous. "Fortunately, he was the only magician employed in the industry."

"The only one you know about," Alex said.

"What happened to Reggie Ferryman?" Gabe asked. "Did he find employment in private stables after being dismissed from here?"

"I'm not sure where he ended up. He was banned from the racing industry altogether. Poor fellow, when you think about it. It wasn't his fault he was a magician."

"It was his fault that he used his magic to cheat," Alex pointed out.

"We don't know for certain if he did."

"You were a jockey then," Gabe went on. "How well did you know Reggie Ferryman?"

"Not at all well."

"What about you, sir?"

Mr. Wellington shook his head. "I never met the man, although the name does ring a distant bell."

Gabe turned back to the former jockey. "Do you know

anyone who may have paid him to use his spell on the horse-shoes he made?"

"No. I had nothing to do with the farriers. I only dealt with the trainers and grooms."

"What about bookmakers?"

"Pardon?"

"Did bookmakers approach you and ask you to lose on purpose?"

Mr. Goreman bristled. "They asked. I refused. Mr. Glass, is there a point to that question?"

Gabe wisely changed the subject. If we wanted to find out the name of the bookmaker who paid Mr. Goreman, we'd have to be smarter. He wasn't going to simply admit it and potentially ruin his reputation in the process. "Did you know a man named Arthur Cody?"

"Oh, yes, I remember him. Nasty piece of work. He used to inject the horses with a cocaine concoction. He was arrested a few years ago and died in prison."

Mr. Wellington had been listening quietly, but his face became animated, twisting with revulsion. "I hope he's rotting in hell."

"You knew him well?" Gabe asked.

"He worked as a groom for one of the trainers who wasn't one of my clients at the time but is now. I didn't hear about the doping until Cody was arrested." He shook his head. "I can't believe he got away with it for as long as he did. Such a cruel way to treat magnificent animals. I'm glad the politicians finally limited the importation and sale of cocaine, but sadly it isn't going to stop doping in this industry. As long as it makes someone money, it will continue."

"What was the name of the trainer Cody worked for?" Gabe asked.

"Arlington."

"You should speak to him," Mr. Goreman added.

The vet frowned at him. "Why? What does he have to do with magic and the racing industry?"

Mr. Goreman shrugged. "You'll find him at Yew Tree Lodge on Derby Stables Road. Don't tell him I sent you. He'll accuse me of trying to start trouble."

Mr. Wellington sighed. "I have another appointment. If you'll excuse me."

Mr. Goreman also made his excuses, but Gabe asked him to stay. "I just have one more question." He waited until the vet was out of earshot, before asking the trainer once again about bookmakers. "I asked you earlier if a bookmaker approached you when you were a jockey, offering you money to throw races."

Mr. Goreman's cheeks flushed, turning as red as his nose. "And I told you, I never threw a race."

"We know that's not true."

Mr. Goreman's jaw worked furiously. His nostrils flared. He looked like a kettle boiling on the stove.

Gabe's charm wouldn't work now, but he tried a calming tone anyway. "Whatever you say to us will remain a secret. We don't want you. We want the bookmaker who paid you."

"How is this related to magic?" When Gabe didn't respond, Mr. Goreman grunted. "This is outrageous. Don't you know who I am?" He jabbed a stubby finger into his chest. "I am the greatest trainer outside the royal stables!"

"You weren't a very good jockey, though. You lost more races than you won. Did you lose on purpose? Did you take payments from a bookmaker who ordered you to lose?"

Mr. Goreman drew himself up to his full height, but given he was short and squat the effect was somewhat comical. "I will not listen to this slander."

Willie grunted. "I reckon you got it wrong, Gabe. I reckon he lost because he wasn't a very good jockey."

"I could have won a lot more races."

"Then why didn't you?"

"I... I have nothing more to say." Mr. Goreman stormed off towards the main gate.

Willie swore under her breath. "He was so close to admitting it."

"What do we do now?" I asked. "Wait for Cyclops to give us the address where Arthur Cody lived at the time of his arrest?"

Gabe nodded at the grand pavilion overlooking the racetrack. "We speak to the manager and ask him for an address for Mr. Ferryman, the farrier magician. Even if he left years ago, they should have a record of him."

The flags on top of the roof were still today and there were no liveried staff on duty at the veranda to keep the riffraff out, unlike on race day. Gabe and Alex headed inside to speak to the manager, while Willie and I remained outside. She sat on one of the chairs on the shady veranda, stretched out her legs, and tipped her cowboy hat over her eyes. Moments later, her snore could have woken the dead; but, somehow, she didn't wake herself up. So much for keeping a lookout for potential kidnappers.

I yawned but didn't succumb to the lethargy brought on by the afternoon's heat. I wouldn't have slept anyway. My mind wouldn't completely rest in a place that could be the hub of the bookmaker's operation.

I was not too surprised when I spotted a man I'd never wanted to see again. The wiry figure of Thurlow stalked past, flanked by his two burly bodyguards, with two more of his men behind. I went very still so as not to draw attention to myself. Thankfully Willie was asleep. It was the only way to ensure her silence.

Thurlow didn't see us, even when he stopped not far away from the pavilion steps. He was focused on the ladies approaching from the main gate. They weren't the usual sort of women who buzzed around Thurlow like flies. They were elegantly dressed in the latest fashions more suited to drawing rooms than the gambling houses where Thurlow liked to spend his days. Both were tall and slim, their comportment suggesting many years of expensive classes. With their straight backs to the pavilion and large hat brims drawn down, I couldn't see their faces, but I had a dreadful feeling I knew them.

After a brief conversation with Thurlow, both women suddenly turned around and hurried off, their pace quick for women dressed in long, close-fitting skirts.

It was Mrs. Hobson and her daughter Ivy, Gabe's former fiancée. They didn't see me as they walked away.

Thurlow, however, did.

CHAPTER 10

I thumped Willie to wake her, then cut her off mid-grumble. "Thurlow's coming."

She shot to her feet, sending her hat tumbling to the veranda floor. She pushed back the flap of her jacket to reveal the gun tucked into the waistband of her trousers. "Turn around and walk away, Thurlow, and I won't shoot you."

Thurlow's condescending smile was all crooked teeth vying for space in his mouth. Both of his men laughed, while the two bodyguards revealed their own weapons. Willie's fingers twitched.

Thurlow bent to pick up her hat then approached her cautiously, hat extended, as if she were a dangerous creature. Once she'd snatched it off him, he stepped back, hands in the air. "Don't startle the wildcat, gentlemen."

The men chuckled.

Willie slapped the hat back on her head. "They ain't gen'lemen. Neither are you. What do you want, Thurlow?"

"I simply want to say hello to the lovely Miss Ashe." Thurlow turned his smile on me. "May I say you look as pretty as ever. That dress is very fetching on you."

Willie made a sound of disgust in her throat.

"Thank you," I mumbled. Too many years of having manners drilled into me meant I couldn't ignore a compliment, even from him.

"I've been weighing up whether to call on you at the library," he went on.

"Lucky you didn't," Willie said. "Gabe doesn't want you anywhere near her. Or any of his friends."

"He doesn't own Miss Ashe. She has a will of her own and a clever mind. Not to mention a classic beauty that— Ah! The man himself."

Gabe joined us, fists clenched at his sides, his body rigid with barely contained fury. Alex was just as tense, but his wary gaze was on Gabe. He was more worried about Gabe's anger boiling over, than Thurlow causing harm. Epsom might be the preferred territory for his gambling operation, but if Thurlow caused a scene on the pavilion veranda, he'd draw unwanted attention to himself. Here, there were other people's rules to play by.

"Step aside," Gabe snarled.

Thurlow hesitated before doing as instructed. He removed his hat and gave me a shallow bow as I passed him. Gabe stayed at my side, ensuring Thurlow didn't get too close.

I stopped on the first step, however, after a brief internal debate. In the end, my curiosity won over my apprehension. "How do you know the Hobsons?"

I felt Gabe's gaze on me, but I focused solely on Thurlow. I would explain to Gabe later.

Thurlow's response was smooth, prepared. "I had business to conduct with them. They chose to meet me here."

"What sort of business?"

"I wish I could tell you, but I'm afraid our agreement depends on confidentiality."

"Who introduced you?" Gabe snapped.

"I don't recall." Thurlow pointed his hat at me. "I do recall your name coming up, Miss Ashe. My, my, you've made an enemy there. I'd be careful if I were you."

"Ivy isn't vengeful," Gabe said.

"Not *Miss* Hobson. I'm referring to her mother. Mrs. Hobson couldn't mention Miss Ashe's name without spitting with rage."

"Why were you discussing Sylvia with them?"

The gold rings on Thurlow's fingers flashed in the sunlight as he waved a hand in dismissal. "Her name came up in passing."

Gabe looked like he wanted to press further, so I touched his hand to get his attention then trotted down the steps. He followed, with Alex and Willie bringing up the rear.

No one spoke until we were out of earshot.

"Why the Hobson *women*?" Alex asked.

"Why *not* the women?" Willie shot back. "They're capable of doing business with pigswill just as much as men."

"The women in that family are more intelligent than the men," Gabe said. "But I can't think of a reason for them to be talking to Thurlow."

"They didn't look happy about the meeting," I said. "If I had to guess, I'd say they didn't want to be here."

"Nobody wants to speak to Thurlow unless they have to," Willie said. "He looks and smells like he crawled out of the sewer."

Alex nudged her with his elbow. "What's your opinion? Did Ivy and Mrs. Hobson seem angry to you? Annoyed? Scared?"

Willie sniffed, then wiped her nose with the back of her hand. "I agree with Sylvia." She glared at me in warning to ensure I didn't tell them she was asleep.

We passed through the main gate and headed for the Vauxhall. Gabe looked a little distracted as we approached the motorcar. "I'll pay them a call and ask—"

"You will not," Alex growled. "Ivy is no longer your responsibility."

Willie agreed. "She and her mother are capable of taking care of their own business. They don't need you, Gabe."

He glared at them both across the vehicle before asking me

for an opinion. "Why do you think they were speaking to Thurlow?"

I wasn't sure I wanted to tell him. He might not like it.

He frowned. "Sylvia? What is it?"

"If you have an opinion, you have to tell us," Willie said. "We can't afford to be in the dark with Thurlow. It gives him an advantage."

"I may be wrong," I began. "It's just a theory."

Gabe urged me on with a nod. "I want to hear it anyway. You have good insights."

"Thurlow was warning me. There must be a reason for that warning."

He cast a look towards the main gate, as if he wanted to march back into the racecourse and force Thurlow to answer his questions. "Such as?"

"Mrs. Hobson has been making enquiries about me, not just with Hope, but with other ladies, too. That in itself isn't that strange, but there's more. My last encounter with Ivy was odd. Looking back, she seemed to be fishing for information about me. At the time, I thought she was making conversation, but the questions she was asking weren't ones you'd ask a mere acquaintance."

"What sort of questions?"

"She wanted to know where I used to live. I mentioned Birmingham, but not the other cities. She even asked me about my father, although she already seemed to know I'd grown up without one."

"Definitely fishing," Alex said. "Those are the sorts of questions you ask someone when you want to look up publicly available records. You have to know where they were born to find the birth records, which will have parents' names listed. It's the first step any private investigator takes when looking into someone's background. The Hobsons must have hired Thurlow to investigate you, Sylvia, but he felt compelled to warn you because—" Alex glanced at Gabe. "I don't know why."

Gabe wasn't convinced. "Why hire a man like Thurlow when a private detective could do the same thing and be easier to control? Hiring Thurlow to investigate Sylvia's background is like using a drill to make a pin hole in fabric."

He waited until I was seated in the motorcar then closed the door. He placed both hands on it. With the Vauxhall's top down, he was able to lean inside. "I'm sorry."

I frowned. "Why? This isn't your fault."

"I brought Ivy and Mrs. Hobson's ire down on you."

"You weren't to know they'd stoop to something like this."

He didn't seem to hear me. "I should have handled the breakup better and kept you well out of it. Mrs. Hobson obviously still thinks you were the reason for it, despite me telling her and Ivy otherwise."

I placed my hands over his. "Gabe."

He slipped free and took his place behind the steering wheel while Alex cranked the engine.

Beside me, Willie was surprisingly silent. Perhaps she wasn't as unsympathetic as she pretended to be. Or perhaps she was relieved he was pushing me away and knew there was no need to pipe up.

I ought to be relieved too. After our kiss at the Buttonhole, I'd decided to keep him at arm's length to keep him safe, so it was hypocritical of me to suggest he didn't need to keep me safe now that our positions were reversed.

But I was not relieved. I hated the distance widening between us. I hated that I might never have the opportunity to touch him or kiss him or simply to talk to him again. He'd become a very dear friend, and more. Cutting him out of my life was going to be painful. But it was a pain I had to endure, for his sake.

* * *

SINCE THE STABLES where Mr. Arlington trained a number of horses for wealthy owners wasn't far from the Epsom Downs racetrack, we went there first. We drove past the gated driveway to the main house, which we couldn't see from the road, and instead followed the signs to the Yew Tree Lodge training facility. The gravel drive led us to a U-shaped stable block surrounding a courtyard. There were at least twenty stalls, all with the top half of the doors opened for air. Behind the closed doors at one end must be the tack room, feed rooms, and staff areas.

The heads of the more curious horses appeared at the sound of our tires crunching on the gravel. Our arrival also caught the attention of several of the staff, two of whom welcomed us with friendly smiles. Given the Vauxhall Prince Henry was an expensive motorcar, they must think Gabe was a wealthy racehorse owner in need of a trainer.

Gabe didn't give them our credentials or mention the reason for our visit. He asked to speak to Mr. Arlington. A stable hand led us to a fenced ring where a horse was being put through its paces while two men and a woman watched on. In the distance, two more horses grazed in a field, and beyond it was a wooded area. After the bustle of the city, it felt peaceful. It made me realize how taxing the previous weeks had been since Gabe's stabbing at Rosebank Gardens hospital.

As we drew closer, it was clear that Mr. Arlington must be the elder of the two gentlemen. The other was middle-aged, as was the woman. She wore clothes similar to that worn by the women who worked in the land army during the war—a belted tunic with deep pockets, brown jodhpurs, and long sturdy boots.

Gabe extended his hand. "Mr. Arlington? My name is Gabriel Glass and this is Alex Bailey. We're consultants for Scotland Yard, specializing in magical investigations. These are our associates, Willie Johnson and Miss Sylvia Ashe."

Mr. Arlington greeted each of us amiably, his curiosity imprinted on his weathered features. The white of his hair, moustache, boater and light summer sports jacket contrasted with his tanned skin and the jade-green neckerchief he wore. He introduced us to the others—his daughter and son-in-law, Mr. and Mrs. Syme. "I train thoroughbreds, Mr. Glass. How may I be of assistance with a magical investigation?"

"You once employed a groom named Arthur Cody. Do you remember him?"

Mr. Arlington shook his head then referred to the Symes. "Do either of you?"

Mr. Syme nodded. "I do. He worked here for a number of years until his arrest."

"*That* fellow. I'd forgotten his name. He was a cocaine addict."

"He imported and sold cocaine," Mr. Syme corrected him.

"You've worked here a while?" Gabe asked the younger man.

"Since I was twenty. That's how we met." He nodded at his wife.

If I had to guess, I'd put her age at about five years more than his. There was an earthiness about her that reminded me of Willie. She wore no makeup, her hairstyle was simple, her clothes practical. Like her father, her face bore signs of years in the outdoors. Her husband was just as practically dressed, with his trousers legs tucked into long boots and shirtsleeves rolled to his elbows. He'd folded his jacket over the fence and loosened his tie. He seemed annoyed by our questions, or perhaps he was annoyed that we were taking him away from his work. The groom leading the horse through its paces in the ring had stopped while we talked.

"Before you ask," Mr. Syme went on, "I had no idea Cody was involved in the cocaine trade until his arrest. I can also categorically say that he didn't dope any of our horses."

"Mr. Glass didn't suggest that he did," his wife pointed out.

"He was about to."

"Do you know any of Arthur Cody's associates?" Gabe asked.

They looked at each other, but it was Mr. Arlington who answered. "He was probably friendly with the other grooms.

That doesn't mean they were involved in his sideline, I must stress."

"The police spoke to all of the grooms, as well as the family, at the time of Cody's arrest," Mr. Syme said. "If there was any doubt about our involvement, someone would have been arrested, but no one was. You can check with your Scotland Yard colleagues if you don't believe me."

"No need," Alex said. "I was one of the officers who arrested Cody at Epsom Downs."

"There you have it. I'm sure your team did a thorough job and would have arrested everyone involved."

"What about Cody's family?" Gabe pressed.

Mr. Syme shrugged. "I don't recall if he had any."

"Do you know if he associated with any bookmakers?"

Mr. Arlington puffed out his chest. "No one from Arlingtons is allowed to associate with bookmakers, whether they're grooms, trainers, or family. We're an honest business, and any suggestion otherwise is slanderous."

Mr. and Mrs. Syme drew closer to Mr. Arlington, flanking him. Closing ranks? Or were they simply offended on his behalf?

Gabe apologized. "Sometimes we have to ask difficult questions. I'm sorry to have caused offence."

Mr. Arlington nodded, although he remained stiff, the amiability gone. His tone was curt as he said, "It's no secret that corruption is rife in our industry, but I get offended when outsiders think all of us are cheats. We pride ourselves on honesty here. That's why the arrest of that fellow came as such a shock. Rumors swirled around the tracks at the time that he was doping our horses, but I can assure you that's not the case. Ask our veterinarian, if you like. Mr. Wellington is a strident opponent of doping. He'd tell you if there were ever any signs that our horses were given cocaine before races."

"He didn't work for us when Cody was here," Mrs. Syme added, her tone calmer than her father's. "Even so, he wouldn't have accepted us as a client if he thought we'd ever doped our horses. He's vehemently opposed to any form of cruelty towards them. I can fetch the address and telephone number of his practice, if you want to ask him yourself."

"It's all right," Gabe said. "We met him earlier."

Had the vet telephoned Mr. Arlington to warn him we might question him about his former employee?

I didn't think he had. Mr. Arlington and the Symes seemed genuinely surprised to see us, as well as offended that we asked questions about their prior knowledge of Arthur Cody's doping. I'd also believed Mr. Wellington when he spoke about the cruelty of the practice. The thought of harming horses was clearly abhorrent to him.

Mr. Arlington narrowed his gaze at Gabe. "Goreman sent you here, didn't he?"

"Father," Mrs. Syme chided.

"He's the one who told you Cody worked here. Admit it! It was that dog, wasn't it?"

"Does it matter?" Mr. Syme asked his father-in-law. "Arthur Cody did work here."

"Goreman can't be trusted!"

Mr. Syme clasped Mr. Arlington's shoulder. "If it comes to another investigation, we'll prove our innocence again. We have nothing to hide."

Mr. Arlington grunted and turned his back on us. He barked orders at the groom studying his fingernails as he stood beside the horse.

Mr. Syme exchanged glances with his wife.

She invited us to walk with her back to the stables, but waited until we were out of earshot of the others before speaking. "My father gets upset about the topic of doping. We had to put up with the rumors swirling about us being in league with Arthur Cody after his arrest. It took a toll on my father."

"On all of you, I'm sure," I said.

"It was a strain. My mother had died a year before that business; without her anchoring him, my father wasn't the same. It was the beginning of the end, really. He has relied on my husband and me more and more ever since. We run the business now. My husband is an excellent trainer, and I take care of the administrative side of things."

"It's just the two of you in the family?" Alex asked.

"We have a twelve-year-old son. He's a delight to my father. He spoils him dreadfully when he comes home for the holidays." She smiled. "The benefit and curse of being the only grandchild."

"When did you say your husband started working here?" Gabe asked.

"In 1890. He's a remarkable man. He used to be a groom, but he had such a rapport with the horses that my father promoted him to assistant trainer, then trainer when a position became available."

There'd been no mention of a Syme in Daniel's invisible ledgers. That didn't mean the name hadn't been there at one point. It was possible it had disappeared once the magic ink faded.

We'd reached the motorcar, and Gabe opened the door for me. I climbed into the back seat, politely thanking him while not daring to look at him. Out of the corner of my eye, I saw him flinch as I brushed past him.

"You worked in the land army?" Willie indicated Mrs. Syme's clothing.

"I did." She admired Willie's combination of men's trousers and jacket, and the cowboy hat. "You must have, too."

Willie pushed the brim of her hat up a little with her forefinger. "I drove ambulances. I wanted to fly Sopwiths but women weren't allowed in the Flying Corps."

Mrs. Syme rolled her eyes. "If only they knew we're capable of more than mothering and answering the telephone." She sighed as she gazed back at her father and husband, their heads bent together as they discussed the horse's progress.

Willie gave her a sympathetic pat on the shoulder before

taking the crank handle off Gabe and cranking the engine in a show intended for Mrs. Syme's benefit.

The Epsom Downs racetrack manager had given Gabe and Alex an address for Mr. Ferryman, the magician farrier who'd lost his position in 1891 after track officials realized he was a magician and grew worried that he was using his iron magic to cheat. According to the invisible ledger, he *was* cheating. It was growing late, however, so we decided not to visit the address. Instead, we returned to the library.

As always, Gabe insisted on walking me along Crooked Lane, and Willie and Alex insisted on escorting him. For once, neither Gabe nor I objected to their company. We were in agreement—we should not be left alone with each other.

Even so, I felt compelled to tell him again that Mrs. Hobson's interest in me wasn't his fault. "Nor do I think she's dangerous," I added.

"Thurlow is."

"She's using him to gather information, that's all. And if the information they find is unfavorable, then I don't care. It's not as though I have any standing in London society worth losing." It would have been laughable if it wasn't for the fact that Gabe's family did have social standing and associating with me could bring scandal to their door.

He seemed to be aware of the thread my thoughts took. He stopped at the library door but didn't open it. "I don't care about that either, Sylvia. But until I find out what's going on, and Thurlow is caught, you and I can't be more than colleagues." He quickly pushed open the door before I could respond.

Willie made sure to step past me and go through next. Where Gabe couldn't, or wouldn't, look at me, Willie was the opposite. The chill from her glare rippled across my scalp and down my spine.

Inside, it was a relief to see Daisy's bicycle leaning against the wall in the foyer. It wasn't her voice booming from the direction of the first-floor reading nook, however, it was Cyclops's. We found him proudly telling Daisy and Professor Nash that Ella was performing excellently in her training to become a WPC. It seemed his reluctance at having his eldest daughter follow him into the police force had vanished. Or perhaps he'd merely suppressed his concerns, for her sake.

The larger of the library reading nooks had enough seats for all of us, but Alex laid claim to the spot beside Daisy on the sofa by standing there. He, like all the men, waited until I'd sat before sitting themselves. Willie sat behind the desk and placed her booted feet on it, until Cyclops growled at her to put them down.

"Show some respect. You're not in your cave."

She poked her tongue out at him, but did as instructed. "So, what are you doing here?"

"I read the file—"

"Not you. Daisy."

Upon hearing her name, Daisy stopped smiling at Alex and blinked at Willie. "Did you say something?"

Willie sighed. "I asked what you're doing here."

"I came to invite Sylvia for cocktails at my place later. Petra is coming. I want female opinions about my designs. I'm not sure if they're any good. Oh! You're a woman. Would you like to come, too?"

Alex chuckled, while his father pressed his lips firmly together to suppress his grin.

Daisy nudged Alex in the ribs with her elbow. "I'd very much appreciate another opinion."

Willie shook her head. "I'd rather sew my eyelids closed with a blunt needle."

Gabe laughed softly. "That was very specific."

"And leaves no room for interpretation," the professor added.

Willie took their comments as compliments. "I'm creative *and* direct. It's a skill."

Cyclops's grin finally broke free.

Willie didn't seem the least upset. "So, are you here because you missed me, or because you've got something to tell us?"

Cyclops reached into his inside jacket pocket and pulled out a small parcel wrapped in brown paper and tied with string. "I read the lead detective's file on Arthur Cody. He was arrested in '16 in the stables at Epsom Downs while working for Arlington the trainer, which you already know. What you don't know is that his belongings were searched, both at Arlington's and at his home address. This was recovered from a small workshop he'd established at his flat and has been in the evidence room ever since."

I expected him to hand the parcel to Gabe or Alex, but he passed it to me.

"It contains pure cocaine," he said. "Can you detect magic in it, Sylvia?"

I untied the string and unwrapped the paper to reveal a cup's worth of white powder. It looked just like ordinary flour or talcum powder and had no smell. "I don't feel any warmth." I took a pinch of it and rubbed my thumb and forefinger together to make sure. "Nothing." I passed the paper and the powder back to Cyclops.

He gave me his handkerchief to clean my fingers, then rewrapped the powder. "So there is no such thing as a cocaine magician. Thank God."

"That cocaine has been in the evidence room for years," Alex said. "The magic may have faded."

"Sylvia should be able to detect traces of it," Gabe said. "Her magic is strong."

"Did Cody have any family?" Alex asked his father.

Cyclops shook his head. "He never married and didn't have children. He lived alone. If he had siblings, he wasn't close to them. No one claimed his body after his death."

"That's so sad," Daisy murmured.

"He injected horses with cocaine to make them go faster," Willie told her. "It would have killed them, but not straight away. Over time, it would damage their organs to the point where they stopped functioning. Not to mention the horses would suffer symptoms of addiction which are bloody awful. Still think he's worth mourning?"

Daisy pulled a face. "How horrible. Is that how he was discovered?" she asked Cyclops and Alex. "All the horses he came into contact with died?"

"Not according to the file," Cyclops said. "Arlington was investigated by the racing authorities and found to be in the clear. None of his horses died suspiciously."

It seemed Mr. Arlington and the Symes had told the truth about that.

"Who informed the police?" Gabe asked.

"Anonymous tip-off," Cyclops said.

"He operated from '90 or '91 up until '16," Alex said. "That's a long time to go undetected. Either he was very lucky or very clever."

"Unless he wasn't actively doping the entire time," Gabe said. "It seems as though a lot was happening in early '91. The existence of magic became public knowledge, Coyle died, Daniel died, his wife and children disappeared... Some or all of those may have caused Cody to stop doping."

"Then what made him start again?"

Willie wasn't usually the voice of reason, but this time, she pointed out something we'd all forgotten. "We don't have evidence that Cody was doping horses, only that he imported and sold cocaine."

"He was in the bookmaker's expenses ledger," I reminded her.

"But we don't know *why*. Maybe he was being paid for information about the Arlington stables. Which horses are training well, which ones are a bit flat, that kind of thing."

Cyclops heaved himself to his feet. "It's something for you all to consider. I'd better go before Catherine gets cross. I told her I wasn't working late."

Daisy rose, too. "I need to prepare for this evening. See you tonight, Sylv."

Alex walked her and his father out. He returned a few minutes later with Juan Martinez, Gabe's Catalonian friend who'd fought with him in the war. I was fond of Juan. Besides helping us decipher the symbols in the Medici Manuscript, he was easy to talk to, and always ready with a smile or joke.

Not this time, however. He looked troubled. "Gabe," he said. "We need to talk."

CHAPTER 11

"$\mathcal{J}$ am worried about Stanley." Juan's accent was as thick as the note of concern in his voice. He was really troubled about their friend.

Stanley Greville had fought alongside Gabe and Juan in the war. His experiences at the Front had shredded his nerves, however, and changed his personality. So much so that he found it difficult to function in society. He'd stopped studying and retreated within himself. The doctors at Rosebank Gardens hospital who specialized in treating shell-shocked former soldiers had helped him a little, and he'd even found work recently. Gabe and their friends were also keeping an eye on him, making sure Stanley didn't spiral into an abyss so deep he couldn't get out of it. The last time I'd seen Stanley, he'd seemed a little better, not quite as anxious, so Juan's concern was a setback.

"We made plans to meet," he went on, "but he did not arrive. I went to the pharmacy, and they say he does not work there anymore. I tried his home, but no one answered my knock."

"You should have broken the door down," Willie piped up. "I would."

"I do not want to get in any trouble."

"Did you speak to his neighbors?" Gabe asked.

"No. It was late."

"He was probably just out," Alex said. "I wouldn't be concerned."

Juan removed a cigarette tin from his jacket pocket, but apparently remembered that the professor didn't like anyone smoking in the library. He fidgeted with a cigarette before tucking it behind his ear. "It is just one time, but... I can't explain why I worry." He tapped his temple. "His mind is not getting better. The war still troubles him."

"I'll speak to him," Gabe said. "I'll call on him tonight."

His words reassured Juan and he relaxed enough to have a friendly conversation with us before it was time for him to leave. Gabe, however, fell into contemplative silence and appeared not to be listening. I worried about him taking on the burdens of his friends, as well as his own. Gabe may be one of the most optimistic people I'd met, but a multitude of problems could wear down even the most cheerful of men.

Gabe asked to use the telephone before he left. We waited for him by the fireplace on the ground floor. Although it hadn't been used since the charwoman had cleaned it at the start of summer, I could feel warmth. It was the warmth of Lady Rycroft's magic in the large clock hanging above the fireplace that I sensed, however. Now that I knew the difference between natural and magical heat, it was quite obvious. Particularly when it came to *her* magic. It was very strong.

Willie stared up at it, as she must have done dozens of times before. "Anyone else get the feeling this mystery is tied to the emergence of magicians in '91?"

"It's just a coincidence," Alex said.

I followed Willie's gaze to the magnificent clock with its brass numbers and hands gleaming in the light of the central chandelier. Without the light, this area of the library was rather gloomy, even in the day. I felt a sense of gloom now. Willie may be right. The timing did make it seem like there was a link.

Gabe rejoined us and Alex asked if they were heading directly to Stanley's flat.

"I didn't telephone him, but we can go there now. It's only four minutes to six, too early for dinner." Gabe hadn't even glanced at the clock or his watch. He always instinctively knew the exact time.

"Who did you telephone?" Alex asked.

"The Hobsons."

Willie swung around to face him, hands on her hips. "You want to visit them tonight, too?"

"I did, but they have dinner plans. I'll see them tomorrow night."

"They agreed to see you?"

"Uh, not quite. I asked the maid who answered the telephone not to tell them I called. She told me about the summer ball they're attending tomorrow night. I was invited, too, but I didn't plan to go. I've changed my mind, however. Meeting them in a public place is much better than calling on them at home. Harsh words won't be exchanged, and everyone present can see that there are no hard feelings between us."

Alex thought it was a terrible idea. "We can't come with you to protect you. We weren't invited."

"I don't need protecting. It's a ball for the wealthy and titled who remained in London for the summer. No one will try to kidnap me or stab me there."

"We can't be sure about that."

Willie had gone quiet, but she now spoke up, her voice heavy with defeat. "I got invited. I threw the invitation away, but I can prob'ly find it again."

Alex's laugh started light but ended in a guffaw that died only when Willie thumped him in the arm. "It'll be up to you to act as his sole bodyguard, Lady Farnsworth."

"*Ugh*. If they use that title to announce me when I arrive, I can't be responsible for my behavior."

"It *is* your title. People will use it, especially if it makes them look good. Imagine having the mad Lady Farnsworth at *their* ball! They'll be the envy of all society. You'll attract a lot of attention, so you need to put a lot of thought into your outfit. Don't embarrass Gabe."

Willie bristled. "I won't. I'll wear my top hat and tailcoat, perfect for a fancy ball."

The reason for Alex and Gabe's grins was lost on Willie.

"You really don't have to go if you don't want to," Gabe told her, still smiling. "I'll be fine."

"I have to go. Someone's got to make sure you're not kidnapped, stabbed, or cornered in a dark room by Ivy when the biggest gossip at the ball just happens to look in and catch you, forcing you to marry or face social ruin. I don't know which is worse, death, kidnap or marriage to that bi—"

"Willie!" Gabe muttered something under his breath as he steered her out of the library.

* * *

DAISY'S FLAT was never particularly tidy, but tonight it was messier than usual with her sketches placed on every flat surface, including much of the floor. It reminded me of when she was trying her hand at painting, but without the easels, and the canvases had been replaced with sketchbooks.

She made cocktails for Petra and me while we studied her designs. "Choose your favorites," she directed us. "I want honest opinions."

Two martinis later, I'd summoned enough courage to tell her I couldn't choose a favorite. "They're not really my style, sorry. But they're all very interesting."

Petra was equally apologetic. "They're not the sort of thing I'd wear either, but you know me, I'm not very adventurous when it comes to clothing." She plucked at the modest ankle-length skirt of her dress belted at the waist instead of the more modern drop-waists of Daisy's designs.

Daisy looked like she wanted to cry. "But they're not supposed to be adventurous! They're supposed to be dresses the average woman would want to wear to a party."

I put my arm around her shoulders. "But *you're* not average, so why are you trying to make things for a type of woman you don't want to be?"

Daisy twisted her long faux pearl necklace around her finger. "I suppose."

Petra started gathering up the sketches. "Let's toss around some new ideas together."

Daisy cheered up a little as she sat with Petra on the faded sofa that looked like it had once graced the drawing room of a country manor. Daisy had inherited a small sum of money from her grandparents, as well as a few pieces of their furniture, although from the mismatched look of them, none had originally occupied the same room. Yet they somehow made the flat feel as welcoming and as cheerful as Daisy.

I poured another round of martinis at the sideboard then joined them on the sofa. By the time we'd finished our cocktails, we'd forgotten about Daisy's sketches.

Somehow, Petra managed to steer the conversation to Huon. "He may have cleaned himself up, but he's still arrogant."

Daisy giggled from her position on the floor. I wasn't quite sure when she'd moved from the sofa to the floor, but she lay flat on her back, her legs crossed at the ankles, her martini glass beside her. "Did you know he was good-looking under all that hair and beard?"

Petra snorted. "I've seen better looking monkeys in the zoo."

Daisy rolled to her side and propped herself up on her elbow. "Don't you think he's handsome, Sylvia?"

"Very much so," I said. "And he smells nice, too."

Petra finally agreed. "I'm glad he washes and shaves these days."

"And gets out of bed before noon," I added. "He's turning

his life around now that he found a purpose with his new business venture."

Petra looked thoughtful.

The wicked side of me couldn't help teasing her further. "It won't be long before a society beauty snatches him up. He's a very eligible bachelor now. If you want him, you should act quickly."

"Me? Want *him*? No thank you. He may be handsome, funny, with quite a clever brain, but he's still conceited. Good luck to the poor woman who ends up with him. She's going to need it."

Daisy and I exchanged grins. Petra failed to notice. She was too busy draining the last drop from her glass.

"Speaking of the men in your life," I went on, "how was your mother's dinner party? You said she had plans for you to sit with a young and handsome guest."

Petra rolled her eyes. "He was young, handsome and dreadfully dull. I prefer men who make good conversationalists."

"You mean funny men with quite clever brains."

Petra pointed her speared olive at me. "You've hit the nail on the head. If only such a man existed."

It was then that I realized she was too drunk to be teased. She was taking me quite seriously.

Daisy grasped my ankle and shook it. "You and Gabe seemed a little tense in one another's company today. What's wrong?"

"It's complicated, but it partly involves his ex-fiancée." I didn't tell them about Melville Hendry possibly being my father and Gabe's family's association with him, mostly because I couldn't quite think of a simple way to explain it. It would seem I was a little drunk, too.

Daisy and Petra pulled faces at the mention of Ivy. "Engagements made during wartime shouldn't count," Petra said. "No one was thinking about the future. It was all about the present moment."

Daisy shook my ankle again. "Gabe isn't keen on her anymore. I know he isn't, because I see the way he looks at you."

I gave her a flat smile. "He's going to see her tomorrow night. At a ball. He wants to talk to her and her mother and tell them to stop investigating me, and to not spread gossip about me."

"Ignore them. They're snobs. Trust me, I know what that sort are like. My parents are the same." She sighed, deflated.

Petra agreed. "Gabe doesn't care about gossip and whether certain people accept you or not. And if it's his family you're worried about, I wouldn't because he isn't. Besides, when they get to know you, they'll adore you."

Daisy sat up with a gasp. "I have an idea. You can borrow one of my gowns and some jewelry and go to the ball, too."

"It's invitation only."

"Don't worry about that. You can use mine. They won't know you're not Daisy Carmichael, daughter of Lord Carmichael."

"You received an invitation to a ball where the hosts don't know you?"

"They know my parents and apparently I met them years ago."

Petra clapped her hands. "Then it's settled. Cinderella *shall* go to the ball. Now, let's put on some music."

Daisy placed a record on the gramophone. When the tune crackled to life, Petra grabbed my hand and took me in her arms as a gentleman would for a waltz. "All the bachelors will want to dance with the lovely, mysterious stranger, and Gabe will be wildly jealous."

If I wasn't so drunk, I probably wouldn't have agreed to the scheme. But after three martinis on an empty stomach, it sounded like a marvelous idea.

* * *

I WAS WOKEN up the following morning by Mrs. Parry knocking on my door and announcing I had visitors. I groaned and rolled over to check the time. It was already ten o'clock!

I pushed off the bedcovers and threw my dressing gown

around my shoulders. Toiletry bag in hand, I jerked the door open and came face to face with my landlady. Behind her stood Gabe, Willie and Alex. Willie sported a smirk, Alex a crooked smile, and Gabe a sympathetic frown.

"I overslept," I said, rather stupidly. "I'd better telephone the professor and tell him I'll be late."

"It's Saturday," Mrs. Parry said.

I pressed a hand to my aching head. That's when I realized I hadn't wrapped my silk scarf around my head to keep my hair in place overnight. I must look a sight. That explained Willie's smirk.

"Looks like you girls had a good night," she said.

Mrs. Parry shooed them out of the way to let me pass.

"Meet us in the kitchen," Gabe said. "I'll make you something to help." As I hurried off to the communal bathroom, I heard him ask Mrs. Parry if she had Tabasco sauce.

"I have a bottle of Crosse & Blackwell's Chili Sauce."

"That'll do."

I wanted to cry when I saw my reflection in the bathroom mirror. My hair wasn't the only thing that looked worse for wear after a night drinking cocktails. Fortunately, a little powder covered the dark circles under my eyes and rouge gave my cheeks some color. I pulled my hair into a simple chignon at the nape of my neck then returned to my room to dress.

When I arrived in the kitchen, Gabe handed me a glass. "It's a Prairie Oyster. Willie introduced it to us after our first hangovers."

Alex smirked. "That was the night we…" His words died on his lips as he caught the sharp end of Gabe's glare.

I peered into the glass. "Is that a raw egg? What else is in it? Oysters?"

"No oysters, but it's best if you don't know the ingredients," Gabe said.

Willie encouraged me with a nod. She'd never looked prouder.

The concoction smelled vile, so I pinched my nose and downed the contents. I almost threw it all up when the egg hit the back of my throat, but I managed to swallow it in one gulp. It burned all the way to my chest and made me cough.

Willie grinned. "Invigorating, ain't it?"

I blinked back tears. "That's not the word I'd use."

Mrs. Parry returned the bottles of chili and Worcestershire sauce to their positions on the shelf. "In my day, young ladies did not need restorative cures after an evening out."

"Then you and I came from different worlds," Willie said.

"She did say ladies," Alex pointed out.

All jolliness ceased as we headed to the motorcar. Alex wouldn't let Gabe leave the building until he'd checked the vicinity, then he and Willie ushered us to the motorcar. Even Gabe continually scanned the area as I tied a scarf around my hair and Willie cranked the engine. They were more vigilant than ever.

"Has something happened?" I asked.

Gabe turned to me from the front passenger seat. "We were being followed this morning after we left the house."

I looked up and down the street, taking note of parked vehicles and passing pedestrians.

"Don't worry. Alex managed to lose them. I'd never lead anyone to your place, Sylvia."

Willie climbed into the back seat with me and passed the crank handle to Gabe. "We should have stayed home today, but Gabe refused on account of wanting to get this investigation over with. He forgets that it's been unsolved for nearly thirty years and a few days lying low ain't going to make a difference."

"Lying low won't change the situation," Gabe told her as Alex merged the Vauxhall into traffic. "It will only delay the inevitable."

"The inevitable being your kidnap?"

"This way we'll draw the kidnapper out."

Willie sulked in silence. I got the feeling this was an argument they'd had multiple times already. Although I had an opinion, I didn't offer it. I didn't want to stoke the embers.

In an effort to ease the tension, I changed the subject. "Did you call on Stanley? How was he?"

"More out of sorts than usual," Gabe said. "He admitted he'd stopped taking his medication because he didn't like the side effects. When I explained that we'd been worried, he promised he'd start taking it again."

Poor Stanley. The war had broken him. How long would it take before he no longer needed his medication? Or would his nerves forever be shattered?

We arrived at the address the manager of Epsom Downs racetrack had given us for the magician farrier. After twenty-nine years, there was a good chance he no longer lived in the modest two-up-two-down house, but the woman who led us through to the parlor introduced the man seated in an armchair as her father, Reggie Ferryman.

He struggled to stand, and when Gabe went to help, he waved him away. "I can still manage."

His daughter stood by the door, twisting her hands together in front of her as she watched her father wince in pain.

Mr. Ferryman indicated his right hand with the gnarled fingers frozen into a claw. "Forgive me for not shaking your hand. This is what happens when you spend too many years on the tools. This and a bad back." He coughed a dry, wheezing cough that turned his face red. "And a bad chest," he added as he eased himself back into the chair with another wince.

Gabe introduced us, then mentioned that he and Alex were consultants on magical investigations for Scotland Yard. Before he could mention that Willie and I were assisting them, Mr. Ferryman interrupted.

"Glass, eh?" He grunted. "So, you're her son."

"India Glass is my mother, yes."

"I met her once." From the sour note in his voice, it was clear what he thought of her.

"Father," his daughter warned. "Don't."

"I wasn't going to. I'm sure she's a very nice person. But she's not every magician's heroine. She and a few others ruined it for some of us."

Willie made a scoffing sound and I worried she'd accuse him of ruining his own life by using his magic to cheat for the bookmaker, but thankfully she kept her mouth shut when Alex glared at her.

"That's why we're here," Gabe said. "You were dismissed from your position as on-site farrier at Epsom Downs because they suspected you were a magician."

Mr. Ferryman's top lip curled with his sneer. "The key word there is suspected. They didn't know for certain, but my work was excellent and I was efficient, so they simply assumed. It all happened suddenly after that bloody book came out."

"Father, language," Miss Ferryman chided.

"You mean Oscar Barratt's book about magic?" Gabe asked.

Mr. Ferryman grunted. "Suddenly the whole world knew we existed. It led to a lot of turbulence. Some magicians came out of that time well and expanded their businesses. Some of us lost our jobs. I lost mine barely even a month after the book was published."

"You landed on your feet," Miss Ferryman said gently. For our benefit, she added, "He found work almost immediately at the Royal Mews, which turned out to be very fortunate indeed. With the increasing number of motor vehicles on the road over the years, there's less need for horse-related work, but the Palace likes its traditions. He only retired six months ago, when the pain became too much."

Mr. Ferryman appeared not to be listening. He was still thinking of 1891. "I was marched out of Epsom like a common criminal."

"They were worried you were using your iron magic to cheat," Gabe said.

Mr. Ferryman grunted again.

"Did you cheat?"

Miss Ferryman gasped. "No, he did not!"

Her father shifted his weight in the chair.

"We know you had dealings with a bookmaker," Gabe went on.

Miss Ferryman drew in a sharp breath. Mr. Ferryman remained silent.

"Who was that bookmaker?" Gabe asked.

Mr. Ferryman pressed his lips together as if daring us to pry them open. He glared directly ahead, not meeting anyone's gaze.

"Was it Thurlow?"

"I don't know that name."

Alex must have been worried that Gabe would hammer the farrier with more questions about Thurlow, so he took over. "What about Arthur Cody?"

"I knew him. He was a groom for one of the trainers. I don't recall which one."

"Arlington."

Mr. Ferryman nodded. "That sounds right."

"Do you know Mr. Arlington?"

"I knew all the regular trainers. The Arlingtons were locals with a facility not far from the racetrack."

"Then you must also know the Symes."

He frowned as he thought. "The name rings a bell."

"Goreman?"

He frowned harder and shook his head.

"He was a jockey at the time you worked at Epsom."

"I didn't know the jockeys. Just the trainers, grooms and some officials."

"Were you ever approached by a bookmaker?"

"No."

Alex was undeterred as he pressed on. "We have it on good authority that one did approach you. Your name is in his ledger. He was paying you—"

"What ledger?" Mr. Ferryman barely got the words out before another cough racked him.

Alex waited for it to subside before continuing. "Who was he, Mr. Ferryman? Who was paying you to do something to the horseshoes?" He waited for an answer, then continued when he didn't get one. "Did you speak your spell into them to make them stronger? Or do you know the iron moving spell and spoke that during the races?"

Mr. Ferryman's face turned red with rage. He pointed his good hand at his daughter, looking stricken as she stood by the door. "See them out."

Gabe and Alex didn't move, but it was Willie who asked the next question. "Did Lord Coyle introduce you to the bookmaker?"

Mr. Ferryman glanced sharply at her. "I don't know that name. Now go. Leave me alone."

Gabe crouched before Mr. Ferryman. "He's still alive, isn't he? The bookmaker."

Mr. Ferryman lifted his chin. "I don't know who you're referring to."

"We understand if you're still afraid of him."

The farrier's eyes flashed. "I have nothing to fear because I don't know what you're talking about. Leave! Now!" Another cough gripped him, causing the veins in his temple and neck to bulge.

His daughter picked up a teacup from the side table and handed it to him.

We took that as our cue to leave. We weren't going to get answers. We were all sure he knew more than he let on, however.

"He's afraid," Gabe said as we drove away. "That means the bookmaker is still at large."

"Or Mr. Ferryman was the mastermind behind the scheme," I added. "Perhaps *he* is the bookmaker."

CHAPTER 12

A lengthy debate ensued between Gabe, Alex and Willie about attending the Saturday races at Epsom Downs. Gabe wanted to go, but the other two were reluctant given that someone had been following them.

"No one has followed us for a while," he pointed out as the motorcar idled in front of my lodgings. "With both of you by my side, nothing will happen. This is one of our best opportunities to observe Goreman and anyone else whose name appears in one of the invisible ledgers. If we see them talking to any bookmakers, we'll add them to our list of suspects." He didn't mention Thurlow's name, but I suspected he was the one Gabe truly wanted to observe.

Willie wouldn't entertain the idea for even a moment. "You're an idiot if you think you'll be safe at a crowded racetrack."

"It's not an important race day. It won't be crowded, and we won't let anyone get too close."

"That won't save you from a bullet."

"Whoever is behind this is not trying to kill me, or he would have told the Rosebank Gardens patient to stab me in the neck, not the shoulder."

I leaned forward from the back seat. "That could have been a random attack, unrelated to the kidnapping attempts."

My voice was drowned out by Willie disagreeing with Gabe. "It's too dangerous. You ain't going to the racetrack."

Alex was swayed, however. "Gabe's right. This is an excellent opportunity to observe Goreman, Thurlow and anyone else on the list we can find."

"Then you and me will go and Gabe can stay home."

"No," Gabe said.

Alex kept speaking as though she hadn't interrupted. "He's also right about it not being crowded and the kidnapper is a kidnapper, not a killer."

Willie threw her hands in the air. "You don't know that!"

"We'll go home to change into racewear, and I'll telephone the Yard. My father said we can have as many resources as we need for this case. I'll request four constables to accompany us to Epsom. No one will come close to Gabe with six of us surrounding him at all times."

Willie crossed her arms and slumped into the seat with a *humph*.

With that battle won, Gabe faced the next one with just as much determination and self-assurance. "Sorry, Sylvia. I don't trust Thurlow when it comes to you. He's up to something with Mrs. Hobson. Hopefully I'll find out more tonight at the ball, but until then..." He shrugged an apology, stopping short of ordering me out of the motorcar.

It was a battle that I couldn't win, so I gracefully surrendered. Besides, I had other plans for my afternoon.

* * *

I HAD GONE over what I would say dozens of times in my head on the bus ride to Smithfield, but as I stood on the front porch of the house where Fred Laidlow lived with the two Hendry sisters, it was as if the words were blown away like autumn leaves on a windy day. When Naomi Hendry opened the door, I tried to gather them up again, but it was hopeless. All I could do was stare at her.

She smiled tentatively. "Are you all right, dear?"

"Uh, yes. I am. I was just...passing by and...and I wanted to ask you some more questions."

Naomi glanced over her shoulder. "I should check with Myrtle first."

Myrtle would probably close the door in my face. Again, I tried to think of something to say that would make Naomi open the door wider.

In the end, I didn't have to. Myrtle appeared behind her sister. "Let her in, Naomi. I want to talk to her."

They led me to the parlor where Myrtle directed me to sit on the sofa and her sister on one of the two armchairs as if she was choreographing a scene in a play. Something cooking in the kitchen smelled delicious.

The two sisters appeared to be alone, but I wanted to make sure. "Your husband isn't in?"

"No," Myrtle said as she sat on the other armchair.

Her sister rose. "I'll make tea."

"No tea. This isn't a social call. Is it, Miss..."

"Ashe."

"I thought that's what you said the other day. Interesting name."

I swallowed heavily beneath her stern glare. She reminded me of a schoolmistress I'd once had who always made me feel guilty, even when I'd done nothing wrong.

This time I did have something to feel guilty about. I'd kept something from Myrtle and Naomi. Even though I simply *suspected* Melville Hendry was my father, I'd still not mentioned my suspicions.

I clasped my hands tightly in my lap and waited for the interrogation to begin. I had a feeling I knew what her first question would be. I wasn't wrong.

"How did you know the book you found in your library contained invisible writing? If you had to take it to an ink magician then you're not one yourself, yet you *knew* it was there. So how could you tell?"

Myrtle's question didn't surprise me, but it did surprise her sister. Naomi frowned at her, then turned to me, her lips parting with a soft gasp as she realized the answer before I gave it.

"I'm a paper magician."

Naomi pressed a hand to her chest. "How wonderful. Another paper magician. Do you know if there are any Ashes in our family tree, Myrtle?"

Myrtle didn't look at her sister as she replied. "There are no Ashes in any paper magician's family tree. Names are important in the magician world. They have meaning. Some have been distorted over the years, many became Anglicized when the family moved here from the continent. But Ashe..." She shook her head. "Fire and paper make ash. Fire is paper's natural enemy."

"Perhaps the paper magic is in her *mother's* family," Naomi said. "It's not her fault she fell in love with a man named Ashe."

I didn't want to hide the truth from these women anymore. It felt important that I be honest. "My mother wasn't a paper magician, nor was anyone in her family."

"Oh? So, if your *father* is the paper magician, perhaps he inherited it from *his* mother who married an Ashe. Family trees are complicated."

Some more than others, I could have said but didn't. "Not every surname has a meaning."

And yet I knew with bone-deep certainty that Myrtle was right, that *my* surname did have a meaning. After discovering that my mother was Marianne Folgate, we realized she'd changed her first name to Alice, so it made sense that she changed her surname too. When considering which name to choose, she'd decided on Ashe, the result of burned paper. The choice was meaningful. Either she wanted to destroy the paper magician who'd fathered me, or she felt destroyed by him.

Either way, her choice of name proved she loathed him.

I felt sick.

When I was a child, I'd made up stories about my father and reasons why my mother wouldn't talk about him. She was too upset after the love of her life died, or he was a foreign king who couldn't acknowledge us and she was protecting his identity.

But the truth was no fairy tale. James and I were the product of a destructive relationship with a man our mother couldn't bear. That man could very well be Melville Hendry. Even his own sisters didn't like him.

One of those sisters was now looking at me with concern in her soft, gray eyes. Naomi offered me a cup of tea again, but I declined.

"I should go."

"But you haven't told us the reason for your visit," Naomi said.

"Right. Yes, of course." I'd tried to convince myself that the reason for calling on the sisters was to ask about the paper rose on the hall table, but that wasn't the entire truth. The real reason was simply to see them again. Did I still think they looked like me? Or had I convinced myself they did because I desperately wanted to know my family, even if my father turned out to be the brother they didn't like?

But this second meeting proved it wasn't hope coloring my perceptions. In fact, I was now surer than ever that the Hendry sisters were related to me. Even so, I wasn't ready to tell them. Myrtle unnerved me.

To account for my visit, I mentioned the paper flower. "I detected magic in it," I told them. "Who did you say made it?"

Myrtle rose, an unmistakable indication she wanted me to leave. "We told you, it was a long time ago and we can't recall now."

"But if neither of you are paper magicians, and you haven't

had contact with either Melville or Rosina in nearly thirty years, why is the magic still very warm to the touch?"

"There are other paper magicians in the family," Myrtle said tightly. "Distant relatives. Now, if you don't mind, we have pies to prepare."

I exited the parlor and passed the hall table with the paper rose in a vase. It was a beautiful, complex piece of art that drew the eye no matter which angle it was observed from. My fingers twitched with the urge to touch it, but Myrtle ushered me to the door before I could. After brief farewells, she closed the door firmly behind me.

I stood on the pavement and blinked up at the rectangle of sky above the narrow street. Should I tell them my suspicions? Would they welcome me as their niece, or tell me I was wrong, that I couldn't possibly be their brother's daughter? Would they want nothing to do with me?

I'd been so lost in my own thoughts that I'd not noticed the door behind me had opened until Naomi whispered in my ear. "Miss Ashe? I want to apologize if we came across as unwelcoming. It's just that your visit the other day dredged up difficult memories for us."

"I understand, and I am sorry that we had to ask those questions."

I thought that would be the end of it, but she didn't return inside. She closed the door softly behind her and stepped closer to me. "It was an awful time. The police wanted to question Melville, but couldn't find him, Rosina and the children went missing, and then Daniel dying... It all seemed to happen at once. It didn't, of course, but that's how it felt."

"Can you clarify the timeline of Rosina's disappearance and Daniel's death for me?" I asked. "As you say, it's all quite jumbled in everyone's memories, but I think you and Myrtle are best placed to offer some clarity. Begin with when Daniel lost his job at Harrods."

She blew out a breath. "Let me see. He finished at Harrods in mid-1890. June, I think."

"It upset him a great deal?"

"He was quite distressed. Fortunately, that didn't last long, merely a few days, then he just got on with it. He perked right up. Rosina, too. They became quite flush with money. Rosina said Daniel found work with a private client who paid well, but she wouldn't elaborate. For the rest of that year, they were both very happy with their lot. We were happy for them too, of course. She's our sister."

"But?"

She sighed. "But Rosina was rather vulgar about their good fortune. They spent money on the most frivolous things. Myrtle called Rosina selfish and said she ought to donate some of it to the poor. They argued over that."

"When did it all go wrong?"

"That's easy to pinpoint. It was early 1891, shortly after that book about magic came out."

"By Oscar Barratt?"

She nodded. "That's when the troubles between magicians and artless started. It didn't affect us, since Myrtle and I aren't magicians, but it was around that time that Melville got into some difficulty with the authorities. Then in February, Daniel and Rosina changed. They became anxious and kept to themselves. After a week or two passed, Rosina and the children suddenly disappeared without saying goodbye."

"And Daniel continued to remain anxious?" I asked when she paused.

"Oh, yes, for a number of weeks. Then in early April, I think it was, his mood changed again. He seemed to relax as if a weight had been lifted. He talked about Rosina and the children coming home. Then the next day, he was dead."

"It must have been a very difficult time, especially with Fred's accident on top of it all."

"It was awful. He couldn't come to Daniel's funeral. For a

man to lose his hand, it's a devastating blow. He had to stop working, and without money coming in, things got desperate there for a while."

"His employer didn't offer financial assistance considering it happened there?"

"The accident didn't happen at the factory. He was here in the shed, fixing a piece of furniture when the saw slipped. He cut himself so badly the hand couldn't be saved." She shuddered. "Don't mention I told you what happened when you see him next. He's embarrassed that his own folly caused it, so he tells people it happened at the factory."

Despite the grim subject, my heart swelled. She'd said *when* I next saw him, not if. She wanted to see me again. Indeed, she expected it.

She must have recognized the emotions on my face because she smiled gently. "I do want to see you again, Miss Ashe. Perhaps we can explore the connection between our families a little more."

"That would be wonderful. Thank you." On a whim, I gave her the address of my lodgings.

It wasn't until later that I castigated myself. What if they were involved in Daniel's death? I wasn't sure how or why they would be, but not only did I suspect they'd lied about not knowing who put the spell into the paper rose, but now I also suspected Fred's accident was tied to our investigation.

I would tell Gabe tonight, when I saw him at the ball.

* * *

DAISY INSISTED I wear her best summer evening gown, a stunning aquamarine column of finely pleated silk with a wide scooped neckline, belted in matching fabric at the waist. The classic Grecian design suited my figure. Once Daisy and Petra finished styling my hair, they added a little color to my lips and cheeks and darkened my lashes and lined my eyes with Lash-

Brow-Ine, a product Daisy had ordered from America after seeing an advertisement in one of her magazines. They were both very pleased with the end result.

I felt more anxious than ever. "I shouldn't go. I wasn't invited."

Petra handed me a small, beaded purse with a silver clasp that Daisy had inherited from her grandmother. "Pishposh. No one will question you when you waltz in with a confident air looking like you just stepped out of the pages of *Les Modes*."

Daisy asked me to perform a twirl. "Petra's right. That gown could have been made for you."

"It's too long."

"It's supposed to be long."

"But I'll trip over the hem."

"Not when you put shoes on."

Daisy insisted on coming with me all the way to the host's house in Belgravia. Although she said it was because she wanted to see what the other guests wore, I suspected she was just making sure I followed through on our plan and didn't back out at the last minute.

We only got as far as the pavement outside the neighboring house, however. I'd spotted the familiar cream Vauxhall Prince Henry parked there, but it was Daisy who approached it when she saw Alex leaning against the passenger door, cigarette in hand.

He was about to take a puff when he saw us. His smile started slow and ended in a grin. It was entirely for Daisy's benefit. I doubted he even saw me until I was directly in front of him.

"What are you doing here?" he asked.

Daisy explained that I was going to the ball as her, using the invitation she'd handed to me before we left her flat. "It'll be a lark," she said.

"It will certainly come as a surprise to Gabe."

I flinched at his warning tone. "I should have mentioned it

this morning, but at that point I'd decided not to go. I changed my mind, but...perhaps I shouldn't. There's really no need for me to be in there and I'll just get in the way."

"Nonsense," Daisy said. "The Hobsons are investigating *you*, and you have every right to question them alongside Gabe."

Alex blew out a puff of smoke. "I can't disagree with her logic."

Daisy looked delighted with his response.

"I'd had too many martinis when the idea was first suggested," I told him.

He chuckled lightly. "Good luck."

"Before I go in, tell me how it went today at the races. Did you learn the names of any new suspects?"

He shook his head, but I got the feeling he had something to say. Something troubling. "What happened? Is Gabe...?"

"He's fine." He angled his chin towards the house. "He's inside with Willie." He drew on the cigarette before lowering it to his side and tapping it to remove the ash. "You're right, something did happen. We must have been followed to Epsom, but we didn't see anyone." He shrugged. "It seemed like nothing, at first. A man at the bar spilled his beer on Gabe. We thought it was an accident. No harm done. Then a while later, in the betting circle, balls of paper were thrown at him."

"Thrown or sent his way by magic?" I asked.

"We think they were thrown. They weren't accurate, but most struck him and not Willie or me. Again, no harm done, and we brushed off the incident. Then someone tripped him up. I caught the fellow and I could tell from the fear in his eyes that it must have been a deliberate attempt, otherwise he'd just apologize and tell us it was an accident. But he tried to run off."

"Did you recognize him?"

"No. We questioned him, and he admitted a stranger paid him. Tall fellow, strong, reddish-brown hair." The description could have fit any number of men, but no one immediately came to mind.

"Why would they do all those things?" Daisy asked.

"We think they were testing Gabe to see if he used magic to avoid the incidents."

"Like he did to avoid bullets in the war? Allegedly," she added quickly. "All those silly reports in the papers have led to this. Those journalists ought to be ashamed of themselves. It's because of their reports that Gabe is now in danger."

"The incidents today weren't dangerous. He was never going to be harmed by them, even if Willie and I weren't there. We think they were experiments that failed."

Failed experiments usually led to a modification of the hypothesis and further tests, and further tests might be successful if the experiments endangered Gabe or someone he loved. It was only a matter of time before the mastermind realized that was the trigger to activate Gabe's time-altering magic.

Perhaps they already knew it, but were just making sure.

CHAPTER 13

$\mathcal{I}$ had no difficulty gaining access to the ballroom. The footman at the door accepted my invitation without a flicker of doubt in his haughty gaze. The footman at the top of the staircase checked the invitation again and whispered to the footman announcing the arrival of guests. The hostess greeted me with a welcoming smile and introduced me to her husband as Lord and Lady Carmichael's "lovely daughter, currently residing in London". He bowed politely, said something about the run of warm weather, then greeted the next arrival.

The only guests who'd taken any notice of me were Gabe and Willie, both of whom looked around in surprise at the footman's announcement. They'd been chatting to some gentlemen at the edge of the dance floor while several couples streamed past them as the ensemble struck up a tune.

Gabe cleaved a path through the crowd towards me, Willie in his wake. Both sported well-cut tailcoats, black bowties and frowns. I braced myself.

"What are you doing here?" Willie snapped.

"Daisy gave me her invitation," I said, trying not to look at Gabe.

"I meant *why* are you here? Do you reckon I can't protect Gabe on my own in a room full of namby-pambies?"

"No. I made the decision last night when I'd had too many martinis. Daisy and Petra wouldn't let me back out."

Willie's frown disappeared, replaced by a nod of understanding. "Since you're here, you might as well stay."

"Kind of you to give your approval."

"She's not staying," Gabe countered. "Sorry, Sylvia, but it's best if you leave."

His cold dismissal was like a punch to my gut. I wasn't sure what I expected, but not that. Not outright rejection.

It even surprised Willie, but she quickly schooled her features. "Come on, Sylv, I'll see you out."

She took my arm, but I shook her off. I squared up to Gabe, determined to get my point across. Daisy was right. This was my fight. I needed to take responsibility for it. "I came tonight because I want to tell the Hobsons to stop investigating me. Although I appreciate you intervening on my behalf, I need to stand up to them, too. If I don't, I'll forever feel inferior."

"Inferior?" he blurted out. "To them? Is that what you think?" He took both my hands in his. Willie forced them apart, but he pushed on. "Sylvia, you are not inferior to anyone, least of all Ivy. I thought I made that clear. You are her superior in character, intelligence, kindness and beauty. It's not just me who thinks that. Look around. Look at all the guests pretending they're not watching you. I can feel every gaze they cast in our direction." His own gaze heated as he took in my dress for the first time. It warmed me from head to toe. "Is it any wonder they're staring?" His velvety voice was barely audible over the music, but I heard it. Or, rather, I felt it, resonating deep within me.

I stared up at him and wondered how I was going to keep my vow to stay away from him. If he continued to look at me like he cherished me, I couldn't be held responsible for my actions, any more than he could control his magic.

Willie pinched my arm, unceremoniously reminding me that we weren't alone. "Everyone's staring because they want to gossip about the son of Lord and Lady Rycroft speaking to a girl no one's seen before. Gabe, have you forgotten that your attention to Sylvia is what got us into this mess?"

"That's not true," I said.

She pointed a finger at me. "And have you forgotten that you might be the daughter of a vile man who tried to kill me and Gabe's mother?"

He rounded on her. "That's enough, Willie. You've made your point." He turned back to me, his gaze cooler. "She's right, though. We can't..." He cleared his throat. "We need to set some rules for the evening before we continue."

Willie tugged on the hem of her gold silk waistcoat and rocked on her heels. I'd seen the owners of winning racehorses look less smug. "Glad you're seeing sense. I have two rules. No dancing together and no going off into a room just the two of you. I don't want wagging tongues forcing Gabe into defending your honor."

"Understood," I said, determined to follow the rules tonight and all nights.

"At least with you here, Poison Ivy won't lure him into a room alone."

"I don't need nannies," he snapped. "She won't lure me anywhere."

A gentleman emerged from the thickening crowd and approached, smiling at me. "Introduce us, Glass."

"Not now," Gabe growled back.

The gentleman swallowed nervously and bowed out.

Gabe's jaw firmed. "I have two more rules to add. Firstly, you don't approach anyone from the Hobson family without me."

"Agreed," I said.

"Secondly, no dancing with the same gentleman more than once."

"Why?"

"Because two dances signals that you like him."

"Do I flatly refuse if they ask? That seems rude."

"Pretend your feet are sore."

Willie threw her hands in the air and muttered something I couldn't hear as the ensemble reached a crescendo in the waltz it was playing.

"Ivy and Mrs. Hobson appear to be here without Mr. Hobson or Bertie," Gabe went on. "They've already seen us, but they're rarely together. I want to wait until they are, and also alone. That way we only have to do this once."

I agreed to his plan.

Somewhat awkwardly, he departed after suggesting to Willie that she stay with me, since I knew no one else in the room. I wasn't sure knowing Willie was an advantage. Everyone seemed to want to avoid us as much as she wanted to avoid them. It gave me the opportunity to study my surroundings, however. The ensemble played familiar classic tunes, so unlike the jazzy ragtime of the Buttonhole and other clubs. The dancers danced the steps they'd learned from expensive instructors, only some of which I knew.

The ladies looked like glittering jewels as they twirled, their beaded dresses shimmering in the light. Gemstones of all shapes and colors adorned throats and ears, as well as their hair and over long white gloves. I was glad I'd borrowed Daisy's dress and necklace. I didn't feel out of place.

That didn't stop people from staring at me. Gabe was right. I was the oddity in their midst, the newcomer nobody knew. Only Ivy and Mrs. Hobson seemed to be ignoring me, or pretending to, but that didn't last. Friends drew them aside and asked if they knew me, since I was clearly known to Gabe and his cousin. It must have pained Ivy to see me, but I no longer felt as much sympathy for her as I used to. Not since I'd learned about their connection to Thurlow and their investigation into me. She was complicit. She must be or she wouldn't have asked me all those questions about my past in the library that day.

It didn't take long before a gentleman summoned the courage to ask me to dance. I started to tell him my feet hurt, but Willie spoke over the top of me and said I'd be glad to. She gave me a little shove in his direction.

I danced with him, then accepted another dance with a second gentleman. I could feel Gabe watching us, but he didn't stand aside and brood. He took to the dance floor too, with a different partner for each dance.

Sometime later, when my feet really did start to hurt, the butler announced that refreshments were being served. The dancers vacated the floor. Guests surged towards the tables set up in the adjoining room and I lost sight of my dance partner as I was caught in the tide.

Before I reached the tables, however, Gabe pulled me aside. "Ivy and her mother are together."

I followed his gaze to see the two tall, regal Hobson women with their heads bent together in earnest conversation. When Ivy looked around, searching the sea of faces, I knew they'd been talking about us. She stiffened as she saw us approach and said something to her mother.

Mrs. Hobson squared her shoulders and thrust out her chin, her pride as obvious as any peacock's. "What an unexpected surprise, Miss Ashe."

"Good evening, Mrs. Hobson, Ivy," I said as politely as possible.

Gabe's greeting held an iciness that I'd never heard him use when addressing them. It made Mrs. Hobson eye him sharply.

"You look *very* well, Gabe," Ivy said breathily. "I'm so pleased to see you out and about again, just like your old self."

"We're only here to speak to you both," he said. "I tried calling on you, but you weren't at home."

"You should have telephoned," Mrs. Hobson said, looking away. "If you'll excuse me—"

"A moment, please," Gabe said. "If you won't stay to hear what I have to say, then I'm afraid I'll have to speak louder."

The muscles in Mrs. Hobson's jaw worked with her frustration.

"You've been speaking to a bookmaker named Thurlow," Gabe went on.

Ivy looked like a startled creature in the moment before it darts away. Despite that, she didn't ask us who we were referring to. Her silence condemned her.

Mrs. Hobson was more composed, but a measure of uncertainty flickered across her face. "Who?" Her delay in asking the question confirmed what we already knew. She hadn't expected to be caught, so hadn't prepared an excuse.

"You need to stop," Gabe went on.

"I beg your pardon." Mrs. Hobson's chin extended further. "You have no right to tell me who we can and can't talk to."

"I can when your dealings with him affect my friend."

Both women went utterly still. Neither spoke.

Gabe pressed further. "Sylvia's background is none of your business."

They remained silent.

Gabe blew out an exasperated breath, so I took over. It was the reason I'd come to the ball, after all. "Thurlow is corrupt and dangerous, and he has Gabe in his sights. Speaking to him about me gives him ammunition against Gabe, because it makes him think I'm important. Please be careful. Thurlow will extract his pound of flesh and then some. We are only warning you in the hope it's not too late for you to end your dealings with him. Tell him you have no interest in my background and he should cease his inquiries. Besides, I'm not all that interesting. I don't understand what you expect to gain from delving into my past."

Ivy's chest rose with her deep inhale. "You think we hired him—this Thurlow fellow—to investigate Sylvia?"

"Didn't you?" Gabe asked.

Mrs. Hobson took her daughter's arm. "Come along, Ivy. The refreshments will all be gone if we don't hurry."

Gabe and I watched them go, all stiff backs and heads held at a lofty angle.

"They didn't know," I murmured. "Were we wrong? Are they dealing with Thurlow for another reason that has nothing to do with investigating me?"

"It's possible; but, if so, what is the reason?"

Willie emerged from the crowd in the refreshment room and handed me a glass of champagne. "What did the Hobsons say?"

"They denied it," Gabe said. "Is that champagne for me?"

Willie sipped from the second glass.

"It seems not. Excuse me, Sylvia, but I think Willie wants me to leave you."

Willie lifted her glass in salute. "Don't scowl at me, Gabe. We had an agreement. I keep Sylvia company while you do whatever it is you like to do at these things."

I watched him join the queue for food. I joined it only when there were other guests between us. It was there that I first heard the whispers and noticed the gazes. They weren't watching me out of curiosity, as they had when I arrived. Some were taking my measure, judging me. Others had already condemned me.

"She's not who she says she is," whispered one, not caring that I was close enough to overhear.

"She shouldn't be here," said her companion. "Does anyone recognize her?"

"Apparently she has no parents, no real home...she could be the daughter of a criminal, for all we know."

"She must be, otherwise why lie? Hold on to your jewels, ladies."

"And warn your sons. Don't let them be hoodwinked."

A third woman who'd been listening now piped up. "We ought to warn the others."

Sympathy came from an unexpected quarter. "Don't listen to them," Willie said. "They're bored toffs with nothing better to do than lick the Hobsons' boots."

"You think the gossip originates from them?"

"Only an idiot would think it didn't, and I know you ain't an idiot, Sylv."

I tried to ignore the gossip rippling around the refreshment room, but when the ripple became waves, it was impossible. Gossip even reached the hostess, although she didn't immediately act. She might be worried that I'd create a scene if she tried to throw me out. That could be worse for her than if I stayed.

I thought her indecision meant she'd do nothing, but by the time the ensemble started playing again, she'd made up her mind. She charged towards me like a bull at an intruder in its field.

I froze. Should I take the wind out of her sails and leave of my own accord, or should I stand my ground?

Willie left me in no doubt what *she* wanted me to do. Not one to back away from a fight, she settled her feet apart and stared down the hostess.

But it was Gabe who rescued me. He took the glass from my hand and swept me out of the refreshment room and onto the dance floor. His firm grip and reassuring smile soothed my frayed nerves. The gossiping ladies pursed their lips tightly and renewed their commentary, but the hostess left me alone. Gabe had stamped his approval on my presence, and the son of Lord and Lady Rycroft had sway amongst this set, even though he didn't attend many society events.

"Don't look at them," he murmured.

I obeyed, but found the only place left to look was at him. It was no hardship. Not in the least. I always enjoyed studying Gabe's green eyes with the flecks of gold, the angles of his jaw, and the way his lips expressed his emotions with the merest twitch. Usually, I had to hide my stares and only study him when no one was looking. I rarely allowed myself to admire him openly.

If I wasn't mistaken, he was admiring me, too. He wasn't merely looking at me to prove a point to the gossips. I could see the flare of heat in his eyes as he held my gaze, feel it in the way his hand took possession of my waist and his body guided mine around the dance floor. We were a single unit, bound together by the music and our mutual desire.

I felt as though we could do anything if we were together.

The music ended too soon. The spell broke. The first person I saw was Willie, glaring at us from the edge of the dance floor.

"We broke her rule," I said.

"Some rules don't make sense." Gabe gave me a tentative smile. When I returned it, he drew in a deep satisfied breath.

Willie wasn't the only one seething on the edge of the dance floor. I was the object of bitter glares and the topic on sneering lips. Dancing with Gabe had allowed me to stay longer at the ball, but it hadn't stopped the gossip. Now it encompassed him, too.

"I shouldn't have come," I said. "I've made everything more difficult for you with these people."

He tilted his head to the side and arched one brow at me.

I got the message. "Right. You don't care. But your parents might."

"My parents spend more time with Willie and the Baileys than they do at these sorts of things. Will you dance with me again?"

I politely declined. He and his parents may not care what others thought, but there was still the matter of Melville Hendry.

I thought Willie would be pleased when I told her I was leaving, but she was a little cross. "Don't let them bully you. You got a right to be here."

"No, I don't. I wasn't invited."

"I'm leaving, too," Gabe said. "I've spoken to Ivy and her mother. There's nothing else for me here. You can stay if you want, Willie."

A young gentleman who'd clearly had too much champagne bumped into her as he passed. He was about to apologize but screwed up his nose as he took in her masculine attire. "Freak."

Willie stepped towards him, closing the gap between them in

a rather intimate move. The man's eyes widened in alarm. A moment later, they filled with tears as he bent forward, protecting his nether region.

Willie stepped back. "There ain't nothing for me here, either."

Whispers followed us as we pushed through the crowd. They didn't upset me anymore. Gabe's reassurances had seen to that.

In the foyer, as we waited for a footman to bring my shawl from the cloak room, Gabe cast a gaze up the staircase. "We wondered what the Hobsons expected to gain from investigating your past, Sylvia. Now we know."

"You reckon they did it just so they can spread rumors about her?" Willie asked. "If they thought to cause you problems, Gabe, they're going about it wrong."

"They don't know that. They think I'll be worried about being cut off from society. They think it will concern my parents when they hear that my new friend has a shadowy past. It just proves Ivy never really knew me at all."

The footman arrived and Gabe accepted the shawl from him. He placed it around my shoulders. His fingers lightly brushed the bare skin at my neck, lingering longer than necessary.

I moved away.

Gabe looked as though he would say something, then his gaze shuttered. He lowered his hand to his side and began tapping his thumb against his thigh.

* * *

MY FELLOW LODGERS peppered me with questions about the ball over breakfast. Coming from middle-class backgrounds, they were familiar with public dance halls but not private ballrooms. They listened intently to my descriptions of the decorations, the food and ladies' dresses, but most of their questions were about the gentlemen.

"Was your handsome Mr. Glass there?" asked one with a sly grin.

"He's not *my* Mr. Glass," I told her.

"How many dances did you dance with him?"

"Just one."

The girl on my left glanced at Mrs. Parry, reading *The Weekly Gazette* at the head of the table. She lowered her voice. "Did you kiss him?"

The landlady gasped, but not because of the audacious question. Something in the newspaper had caught her eye. "Sylvia, you should read this. It's about Mr. Glass."

Not again.

She passed the newspaper to me. The article wasn't very large, but its accusation was powerful. It stated that "sources close to Mr. Gabriel Glass admitted he could heal himself with magic."

"It's not true," I told her. At least I didn't have to lie.

"I never thought it was," she said with utmost conviction. "Journalists will write anything these days. There's nothing to stop them making things up and passing it off as truth."

"Who is the source?" asked the girl beside me reading over my shoulder.

"Nobody, silly," said one of the others. "The journalist made it up, like Mrs. Parry said. Poor Mr. Glass, having to continually deny claims like this. It must be taxing."

"You ought to see if he's all right, Sylvia," said another. "He'll be in need of comforting." She sighed. Three others sighed, too, as they tucked into their sausages and eggs.

Mrs. Parry urged me to finish my breakfast quickly then call on Gabe.

I hesitated, however. I shouldn't go. Visiting him would be against my own self-imposed ban. We were supposed to keep our distance unless working on the investigation. Besides, he didn't need me asking after his well-being when he had good friends under the same roof to check on him.

So, I wouldn't call on Gabe to see if he was all right. I would call on him to tell him my suspicions about Fred Laidlow's accident. There. No one could argue with that reasoning. Not even me.

* * *

IT JUST HAPPENED that my first question to Gabe when I saw him in the library at his house was to ask whether he'd seen the newspaper article. He was surrounded by the Sunday morning papers but hadn't yet seen the article in *The Weekly Gazette*. I opened it to the relevant page.

As he read, Alex arrived. He stopped just inside the doorway. "Something's wrong, isn't it?"

Gabe showed him the article. "Another one. They're getting more inventive with their theories."

"And further away from the truth," Alex said as he read. "Who do you think the source is?"

"It's probably no one. The journalist made that up along with the rest of it."

Murray arrived carrying a tray with coffeepot and cups. "Mrs. Bristow thought you might need this, Miss Ashe, after Mr. Bristow told her you looked tired."

In my experience, saying someone looked tired was a polite way of saying they looked dreadful. "Please thank them for me."

"You do look like you could do with a cup," Murray said as he poured the coffee. "Late night, eh?" He winked and smiled as he handed me a cup.

"Don't you have work to do?" Gabe asked him.

"Not really."

Gabe crossed his arms over his chest. Murray saluted him lazily before leaving, passing Willie as he went.

She yawned without covering her mouth. "Is that coffee I smell?" She grasped a cup in both hands and breathed deeply. "I reckon I'll need a second one of these if I'm going out today."

"We didn't stay very late last night," I said.

"I made sure Gabe got home safe, then I went out again."

"To see Nurse Tilda?"

She grinned into her cup.

Alex hesitated before passing the newspaper to her. "You won't like this."

She swore as she read the article. "Who is this idiot?" She checked the byline. "He calls himself an inquiry journalist who exposes the truth, but there ain't a hint of truth in any of this. It's all hogwash."

"It doesn't matter that it's false if people believe it," Alex said. "The theory that Gabe can magically heal himself gives the kidnapper another reason to run tests on him."

"Damned Jakes," Willie spat.

"We don't know if it's him," Alex reminded her.

She tossed the newspaper onto the table. "I'll pay the journalist a visit and find out the name of his source, then make sure he prints a retraction."

"How will you get him to do that?" I asked.

"He won't be able to resist the charms of my Colt."

Gabe stood, coffee cup in hand. "You're not going to visit him, Willie."

"Fine. I'll call on the Hobsons and make sure they tell the journalist they made it up."

"We don't know if they're the source."

"Course they are, Gabe."

For once, I agreed with Willie, but before I could advise Gabe to listen to her, Alex chimed in. He also believed the Hobsons were the journalist's source. "Who else wants to get their revenge on you? You told us what happened last night, so you know they're capable."

"That was different," Gabe said. "That was gossip. This is more direct and more dangerous."

We watched him war with himself over the notion that a family he'd once held dear was now stooping to a low act that resulted in his life being upended and his freedom curtailed. He liked to think the best of people, but even he must see the

Hobsons now hated him enough to be behind this latest rumor.

I indicated the newspaper on the table. "This is gossip, too, Gabe. It's a larger, more public platform than the ball. To be fair, if it is the Hobsons, they don't know that these sorts of articles could fuel the kidnapper's interest in you further. They might simply believe they're making you unhappy."

Willie snorted in disagreement.

Alex was on her side. "You give them too much credit, Sylvia. I don't believe they're as innocent as that."

Gabe picked up the newspaper and flipped the pages to return to the front. "Whatever you all believe, no one is going to confront the Hobsons. Is that understood? They'll eventually lose interest if we ignore this."

Willie sat on a chair and poured herself another cup of coffee from the pot. Her morose silence left us in no doubt of her thoughts.

Gabe offered me another cup, too. "By the way, you don't look tired." He gave me a small smile.

Willie grabbed the cup before Gabe could pass it to me. "Last night, you made it clear you would stay away, Sylvia."

"And I will," I said. "Except when it involves the investigation, since it is my investigation, too."

Gabe plucked the cup out of her hand and gave it to me. "Sylvia came to warn me about the article."

"She could have done that over the telephone. And that article ain't got nothing to do with the investigation."

I thought I ought to speak up before one of them mentioned the real reason I'd come was because I wanted to be with Gabe. "I do want to discuss the investigation, as it happens. I forgot to tell you last night, but yesterday, while you were all at the race-track, I called on Myrtle and Naomi."

"That may not have been wise," Alex said. "Fred might be a suspect."

"Yes, I know. Naomi told me something interesting. He

didn't lose his hand in an accident at the factory. He lost it in the shed at home. He told his wife and sister-in-law that he was fixing furniture, but I have my doubts about the story. For one thing, surely it's impossible to almost saw off your own hand."

"A bad cut could have gone gangrenous," Alex suggested.

"Within a day?" I shook my head. "Then there's the timing. It happened just after Daniel died and before his funeral. We know someone was looking through Daniel's belongings immediately after his death. The sisters told us the house was in a dreadful state. Someone was searching for the ledgers. When they didn't find them in the house, perhaps they threatened Fred. When he couldn't deliver the ledgers because he didn't know where they were, the attacker followed through on his threat. Why would he do that if Fred knew nothing about Daniel's ledgers? He wouldn't. So not only must Fred have known *something* about the ledgers, he must also have known who wanted them. I think he knew Daniel's killer."

Alex and Willie exchanged worried glances, but it was Gabe's reaction that concerned me. His grip tightened around his coffee cup, turning his knuckles white.

"Gabe?" I asked. "What is it? What's wrong?"

"Do you recall that Fred told us he didn't know Thurlow?"

"I do. He claimed he'd never heard of him, but we doubted that considering he's a gambler and Thurlow is a well-known bookmaker."

"We saw Fred yesterday at the races. He didn't see us, nor did the man he spoke to. Thurlow."

My heart skipped a beat. It was proof of a connection between them. "Fred lied that day because he didn't want us to link the two of them."

"Or he didn't want *Thurlow* knowing he'd spoken to us. Perhaps he already lost his hand because of that link. Next time, he might lose his life."

CHAPTER 14

It was Sunday, which meant Mr. Jakes wasn't at work. Paying him a visit would have to wait for the following day.

We hit a similar problem at Fred Laidlow's house. No one was home. A neighbor said they'd gone to church and wouldn't be back for some time, since they often paid calls on friends after the service.

With nothing further to do for the investigation, Gabe and the others drove me home. In the past, I would have spent the day with them. Not anymore.

Mrs. Parry met me in the entrance hall and informed me that I had a visitor in the front parlor. My landlady was usually unruffled, but she flapped her apron at me and hissed at me to hurry. "She's already cross that you weren't here to receive her. Don't make her wait any longer."

For a heart-stopping moment, I thought Mrs. Hobson or Ivy had come to confront me, but I wasn't entirely surprised to see Lady Stanhope instead. The tea and cake Mrs. Parry had laid out remained untouched, and the expression of snobbish indifference was firmly in place. She did not rise to greet me.

"Good morning, Lady Stanhope," I said. "If you came here looking for Gabe—"

"Why would I assume he was here?"

"I'm merely surprised that you wish to see *me*. How may I help you?"

Lady Stanhope fidgeted with the rings on her fingers. Her black lace gloves lay on the table beside the teacup and saucer. Could she possibly be second-guessing herself? I should have known better. Hesitation and doubt were foreign to her. She broached the topic on her mind as directly as ever. "I heard about last night."

"Anything in particular about last night, or the evening in general?"

"Don't pretend stupidity, girl. You know I'm referring to your attendance at the ball when you weren't invited."

"I attended because I knew the Hobsons were going and I wished to speak to them."

"You could have left that to Gabriel."

"Gabe was kind enough to offer his support, but since it concerned me, I wanted to be the one to confront them."

She surprised me by giving me a nod of admiration. "You're different when not in Gabriel's company."

"As are you." I could have said she was less sycophantic, but I kept my opinion to myself. Indeed, I decided not to talk again unless absolutely necessary. Lady Stanhope was the sort of woman who knew how to draw out a response I might later regret making.

"I sympathize with you, Miss Ashe. Mrs. Hobson has you in her sights, and that is not a good place for a friendless young woman to be."

Since meeting Gabe, I felt very far from friendless, but I maintained my conviction and refrained from retorting.

"Of course, if what she says is true..." She waited, but I didn't fill the silence. "Society will never accept you, Miss Ashe. You must see that after the reception you received last night."

I gave in. I could stay silent no longer. "And by continuing to associate with Gabe, I am dragging him down to my level. Is that what you came to say?"

She fidgeted with her rings again. "That is *your* assumption, not mine. I am aware that he has taken you in as a colleague, of sorts, and I accept it."

Somehow, I managed to refrain from rolling my eyes.

"It's because of your association with him that I'm appealing to you now. Tell me, Miss Ashe, is the article in the latest edition of *The Weekly Gazette* accurate?"

I kept my features schooled and answered smoothly. "I haven't seen it, but considering none of the newspaper articles written about Gabe have been true, I doubt this one is."

"Don't you want to know what it says?"

"No."

"It states he can heal himself using magic, that he survived the war by magically healing his wounds."

"As I said, it's nonsense."

"Are you quite sure? Perhaps he hasn't confided in you."

"Then why are you here, if you think I don't have the answers?"

Her lips thinned in what I suspected was an attempt at a smile. "You are a smart girl. It must be from all those books you read."

"Is that all, Lady Stanhope?"

"I am not finished." She picked up the teacup and sipped.

I suppressed my sigh of frustration and waited.

She returned the cup to the saucer with a slow, deliberate action. "I've thought about it all morning, and I believe the article to be true."

"Why? Because a so-called source close to Gabe says so? I can assure you, no one close to Gabe would speak about him to the newspapers, whether he was a magician or not. The journalist or his source is simply trying to stir up trouble."

"They may achieve their aim. We all know someone

attempted to kidnap Gabriel some time ago. If that person is still at large, it stands to reason they may try again. You see, I believe someone wants to study him to see what magic he possesses. Perhaps the government or a private enterprise that wishes to replicate the magic. Whoever it is, I think they believe that conducting experiments on Gabriel will reveal the truth of his miraculous survival."

Experiments. Studies. She was using the same words we used, yet she had only half the information. She didn't know he'd been stabbed at Rosebank Gardens hospital. She only knew about the kidnapping attempt that had been reported in the newspaper, not all of them.

How had she reached the same conclusion?

"Believe what you want, but it sounds like fiction to me," I said. "Is that all, madam?"

"Not quite. I want you to advise him to confide in me. I can protect him from further kidnapping attempts."

"How?"

"If I told you, I'd have no leverage, would I? Leverage, Miss Ashe, gives one power and power is everything."

"You've wasted your time coming here. I have no influence on Gabe. Alex is his closest friend. You should approach him."

She sniffed. I wasn't sure if she thought Alex was beneath her or she thought I was the easier target. "You do have influence, Miss Ashe. Perhaps more than his other friends. You just haven't realized it yet." She gathered up her gloves from the table. "Do this for me, and I'll put in a good word for you with my friends. You won't experience another evening like last night. They'll accept you if I tell them to."

"I don't need their acceptance."

"*You* may not, but Gabriel does. He'll tell you it doesn't matter, but that's not true. Acceptance from his peers will make his life a great deal easier." Anyone who knew Gabe knew she was quite wrong. She was projecting her own needs and wants onto him.

I couldn't help the bubble of laughter escaping at her ridiculous statement. I tried to cover it with my hand, but wasn't quite successful.

Lady Stanhope narrowed her gaze at me as she shoved her hand inside her second glove.

I showed her to the door to make sure she left. After closing the door, I leaned back against it and expelled a measured breath. She might be wide of the mark regarding Gabe's need for society's approval, but her assumptions about the kidnapping attempts were very close to our own. Suspiciously close.

* * *

THAT AFTERNOON, Daisy and Petra arrived together with the same purpose—to find out how the ball went. I suggested we go out, instead of sitting in the stuffy parlor with Mrs. Parry listening in to our conversation.

Daisy wanted to take a leisurely stroll along Bond and Regent Streets to admire the fashions we couldn't afford in the windows of the exclusive shops. Petra and I protested that it was too hot for walks.

"Besides," Petra added, "you're supposed to be creating unique styles, not seeing what other designers are already doing this year."

Daisy sighed. "I suppose."

"We should find somewhere out of the sun, like a museum or gallery."

I liked the idea, but Daisy wasn't keen. We settled on a teahouse near the British Museum with daffodil-yellow tablecloths and pink daisies in small glass vases decorating each table. Their questions came thick and fast from the moment we sat down. They were sympathetic when I told them about the gossip, but Daisy's sympathy quickly turned to triumph.

"It was worth it just to have Gabe rescue you."

"She doesn't need rescuing," Petra said. "Sylvia is a modern woman and doesn't need a man to take care of her."

Daisy poured the tea into blue-and-white china cups from the matching pot. "But it is nice, particularly when she's keen on him."

"At least you didn't kiss him, Sylvia."

Daisy wrinkled her nose at her. "I think it would have been wonderful if they kissed."

"She might have regretted it the following morning." Petra picked up her teacup then lowered it again. "Particularly when the gentleman *presumes*." She sipped her tea, staring into the distance over the rim. "These things can't always be helped after a few martinis."

"I wasn't drinking martinis, and I was quite sober." I raised my brows at Daisy to see if she could shed any light on what Petra was saying. She shrugged. "Petra, is there something you want to tell us?"

"No." Petra placed the cup in the saucer with a sigh. "Yes. I kissed Huon Barratt last night."

Daisy choked on her mouthful of tea.

I stared at Petra. "Oh. Well. That is...an interesting development."

She sighed again. "We met at the Buttonhole. I rarely go, but I felt like dancing so went with a cousin after hearing you both talk about it. Huon was there. We said hello when we first saw one another, but didn't speak for the rest of the night. My cousin kept buying me martinis, and I blame that for my lapse in judgment. Just as I was about to leave, Huon approached. We kissed. I'm not even sure what led to it. It just happened." She made a face. "He's the last man I thought I'd kiss. I blame the fourth martini."

Daisy wasn't convinced by the excuse. "You *must* have wanted to kiss him, or you wouldn't have done it. I believe that drunkenness makes us do what our heart desires, but our mind would usually stop us. It helps us shed our insecurities and doubts."

"No. Absolutely not. I did *not* want to kiss Huon, consciously or subconsciously, not last night, and certainly never again. I won't make the same mistake twice."

The devilish part of me couldn't help teasing her. "He is rather good-looking though."

Petra blushed. "That's beside the point. The point is, he's arrogant and obnoxious."

"But is he a good kisser?" Daisy asked, grinning.

Petra glared at her.

I placed a hand over hers. "Sorry. We'll change the subject."

The rest of the afternoon passed with laughter and chatter, helping remove the bitter taste left in my mouth after Lady Stanhope's visit.

* * *

The following morning we had an easier time trying to see Mr. Jakes than the last time we'd visited him at the Directorate of Military Intelligence within the War Office building. His assistant remembered us and invited us to wait. Twenty minutes later, when we'd all reached the end of our tether watching Willie pace across the carpet, Gabe and I were allowed through. Mr. Jakes asked Willie and Alex to wait outside. That didn't stop her, however, and she barged past him and planted herself on one of the chairs as if setting down roots.

"We ain't leaving," she declared. "We're Gabe's bodyguards. If you don't like it, that's too bad."

Mr. Jakes gave in and closed the door. "He'll be safer in Military Intelligence than anywhere."

"Not if you're the ones trying to kidnap him."

"We're not trying to kidnap him."

"That's what a guilty person would say."

Alex positioned himself near the door. "Don't bother arguing with her. It's a waste of breath."

Mr. Jakes sat behind the desk and opened his gold cigarette case. He offered each of us a cigarette, before taking one himself. He lit it and took a puff, drawing the smoke in deeply as if it were his first for the day. He blew out a smoke ring towards the ceiling, away from us, but kept his gaze on Gabe.

"I'm glad you called on me, Glass. You saved me a visit."

"Let me guess. You want to speak to me about the latest article in *The Weekly Gazette*. It's all bollocks. I can't magically heal myself."

Mr. Jakes puffed on his cigarette again, giving nothing away.

Willie fell into the trap he set and filled the silence. "That journalist is either desperate for a story or someone's pulling his leg. We have our suspicions, but that ain't the reason we're here. We're here because we know you're behind the kidnapping attempts and we want to make sure you know that we know and tell you not to try again. Understood?"

Smoke billowed from Mr. Jakes's nose. "Are you finished?"

"Yes," she muttered.

He addressed Gabe. "I wanted to ask you about Hobson."

"Ivy's father?" Gabe sighed. "Is this about him not placing a spell on a batch of army boots again? Because I told you last time, it's nothing to do with me."

Bootmakers, Hobson and Son, had won the contract to kit out the entire British army during the war, after Mr. Hobson proved his boots would withstand the harsh conditions at the Front, thanks to his spell.

But something had gone wrong, and some soldiers suffered trench foot when water leaked into their boots. The worst cases resulted in lost limbs. The Hobson family denied any wrong-doing and asked Gabe to vouch for the magic in the boots, but he refused.

The War Office had shown an interest in understanding what really happened, and it wasn't the first time Mr. Jakes had asked

Gabe questions about the business and the family. Despite Gabe's reluctance to get involved, Mr. Jakes and the Hobsons continued their attempts to draw him in.

"Hobson is ill," Mr. Jakes said. "He's bedridden."

Gabe's gaze sharpened.

"Is he dying?" Willie asked.

"We're not sure."

"You're still spying on them?" Gabe asked.

Mr. Jakes placed the cigarette between his lips and left it there as he used both hands to sift through a stack of files on the edge of his desk. He found the one he wanted and flipped it open. "He's suffering unexplained chest pain."

"You shouldn't be telling us his private medical details."

Mr. Jakes closed the file and removed the cigarette from his mouth. "The doctor he is seeing now is not the same doctor he used to visit. Getting hold of Hobson's earlier records is proving difficult."

"Why do you need them?"

"Because we want to know if this is the first time he has been absent from work for any length of time."

Now I understood. He wanted to know if Mr. Hobson had been ill during the war—too ill to cast his spell. Something scratched at the back of my mind, a niggling thought that wouldn't go away. I couldn't quite capture it, however.

"You want me to tell you if he was sick at any point in the past," Gabe said.

"If he was, why not just admit it?" Willie asked.

It was Mr. Jakes who answered. "Because if he was absent from work, and the boots manufactured in that time never received a spell, it would open the company up to litigation by the government and the affected soldiers. The contract between the military and Hobson and Son stated that *every* army-issued boot would receive the strengthening spell."

"I don't know if Hobson was ill during the war," Gabe said. "I was rarely back on home soil."

"Your fiancée would have written to you."

"Ivy never mentioned her father was ill to me."

Mr. Jakes studied Gabe, trying to get his measure and determine if he was lying for Ivy.

Gabe knew it, too. "If Hobson and Son's failure to put a spell on some of the boots resulted in trench foot, I want them to face up to their mistake and compensate those men. They're in for a hard road ahead and some money would help ease the way a little. So no, Mr. Jakes, I am not lying to you. I genuinely don't know if Hobson was ill during the war."

I wasn't sure if Mr. Jakes believed Gabe, but I did. If I was unsure, if I thought he wanted to protect the Hobsons, I would have kept quiet. Instead, I finally captured the thought that had bothered me. "He has been ill before. Ivy told me so a few weeks ago. It was when she asked me questions about myself," I added for Gabe's benefit. "I don't know whether his illness was during the war or not, though."

Mr. Jakes's smile didn't reach his pale blue eyes. "Thank you, Miss Ashe. Did Miss Hobson also tell you who took over in her father's absence?"

"No."

It was likely the son in Hobson and Son had, but he didn't need me to tell him that.

Realization dawned, slow at first, then coming at me like a flood. Ivy's older brother had been a patient at Rosebank Gardens before the war. At that time, the hospital was a private clinic that specialized in drawing out magic from the artless children of magician parents. The doctors theorized that their magic lay dormant within them, and they simply had to be treated to activate it.

If Mr. Hobson was ill during the war and the factory relied on Bertie to infuse the army boots with the strengthening spell, it was no wonder that batch of boots failed in the muddy conditions at the Front. They never contained magic in the first place, because Bertie was artless.

It also meant Bertie's parents knew the boots wouldn't receive magic. They, and he, *knew* he was artless.

I didn't mention Bertie's stay at Rosebank to Mr. Jakes. It would be best for him if he came clean himself.

Gabe must have agreed because he also stayed quiet. Afterwards, as we drove away, he confirmed it. "I'll tell Bertie to talk to Jakes before this gets out of hand."

"It already has," Alex said. "You shouldn't get involved."

"It ain't none of your business, Gabe," Willie added. "Let the Hobsons deal with it themselves. It's a problem of their own making."

Gabe turned to me, seated in the back. "What do you think, Sylvia?"

"I think the real question is, why did Jakes mention Mr. Hobson's illness at all? Surely a senior officer in Military Intelligence can find out for himself whether Mr. Hobson was absent from the factory for any period of time during the war. So why involve you? Is he truly in the dark, or is he deflecting?"

"From the kidnapping attempts?"

"And his involvement in them." I held up my hands in surrender. "I'm not convinced either way, just as I'm not convinced of Lady Stanhope's innocence or guilt." I'd told them about her visit when they collected me from the library, and how she'd jumped to the same conclusion as we had, but with less information.

Brow furrowed, Gabe faced forward again.

Willie and I turned to look out the back of the motorcar, to make sure no one followed us.

* * *

ALEX WAS PARKING the motorcar at the curb a few doors down from Fred Laidlow's house when the front door opened. The two sisters emerged, each carrying a basket over their arm.

"Good timing," Willie said. "We can question Fred without his wife interfering."

Gabe, however, had another plan. "

"I want to follow them. It's likely they know more than they've told us. I personally don't believe Myrtle was entirely ignorant of the events unfolding with her own sister who lived next door."

"Myrtle ain't going to admit anything. She's too wily." Willie sounded impressed. Under normal circumstances, they would probably be friends.

We followed Myrtle and Naomi as they walked. Although we stayed well back, they would have seen us if they turned around. We were conspicuous, with two tall men and Willie in her cowboy hat. The sisters forged ahead, however, neither looking back nor stopping.

We almost lost them on a busy road where local housewives came to do their Monday shopping for weekly essentials. We passed fishmongers and butcher's assistants shouting their specials from the doorways, and children playing on the pavement as they waited for their mothers to finish inside the grocer's. The smell of coffee wafted from a café where olive-skinned men sat on stools, chatting in their own language, and my stomach grumbled at the sight of the small cakes in the window of a bakery.

There were more horse-drawn vehicles in this part of London than Mayfair, where expensive automobiles ruled the roads. They slowed down traffic along the main thoroughfare, allowing our quarry to quickly cross it and disappear down a side street.

I recognized the area. We weren't far from the old house in Whitechapel where we'd found the ledgers buried in the cellar. It couldn't be a coincidence, surely.

My suspicion was confirmed when Myrtle knocked on the door of the same house in the dead-end court. The same worn-out housewife who'd greeted us opened the door. Naomi reached into her basket and handed over what appeared to be a pie covered with a red-and-white checked cloth. The woman accepted it and exchanged a few words with the sisters before they moved on to the next house.

"The sisters are the connection," Alex said. "Daniel knew the man who was after him would never look here for the ledgers."

"He must have come here once with them," Willie added.

"That's one possibility," Gabe said. "The other is that he gave them the ledgers to hide, and they brought them here themselves."

It was certainly worth asking them. Myrtle might give nothing away, but I planned to watch Naomi. Her face was the more expressive of the two, and she was less devious.

CHAPTER 15

I was very aware of how formidable the four of us appeared, waiting near the entrance to the courtyard. While we weren't blocking the sisters' exit, we presented a united front.

Even so, Myrtle marched up to us. With her basket resting on one hip and her hand on the other, she confronted me. "Why have you followed us?"

My guilty conscience got the better of me and I apologized. "Sorry, but we wanted to ask you some questions."

"You could have done that at home. I'll ask again, why follow us?"

"I had an inkling you would come here," Gabe said. "I had a theory and I wanted to see if I was right."

"A theory about what?"

"Do you recall our first meeting, when we told you Daniel wrote an invisible message in a book to his cousin? The message gave an address where he'd hidden evidence of crimes committed by a corrupt bookmaker." Gabe nodded at the house. "We found the evidence in there."

Naomi gasped. "But Mary Philpot lives there. Surely you don't think she had something to do with Daniel's death?"

Myrtle clicked her tongue at her sister, but kept her gaze firmly on Gabe. "Don't be a fool, Naomi. He's accusing *us* of hiding something there for Daniel."

Naomi gasped again and pressed a hand to her chest.

"That's not what he said," Willie snapped.

"It was implied," Myrtle shot back.

Gabe shook his head in warning at Willie and she closed her mouth. She grunted to signal she did so reluctantly.

"You give charity to these families?" Gabe asked.

"We're not answering your questions," Myrtle said. "Move aside."

"You're free to go at any time. But I warn you that will make you look guilty."

Myrtle's grunt was remarkably similar to Willie's. Like Willie, she also complied, however. "Yes, we provide charity to all the families in this yard."

"Some of the wives lost their husbands in the war," Naomi added. "Or their husbands came home too damaged to work. In two instances, the man of the house is on strike, so there's no money coming in. Most rely on charity just to survive."

"You've been coming here for years?" Gabe asked. "Since before Daniel died?"

Naomi glanced at her sister, no longer sure if she should answer.

"Yes," Myrtle said. "There has always been a need for charity in these homes, for one reason or another. The cycle of poverty continues from generation to generation because every government fails to end it."

"How did Daniel know about this address?"

"He must have followed us one day."

Naomi hefted the basket higher on her hip and studied the ground at her feet.

"We have nothing to hide, Mr. Glass," Myrtle went on. "Not from you or the police. Now, if you'll excuse us, we have hungry families to feed."

Myrtle marched off with long, purposeful strides. Naomi trotted behind. As she passed, she cast me an uncertain half-smile.

I watched them go. "I think they spoke the truth. They have nothing to hide from us or the police. But I believe they did have something to hide from the bookmaker—those ledgers. They're still afraid of him."

Gabe indicated that I should walk ahead as we left the court-yard. "I wish we could tell them not to be afraid, but I can't guarantee them safety when I can't even guarantee my own."

It took all my self-control not to take his hand and give it a reassuring squeeze.

We left the airless courtyard behind and returned to Fred's house in Smithfield. Myrtle and Naomi had headed in the oppo-site direction, so it was safe to assume they would be gone for a while.

I, for one, was grateful that Myrtle wouldn't be present when we questioned her husband.

We caught Fred about to leave. A newspaper was tucked under his arm, and he rested his hat on his wrist stump as he stepped onto the porch. "Hello again. The girls aren't home, I'm afraid. They're out fixing the world's problems with their pies."

"Actually, we came to see you," Gabe said. "May we come inside?"

"I was about to leave."

"This won't take long."

Fred paused before taking a step back. "Come into the parlor."

As I passed, I noticed the newspaper was opened to the racing pages. He'd circled several horse names in pencil.

Gabe and I sat, but Alex stood by the door and Willie near the window. I thought they were there to guard Gabe from intrud-ers. When Fred eyed them with suspicion, however, I realized they'd deliberately positioned themselves to cut off his escape routes.

Despite his suspicion, Fred maintained a cheerful disposition. "I'm not sure how I can help your inquiries further, but I'll try."

Gabe took the direct approach. "We saw you yesterday at Epsom, speaking to a man named Thurlow."

Fred made a show of gazing to the ceiling and puckering his lips in thought. "Thurlow... Thurlow... Sorry, it means nothing to me."

"Come now, Mr. Laidlow. You're a gambler and he's a long-time bookmaker there. This meeting will go faster if you tell us the truth the first time."

Fred's forehead beaded with sweat.

Willie huffed. "We could threaten you if we wanted to. You're real familiar with how threats work, aren't you?"

Fred tugged on his cuff to cover the stump. "I know Thurlow. What of it?"

"Why did you lie and say you didn't?" Gabe asked.

"Because I know he's a thug. You were asking about him at the racecourse, so I assume you think he has something to do with your investigation. I didn't want to get involved. I owe him money, you see. If he finds out I helped you..." He removed a handkerchief from his pocket and wiped his forehead. "Let's just say he won't like it. Not that he had anything to do with Daniel's death," he added quickly. "That's not what I'm saying. He was young then. Thurlow, I mean. His business had barely begun in '91."

"Are you implying he conducted himself honestly in those days?" Gabe asked. "As a bookmaker?"

Fred winced. "More or less."

"Or is that simply when his business became more successful?"

Fred pocketed the handkerchief. "I've answered your question. I knew Thurlow then. Now, if there's nothing else..." He rose to leave.

Alex moved to block the exit. "Sit down, Mr. Laidlow. We'll let you know when we're finished."

Fred sat. "This is harassment."

"This is interrogation," Gabe said. "We can do it here or at Scotland Yard. Of course, if you choose the latter, the neighbors will see you leaving with us and will tell anyone who comes looking for you. Thurlow, for instance."

Fred blew out a shuddery breath. "Look. I admit I lied about knowing Thurlow. I didn't lie because he's guilty of killing Daniel. I did it because he terrifies me. He wouldn't want me speaking to the police, even if I was telling you he's innocent." He wiped away a trickle of sweat running down the side of his face with his shoulder. "I wasn't even in debt to Thurlow in those days, so he had no leverage with me back then."

"Who were you in debt to?"

Fred shook his head. "None of this makes sense."

Gabe leaned forward and rested his elbows on his knees, his hands loosely clasped. "Look at me, Fred."

Fred lifted his teary gaze to Gabe's. I knew how compelling Gabe's eyes could be, how his gaze drilled into you and made you feel seen. For me, it was a comfort. For someone with something to hide, I suspected it was alarming to find oneself confiding things they planned to keep secret.

Gabe's tone gentled. "Let me tell you what we know. We know you knew Daniel went to work for a bookmaker after he lost his job at Harrods. Presumably Daniel told you because, as a regular racegoer and gambler, you were familiar with the fellow."

"That's the gist," Fred muttered.

"Then Daniel had a change of heart. He wanted to stop. But he knew too much. He could bring the bookmaker's entire operation crashing down. Daniel knew the only way to stop working for men like that, men of the same ilk as Thurlow, is to either hide or attack. He used a combination of both. He hid his wife and children, and he hid some evidence. He then wrote to his cousin, telling him he feared for his life, and to avenge his death using the evidence the book would help him find, if it came to that. The problem was, Oscar never saw the message. The book-maker went after Daniel. He threatened him, telling him to return the evidence. When Daniel didn't, the bookmaker put pressure on him. That pressure must have killed him."

Fred sniffed. He wiped his nose on his sleeve but didn't inter-rupt. It was a sign that Gabe was on the right path.

Gabe continued. "He searched Daniel's house but didn't find the evidence. So, he came to you. As Daniel's brother-in-law, neighbor, and a man who was in debt to the bookmaker, he presumed you would know where the evidence was hidden."

"I didn't," Fred spluttered.

"He didn't believe you, though, did he? He threatened to maim you. When you didn't deliver the evidence, he had to follow through on his threat. For people like Thurlow and this bookmaker, threats have to be carried out when delivery fails, or no one will fear him ever again. So he cut off your hand."

Fred rubbed the stump where his hand used to be. "I told him, I didn't know!"

"Who? Who did you tell?"

"It no longer matters."

"Why not? Is the bookmaker dead?"

Fred wiped damp cheeks with his sleeve. "Last I heard, he was still alive. But he's been in an asylum for years."

"Asylum?" Alex asked. "Like Bedlam?"

"Not Bedlam. A private one."

The news took us all by surprise. Gabe took a few moments to process it before coming up with more questions. "How long has he been there?"

"That's the thing. That's why he couldn't have killed Daniel. His riding accident was in March '91, a month *before* Daniel died."

Gabe slowly sat back, not taking his gaze off Fred. "What's the bookmaker's name?"

"Arlington."

I bit the inside of my cheek to stop myself blurting out that we'd met the trainer, Mr. Arlington, and he was perfectly well.

Gabe's features remained schooled. "Which Arlington?"

"Ambrose. He was only twenty-three at the time, but he was already ruthless. Thurlow modeled himself after Ambrose. You could say he took over from him."

"Thurlow worked for him?" Willie asked.

Fred shrugged one shoulder. "I meant Ambrose Arlington's accident led to his absence from the bookmaking business, and that left a hole. Thurlow swooped in and filled it. The rest is history."

"Is Ambrose any relation to Arlington the trainer?"

Fred drew in a deep breath. "His son."

"He doesn't have a son," Willie said.

"He does. He just pretends he doesn't. He never talks about him. From what I hear, Ambrose is as helpless as a baby. For a successful, proud man like Ignatius Arlington, he must find that embarrassing."

When put like that, it was a double tragedy. First, when the accident happened, and then when Ambrose's own father stopped caring.

Perhaps I shouldn't feel sympathy. At the very least, Ambrose was a bookmaker on the sly. According to Fred, however, he wasn't responsible for murdering Daniel. His accident had sent him to the asylum a month earlier.

Something about the timeline didn't ring true. "If Ambrose was in the asylum in March, and Daniel died in April, just a day or two before your hand was cut off...Ambrose wasn't the one who threatened you, was he? He couldn't have. So who did? Who removed your hand, Mr. Laidlow?"

"I don't know. I never saw his face."

Willie snorted and Alex made a scoffing sound.

"It's true! He wore a mask made of black cloth that covered his entire head. He cut out eyeholes so he could see."

"Was there anything unusual about him?" Gabe asked. "His height? Girth?"

Fred shook his head. "I didn't even recognize his voice."

With no further questions, we filed out of the house with Fred. He locked the door before walking off, head sheepishly bowed, the newspaper tucked under his arm. We sat in the motorcar with the engine idling, watching until he disappeared around the corner.

"Thurlow is in the clear for this," Alex said to Gabe.

"*If* Fred's telling the truth," Gabe said. "We can't take his word about anything, but particularly that. He's afraid, and fearful men tell lies. We should check whether Ambrose Arlington is actually in an asylum. He may have simply had a falling out with his father and left the family home."

"The timing matches," I pointed out. "The sisters told us Daniel stopped being afraid leading up to his death. The book-maker's accident or disappearance would explain that. Daniel thought he was safe. He didn't consider anyone else a threat."

"The killer could be the bookmaker's business partner," Alex suggested.

Willie pulled aside her jacket to reveal the gun at her side. "Want me to go after Fred and ask about a partner? I reckon this will make him answer."

"Put it away," Gabe growled. "We'll verify his claim first by learning what we can about Ambrose Arlington. We'll ask his father where he is."

Alex pulled the Vauxhall away from the curb into the traffic. "Ignatius Arlington and the Symes let us believe he only had the one child, Mrs. Syme. They didn't lie, they merely didn't give us the entire truth."

Willie clicked her fingers as a thought occurred to her. "Syme started working there in 1890 and got promoted to trainer when a position became available. That must have been when Ambrose had his accident."

I recalled the conversation with the family at their training facility. There'd been no mention of Ambrose. It was as if he never existed. I also recalled Mr. Arlington's vehement denial that his employees associated with bookmakers. How would he react when we accused his son of being an illegal bookmaker, and a cheating one at that?

"I don't think we should confront Mr. Arlington directly," I said, raising my voice to be heard over the engine. "I doubt we'll get an honest answer. In fact, we may cause him to completely shut us out if he thinks we're accusing his family of wrongdoing."

"I reckon she's right," Willie said. "I reckon we don't confront them. Not yet. We don't want to let them know that we know about Ambrose."

Alex nodded as he slowed the motorcar to stop at an intersection. "We don't want them destroying evidence. We need to find Ambrose without asking them where he is."

"Any suggestions?" Gabe asked.

"You won't like it."

"When has that stopped us?"

Willie let out a *whoop* and slapped her knee. "This'll be fun!"

"What will?" I asked, looking at each of them in turn. "What are we going to do?"

"Not you," Gabe said. "It might be dangerous."

"Aw, let her come," Willie said. "She'll be less conspicuous than either of you two, and it ain't fair to leave her out of the investigation now."

I hadn't expected support from that quarter, given she wanted me far away from Gabe. Her sense of female solidarity must be strong indeed. "Are you suggesting we break into the Arlingtons' home after dark? Can we not just ask Scotland Yard to authorize a search?"

"That'll take too long," Gabe said.

"We don't have enough evidence for a search warrant," Alex added.

"And it ain't as much fun." Willie plucked at my cream-colored skirt with the navy piping around the pocket. "Wear black."

* * *

IT WAS a good thing that I spent the rest of the day working in the library. Being surrounded by books helped settle my nerves. Professor Nash and I stopped to have tea with Evaline Peterson who called on me in the afternoon. Although she claimed she was simply in the area and her visit was unplanned, I got the feeling she was curious about me and wanted to see where I worked.

Her visit was fortuitous. I'd been considering whether to ask her and Walter about Rosina Barratt. I broached the topic as I handed her a teacup and saucer.

"Are you familiar with a paper magician named Rosina? Her maiden name was Hendry, and she married an ink magician, Daniel Barratt."

Evaline's thin, straight eyebrows furrowed with her thoughtful frown. "The name Hendry is familiar, but not Rosina. There was a magician named Hendry who knew a spell to make paper fly. I believe we mentioned him to you. His spell caused some trouble and the police had to intervene. I was only thirteen or fourteen at the time, so I don't know the particulars."

"Rosina disappeared around the time of the incident you're referring to. I thought you might know her."

"There are a number of paper magicians," she said, wryly. "We're not all related."

I laughed softly. "I know."

"Are you looking for her, this Rosina Hendry?"

"We are."

"Because you've learned she's your relative?"

"Oh, no," I said quickly. It was too soon to tell her my suspicions about my relationship to the Hendry family, and Melville

Hendry in particular. Until I was sure, I must continue to deny it. For Gabe's sake, as much as my own.

Evaline changed the subject and asked the professor and me to tell her about the library and our work. She was an excellent listener given the topic was one that bored some people. Perhaps that was because her paper magic made her more inclined to like anything to do with books, as mine did.

It wasn't until after she'd left that I wondered if she'd encouraged me to talk because she was studying me. Indeed, even when the professor spoke, Evaline continued to cast me surreptitious glances.

I'd been in her company several times since meeting her and Walter, so why did she take so much interest now? Did she know more about Rosina than she let on? Or had she come to the library with the sole purpose of studying me?

* * *

FOR SOMEONE who liked to follow the rules, I was becoming quite the expert at breaking and entering. I told myself we were on official police business, and if we were caught, we would be let off with just a warning. Unsurprisingly, that imaginary voice sounded a lot like Willie's. The voice warning me that this time might be different sounded more like mine.

Alex stayed with the Vauxhall, parked amongst some trees at the side of Derby Stables Road between the two gated driveways. We'd taken one of those driveways to the training stables on our last visit, but this time, Gabe picked the lock on the iron gate across the driveway that led to the main house of Yew Tree Lodge. Moments later, he opened it for Willie and me.

From Alex's vantage point, he could see anyone entering the estate. He told us he would warn us with a hooting sound mimicking a tawny owl's call. Conversely, if we needed to be collected in a hurry, Gabe would make the same noise and Alex would bring the motorcar to the end of the driveway. With the clear, still night, the sounds would carry.

Willie, Gabe and I walked along the verge to avoid the crunching gravel. We'd decided to look through the main house. While it was possible that records were kept in an office near the stables, we assumed those files would be for the business. We were after more personal information.

The large, symmetrical manor looked like a dollhouse set in the middle of a vast smooth lawn bordered by a low hedge. We took the path that led around the side to the backyard; more lawns and hedges were swallowed in the distance by the trees.

We crept across the paved courtyard where a number of French doors presented different entry points into the house. Gabe signaled that we should try each of them. If one was open, we'd use that instead of picking a lock.

I found one of the glass doors to what I assumed to be a conservatory unlocked. I waved to get the attention of the others before entering. Moonlight flashed on an expanse of water. At first, I thought it was a pond, but closer inspection proved it to be an indoor pool.

Gabe signaled for Willie and me to follow him through to the main part of the house.

It was two AM. Everyone should be asleep. Both the family and their live-in staff would rise early for work, so had probably been in bed for hours. The large size of the house gave me a little more confidence that we wouldn't be overheard. Even so, every creak of the floorboards and every bird call made my heart leap into my throat.

Willie was in her element. It was as if she was born for criminal activity. She stepped confidently yet quietly, and soon drew ahead of Gabe to lead us into each room on the ground floor. We studied photographs by moonlight and rifled through drawers, searching for something—anything—about a son named Ambrose.

We found nothing in the formal reception rooms, nor the

library or informal sitting rooms, although there were many photographs of Ignatius Arlington's other family members, particularly his grandson. Horses also featured prominently. I expected to see a family portrait hanging above a fireplace, but there were none. Instead, there were paintings of proud race-horses with Yew Tree Lodge in the background. In the dining room, I struck a match to provide enough light to read the brass plaque of the painting. It was inscribed with the horse's name.

I recognized it.

I returned to the other rooms where paintings of horses occupied pride of place above the marble mantelpieces. I recognized one other name on the plaques.

There was no time to inform the others. Gabe signaled to us to follow him back to the grand entrance foyer where a sweeping staircase curved upwards to a gallery on the next level. He placed his foot on the bottom step, but hesitated.

I understood his concern. It was likely the information we needed was kept on a bedside table or in a dressing table drawer in the room where Mr. Arlington slept. Although Fred had told us Ignatius was too proud to care about his son after his accident, I suspected that was merely the facade he presented to the world. A parent would still love their child, no matter what. If we couldn't find a photograph or paperwork in one of the unoccupied bedrooms, we'd have to sneak into Mr. Arlington's.

But that wasn't why Gabe hesitated. He'd changed his mind. He indicated we should follow him, but instead of going up the stairs, he took the door to the right. It led through to the kitchen and other service rooms, including an indoor bathroom used by the staff. Beyond that was another door that led to a large room at the furthest point of the house.

It was an office with French doors leading out to a private courtyard. Gabe's instinct had proved to be right. The office was located on the lowest level with direct access to the rear of the house, allowing trainers and grooms to come and go without traipsing through the formal areas. There was even a covered porch outside for their muddy boots.

The abundance of moonlight streaming through the tall windows made it easy to search the desk, bookshelves and filing cabinet drawers. I studied all of the photographs but came to the conclusion that none featured Ambrose Arlington. The men in them were either the wrong age, or the photograph was too recent, based on the clothing styles.

I moved to one of the filing cabinets next. It was labeled HORSES, so Gabe and Willie had overlooked it in favor of the desk drawers and the other, unlabeled cabinet. I found the files for the two horses whose names I'd recognized on the painting plaques. Both files contained official certificates, letters exchanged with breeders, and details of training regimes, and races they'd competed in.

I tapped Gabe on the shoulder and pointed to Ambrose Arlington's name, listed as trainer for both horses. Other than Fred's word, it was the first piece of evidence we'd found that he existed.

I returned the files to the cabinet and was about to help Gabe look through the desk drawers when Willie clicked her fingers to get our attention. She clutched a stack of papers that she angled towards the moonlight so we could read them.

The topmost letter was from a surgeon at St. Thomas's Hospital dated May 1891 and addressed to Mr. Ignatius Arlington. The surgeon said Ambrose had survived his second surgery and to pray for his full recovery. The next letter, dated July, was from the governor of the hospital writing to say that Ambrose's situation hadn't improved and that he still needed assistance for simple daily tasks. If he continued to show no sign of improvement, he would be transferred to Putney Private Asylum for Incurables once his wounds completely healed.

A third letter dated a month later was written on Putney Private Asylum for Incurables letterhead and stated that Ambrose had settled in, and treatment would begin the following week. The governor claimed their treatments were based on the latest medical science, but were unlikely to work on Ambrose with his extremely limited mental capacity.

The next letter, dated six months later, said Ambrose had been moved to the wing for patients who were not expected to make any further progress. He would require full-time care for the remainder of his life. The governor listed the monthly sum necessary for the care and asked for the first month to be paid in advance. The paper on which that letter was written was crumpled. It was easy to imagine a distraught Ignatius Arlington screwing it up in despair before flattening it out again and filing it with the rest of the letters relating to his son's accident.

Willie returned the letters to the filing cabinet then softly closed the drawer. We exited the office and headed past the bathroom and service rooms, through to the kitchen. Gabe stopped suddenly in the doorway. He waved us back.

I couldn't see past him, but I could just make out the flickering glow of candlelight coming from the kitchen. I heard a cupboard door close. A tin or jar knocked against the bench. A man coughed, then his gravelly voice filled the silence.

"Is someone there?" It was Mr. Syme. "Ignatius?"

I froze.

CHAPTER 16

illie grabbed my hand and pulled me away from the kitchen door. We ran back to the office, Gabe on our heels. He closed and locked the office doors as Willie tried the French door leading to the covered porch.

They were locked.

The handle of the main door rattled as someone tried to get in from the other side. "Who's there?" Mr. Syme called out.

Gabe removed his lock picking tools and crouched down to get to work on the porch door lock.

Mr. Syme shouted for help. "There's an intruder! I've trapped him!"

Floorboards above us creaked as the household awoke. Soon, they'd be charging down the stairs with a key to the office door.

"Hurry up," Willie hissed at Gabe.

"Ignatius, fetch a gun!" Mr. Syme's command was directed at his father-in-law, but Willie decided it was a good idea and withdrew hers from the holster strapped to her hip.

We needed to get out before blood was shed.

Gabe finally unlocked one of the French doors and pushed it open. We ran outside. I was about to head back the way we'd come, to the front of the house and the driveway, but Gabe gripped my hand and directed me towards the nearest hedge.

We ducked behind it. It came to Gabe's waist height. He had to crouch low, but Willie and I didn't have as much difficulty. For once, being short was a blessing. We followed the length of the hedge in single file then, when it ended, crossed a section of open lawn, aiming for the woods in the distance.

The crack of a gunshot tore through the night air, rousing sleeping birds from their nests in a cacophony of screeches. My instinct to fling myself onto the ground and make myself as small as possible was thwarted by Gabe. He took my hand again and urged me to continue.

"It's unlikely they can shoot accurately in the dark."

If I wasn't so out of breath, I would have told him that wasn't at all comforting.

We didn't slow even when we finally reached the trees. Gabe led the way with Willie bringing up the rear, still clutching her gun. The woods were darker than the garden, with the moonlight reaching the floor in dappled patches. Every snapping twig and thudding footstep made my heart beat faster.

The trees thinned then finally stopped altogether at the wooden fence at the edge of the estate. Gabe easily scaled it and balanced himself on the top to assist me. Once I was alongside him, he cupped my cheek as if checking to see that I was all right, before dropping softly to the ground. He grasped my waist and helped me down.

My breaths were ragged, but I wasn't entirely sure if it was from exertion or from the way the moonlight reflected in his eyes. I wanted him to keep touching me, but he quickly let me go, balling his hands into fists at his sides.

The rumble of an engine approached along the road from the direction of Yew Tree Lodge's main gate. We melted back against the fence. The vehicle drove slowly, the lights off, but we waited until we were sure it was the Vauxhall before stepping out.

Alex's white teeth flashed with his grin. "Willie, what's wrong? I only heard one gunshot and it wasn't from a Colt."

She flung herself onto the back seat and watched the road behind us. "I'm more responsible now. I only shoot when necessary."

"Ha!"

"Drive!" Gabe barked as he closed his door. After a few moments, he asked Willie if we were being followed.

"Nope." She turned to face the front and holstered her gun. "*Woo hoo!* That was more fun than the time your two pappies got drunk and accidentally set off firecrackers inside the Broken Creek Saloon."

Gabe flicked the switch on the dashboard to turn on the headlights. Now that he could see the road better, Alex sped up.

"Were you seen?" he asked over the noise of the engine.

"Only in silhouette," Gabe said. "We were in a dark corridor, so Syme wouldn't have seen my face."

"Learn anything?"

"Ambrose was placed in Putney Private Asylum for Incurables a few months after his accident. Despite undergoing two surgeries, he was permanently affected."

"The asylum changed its name years ago to the Putney Hospital and Home for Incurables. I've never been, but I've heard it's expensive. He should be well cared for there."

That didn't endear me to Ignatius Arlington. Aside from those letters, the only other record of Ambrose was the paperwork mentioning him as trainer. There wasn't even a single photograph.

"There were paintings of two horses that were mentioned in Daniel's ledgers," I told Alex.

"It all fits," Gabe said. "Ambrose was operating as an illegal bookmaker. He paid Arthur Cody to dope his two horses before races to make sure they won, then raked in the prize money. He then stopped doping them, so they stopped winning, and as a bookmaker, he collected."

"Don't forget he paid Ferryman the iron magician, too," Alex added. "Probably just to make sure."

That explained something that hadn't made sense to me. I'd recognized the names of the horses from the ledgers, but they'd been written alongside jockey names. The only reason a book-maker would pay a jockey would be to throw races, so the horses *must* have lost. If they were champions at that point after winning races thanks to being doped with cocaine, or wearing shoes containing magic, then the bookmaker who collected bets on them would have made a fortune when they later lost. I assumed the punters didn't know the identity of the illegal book-maker or they never would have trusted him, given he was also the trainer.

We returned to London where a few merry souls enjoyed the sound of their voices echoing on the otherwise empty streets. Willie joined in the merriment with a cheer every time we passed a group of young men stumbling along the pavement. She even sang the chorus of *It's a Long Way to Tipperary* with four drunk-ards who could hardly stand, let alone sing in tune.

Gabe shushed her when we turned onto my street. "You'll wake Sylvia's landlady."

Mrs. Parry didn't know I'd left after curfew, wearing a pair of black trousers I'd borrowed from Willie. Although she didn't mind her lodgers staying out after curfew if we'd left earlier in the evening, she didn't like it when we left the house after she'd locked up. She wanted to know where we were and when we'd be home. Although her rule could be restrictive at times, I quite liked having a motherly figure fuss over me.

Gabe opened his door to escort me to the house, but Willie grabbed his shoulder from behind and pinned him to the seat.

"Stay there," she said. "I'll go."

Previously, Gabe would have insisted. Not this time. He was still determined that we should keep our distance where possible.

Before I closed the motorcar door, I asked him to bring the

transcribed ledgers to the library in the morning. I wanted to check something.

He had a better idea. "Come directly to Park Street first thing, instead of the library. We'll travel from there to Putney."

Willie looped her arm through mine and walked with me to my front door. She hummed *It's a Long Way to Tipperary* softly, and in the light from the streetlamp, I could see her smile.

"Did you have a few nips of brandy while we weren't looking?" I asked.

"I'm drunk on adventure and danger."

She would have been an excellent ambulance driver in the war with an attitude like that, although she would have been an equally good soldier. The British army missed out by not allowing women to enlist.

* * *

I TELEPHONED the professor from Gabe's house to tell him I would come in to work later. He told me to take the entire day to investigate if necessary. I returned to Gabe's library where he waited with a leather document holder. Alex sat in one of the armchairs, his long legs outstretched, and his eyes closed. I thought he was asleep, but he opened them upon my return and yawned.

"Where's Willie?" I asked. "Did she oversleep again?"

As if I'd summoned her, she strode into the room, muttering some colorful words under her breath. "We got a visitor."

Gabe shrugged at me. "Yes, I can see that. Sylvia's right—"

"Not her. Coming up the steps now. It's Miss Hoity Toity herself. I saw her through the window."

"Ivy?" Alex asked.

"That'll save me a visit," Gabe said. "I was going to call on them later and advise them to admit that a batch of boots missed receiving magic when Bertie was in charge during the war."

The door knocker banged just as Willie told Gabe that she

thought it was a bad idea to warn the Hobsons. Her colorful language left us in no doubt that she didn't like his plan. Alex also shook his head.

While I could see their point, I could also see Gabe's. He had a history with the family. He'd once cared for Ivy. His conscience wouldn't allow him to stand by as they dug a deeper hole for themselves.

Moments later Murray announced Ivy then stepped aside. She swanned into the library, blinking long lashes darkened with makeup, only to stop when she spotted me. She forced a smile and we all managed to politely exchange greetings.

With that over, she turned to Gabe. "May we speak in private?"

He refused. "I'm just going to tell them what you tell me anyway, so let's save time and talk in here."

Her spine stiffened at his tense tone, rippling the delicate chiffon fabric of her sleeves. Daisy would have admired Ivy's dress, while simultaneously ridiculing her for wearing such an elegant outfit for a social call. It was the sort of dress one wore to a day at the races attended by a member of the royal family. The drop-waist suited Ivy's tall, slim figure, and the silver leaves embroidered down the front panel must have taken a piece-worker several days to complete.

Ivy blinked her lashes at Gabe again, perhaps hoping that would soften him. "I came to apologize for my mother's behavior at the ball the other night."

Gabe indicated me. "How fortuitous that Sylvia is here to hear it."

Ivy stopped blinking. "It is." She reached out a hand to him but changed her mind and quickly returned it to her side. "I'd like to say how sorry I am that my mother spoke rudely to you. To you both," she added with a nod for me.

Gabe waited. The room fell silent.

Ivy cleared her throat. "You seem to be waiting for more. I know why, and I'd like to assure you those rumors were not started by my mother. Or me. Someone must have learned those things about Sylvia from someone else, and once they learned she'd attended the ball under a false name, they began to talk. They were upset at the presence of an uninvited guest."

"The name wasn't false," I said. "But I see your point. I'll write a note to the hostess and apologize." I doubted it would do any good except to make me feel a little better.

Ivy glanced my way, but I might as well not have spoken. She all but ignored me. "I also came to tell you that my father is ill."

"I'm sorry to hear it," Gabe said. "I was going to call on him later. There's something I need to tell him."

"He's too ill for visitors."

Willie grunted, clearly not believing her.

"You may tell me," Ivy added. "I'll pass on your message."

Gabe invited her to sit. "You need to encourage your father to come clean to the police about the batch of boots that missed their spell."

I wondered why he'd mentioned the police and not Jakes, but then I realized he probably thought it best to leave Military Intelligence out of it. The police would inform them of any necessary developments.

Ivy shot to her feet. "As my parents have said, we did our bit for the war effort. These accusations are unfair and unfounded."

"The authorities know Bertie is artless."

She started to laugh but stopped when she saw he was serious. "Bertie *is* a magician. Gabe...why are you saying such things? You never used to be like this." She didn't look at me, but she seemed to blame me for influencing him.

"During one of our investigations, we discovered he was a patient at Rosebank Gardens Hospital in 1913. At that time, the doctors there claimed they could draw out the magic from the artless children of magicians."

The rapid blinking returned, but this time it was less flirtatious and more confusion. "He went there to rest. He'd been having a difficult time of it at school and needed somewhere quiet for his nerves. You know him. He's always been shy. The world isn't a kind place for men with nervous dispositions, and boys can be particularly cruel. I can assure you he wasn't there to draw out his magic. He already possessed it."

I believed her. Or, more precisely, I believed that *she* believed it. Her parents would have told her only what they thought she needed to know, and she had no reason to doubt them. She truly thought Bertie had been admitted to Rosebank simply to rest.

Did she also believe he was a magician? Or was that part a lie? I wasn't quite sure.

She made her excuses and Murray showed her out. After she'd gone, Willie gave her verdict without being asked. "She's as cunning as her mother. You can't believe anything either of them say. There ain't no one else who would attack Sylvia's character at the ball. Mrs. H must have started the rumors and Ivy knew it. If Ivy lied about that, she prob'ly lied about other things." She poked a finger at Gabe's chest. "Don't you fall for her fluttery eyelashes."

"There's not a chance of that." Gabe leveled his gaze with mine. "Not a chance."

My face heated and my pulse quickened. My determination to keep him at a distance wasn't going well. I could feel my resolve crumbling a little more every time he looked directly at me.

Willie stepped between us, severing the connection. "Sylvia wanted to see the transcripts of the ledgers."

Gabe cleared his throat. "Yes. Right." He handed me the leather document holder. "Are you looking for the names of those horses?"

I nodded as I removed the transcribed pages covered with Huon's untidy writing. I flipped through the ones listing the bookmaker's expenses until I found the horse names scrawled alongside other names that we suspected were jockeys.

I pointed to the entries as I read. "Macintosh riding Arabian Prince. Macintosh riding My Tribune. Goreman riding My

Tribune. And here, Goreman appears again beside Arabian Prince. Those were two of the horses that Arlington trained."

"Goreman!" Willie slapped a hand on her thigh. "We knew it! This is proof he was part of the bookmaker's scheme."

"Not quite proof," Alex said. "These pages only prove that he rode a horse trained by Arlington stables, not that he took money to throw the race."

Willie flicked the pages I held with the back of her hand. "But why would the bookmaker pay him if not to throw the race?"

"It won't hold up in court."

"It's enough to question him."

"It is," Gabe agreed. "But first, we need to see if Ambrose Arlington is still alive. If he is, perhaps he can shed some light on who killed Daniel. He managed the operation. He's the key."

"Those letters we found at Arlington's suggested he can't speak," Willie said.

"They were written years ago. His condition may have improved. Or he could be dead by now. Either way, I want to know for sure."

* * *

PUTNEY HOSPITAL AND HOME FOR INCURABLES reminded me of Rosebank Gardens, but without the extensive grounds. Like Rosebank, the manor had once been a private home. A family crest of two crossed swords and a lion still appeared above the colonnaded entrance. Inside, the homeliness continued with a portrait of a dapper gentleman hanging above a stunning bouquet of blue hydrangeas in a vase on the sideboard. The plaque stated the gentleman had bequeathed the house to the asylum in 1801. Brightly colored oriental rugs and wooden wall paneling exuded warmth, and the pretty nurse dressed in a crisp white uniform seated at the desk gave us an equally warm smile.

It disappeared when Gabe introduced us as consultants for Scotland Yard.

"Can you confirm whether you have a patient here by the name of Ambrose Arlington?" he asked.

"We do," she said, hesitantly.

"May we see him, please?"

"Why?"

"We need to ask him some questions."

"He can't answer you. He doesn't speak."

"Can he communicate using a different method?"

"No, Mr. Glass, he cannot. Mr. Arlington, like many of our patients in the West Ward, is entirely dependent on the staff."

"May we see him anyway?"

"Why? He won't be of any use to you."

"I insist."

Her lips thinned. "Wait here." She pushed open an adjoining door, revealing a man seated behind a desk.

At her request, he emerged from the office and greeted us, somewhat warily. He introduced himself as the governor, Mr. Finley-Cross. He wasn't the same governor who'd written the letters to Ignatius Arlington in 1891. "I understand you want to see Ambrose Arlington."

"We do," Gabe said.

"As the nurse told you, he can't help you. He hasn't spoken in twenty-nine years."

"Even so."

"Very well. But I request just two of you come with me and the other two stay here. We don't want to frighten the residents with a large group."

Alex volunteered to stay, but Willie clearly wanted to go with Gabe. When he told her to remain behind with Alex, she protested.

"Sylvia ain't going to protect you in there."

"You saw on the way here that nobody followed us. I'll be fine."

"Remember what happened last time you went to a hospital with just her," she grumbled.

Mr. Finley-Cross indicated the open register on the desk. "All visitors must sign first."

Gabe signed his name and wrote the date and the name of the patient we came to visit, then handed the pen to me to do the same.

The governor headed up the stairs. "Mr. Arlington's room is on the upper floor."

"Isn't he immobile?" Gabe asked. "Wouldn't it be easier to give him a room on the ground floor given he's wheelchair-bound?"

"He doesn't leave his room."

"Not even for fresh air?" I asked.

"There's no point. When you see him, you'll understand. May I ask why your investigation has led you to Mr. Arlington?"

"It's confidential," Gabe said.

The governor led us up two flights of stairs and along a corridor. The hospital was eerily quiet given it must house dozens of patients as well as staff. We passed young nurses doing their rounds. Their greetings to Mr. Finley-Cross were cordial, but their smiles were for Gabe's benefit.

We stopped at a door numbered twenty-eight. Mr. Finley-Cross entered without knocking and stepped aside so we could see the man in the bed.

He sat up, two pillows at his back. His head lolled forward, as if too heavy to be held up by his neck, and his arms lay loosely on the bedcovers, the palms up and fingers curled. He was dressed in striped pajamas and needed a shave, but his gray hair had been neatly combed.

"This is Ambrose Arlington," Mr. Finley-Cross announced. "As you can see, he can't help you with your inquiries."

"Good morning, Mr. Arlington," Gabe said.

"Don't bother. He won't respond."

"Can he hear me?"

"We don't know. If he can, he's incapable of showing a sign."

Gabe sat on the edge of the bed as there was no chair. "My

name is Gabriel Glass, and this is Miss Ashe. If you can hear me, can you give me a sign? Can you make a sound? Or move your fingers?"

Ambrose didn't move. Not even a hiss passed his lips. He was utterly still and silent except for the occasional blink.

Gabe didn't persist and we left the soulless room with its lonely patient. I was no medical professional and didn't know whether Ambrose could have recovered if he was in a more stimulating environment, but it wouldn't hurt to try. At the very least, position him by the window so he could look out of it.

"Does anyone visit him?" I asked as we walked back along the corridor.

Mr. Finley-Cross shook his head. "Not since his mother died. She used to visit on his birthday."

One visitor, once a year. No matter what illegal activity Ambrose had been involved in before his accident, he didn't deserve this.

Gabe must have been thinking the same thing. "Some medical professionals are making remarkable progress with returned soldiers suffering head injuries. Their methods might work on the patients here."

"Those institutions are funded by the government. Ours is privately funded. Our clients pay for the day-to-day care of their family members, not experimental therapies that are unlikely to help and will only cost more."

As much as I wanted to protest, I knew it would change nothing. Men like Ignatius Arlington, who kept no visible reminder of his son at home, wouldn't pay unless a full recovery was guaranteed. Ambrose was lost to him long ago.

We rejoined Alex and Willie in the foyer. At their questioning looks, Gabe merely shook his head.

He turned to Mr. Finley-Cross. "May we look at the visitor records for Ambrose Arlington, going back to his admission in '91?"

"Of course." He pointed at the register on the nurse's desk.

"At the end of each day, the nurse on desk duty transcribes each name from the visitors' book to the patient files. Some patients show signs of recognition when they have a particular visitor, you see, and that helps give us a clearer picture of the extent of their condition. In Mr. Arlington's case, there has never been a sign, but we keep a record of his visitors nevertheless."

He led us through to his office where he plucked a slim volume from a bookshelf containing dozens like it. Ambrose Arlington's name and date of birth were written on labels stuck to the spine and front cover. Gabe scanned each of the pages before handing it to me. Only the first few pages had writing, the rest were blank.

Given Gabe's perusal had been so quick, I assumed it contained nothing of interest. But that wasn't the case.

In twenty-nine years, Ambrose received only two visitors. The repetition of Mrs. Arlington's name, appearing on the same day every year, was broken only once.

In 1916, the same year he was arrested for importing and selling cocaine, Arthur Cody visited.

CHAPTER 17

*A*s we drove away from the hospital, Alex confirmed that the date of Arthur Cody's visit to Ambrose occurred mere weeks before his arrest. The question was, why did he visit?

Given Ambrose was the bookmaker behind the entire operation, and Cody doped horses for him, it was likely the two worked closely together. Perhaps Cody wanted to verify whether Ambrose would tattle. Perhaps he only learned where Ambrose was living in 1916. The timing was even more curious when his arrest was taken into account. Had his visit to the hospital triggered his arrest somehow?

I felt as though all the details were there, just jumbled. We needed some clarification.

Hopefully Mr. Goreman could provide it. As a jockey in 1891, he was listed in the ledger as accepting payments. As a trainer now, he knew all the players in this dangerous game.

* * *

WE FOUND the jockey-turned-trainer at his stables, west of the city. It wasn't as large as Yew Tree Lodge, and not all stalls were occupied, but it was well maintained. Just like the last time we'd spoken to Mr. Goreman, he was with the veterinarian, Mr. Wellington. The two men were giving their full attention to the same horse they'd been watching at the racetrack and didn't see us approach. I overheard Mr. Wellington lament that the horse may never fully recover. As if it understood, the horse nudged him with its nose. Mr. Wellington rubbed it, murmuring words of comfort.

Mr. Goreman kicked something over. With the lower half of the stall door closed, I couldn't see what. "Why the devil am I paying you then?"

Mr. Wellington spotted us and jutted his chin in our direction.

Mr. Goreman followed his gaze. A flicker of irritation registered on his face before it was replaced with a smile. He greeted us warily. "I answered all your questions. I doubt I have anything useful to add."

"We have a confession," Gabe said. "We're not researching the use of magic in the racing industry for my mother. We're consultants for Scotland Yard, investigating the death of Daniel Barratt."

"I knew it! Your questions about throwing races were highly suspicious, not to mention offensive. Anyway, my comments stand. I can't help you any more than I already have. I don't know the fellow you speak of."

"He was involved in the same scheme as Arthur Cody, the groom from Arlington Stables who was arrested for cocaine dealing."

Mr. Wellington grabbed his bag from the back of the stall and pushed open the door. "I'll check on the other horses."

Mr. Goreman emerged, too. "Did you confront Arlington? I'm sure he didn't admit to being in league with Cody, but hopefully you scared him a little."

"Why hopefully?"

"Just in case he's still cheating. He'll stop if he thinks you're onto him."

"Do you have any reason to believe Arlington is, or was, doping his horses?"

"I would never accuse a fellow trainer of such a thing."

Willie barked a protest. "You didn't accuse him, but you did imply."

"We've learned a thing or two since we last spoke to you," Gabe went on. "We now know that Arthur Cody was being paid by an illegal bookmaker to dope horses in 1890 and '91."

"Which bookmaker?"

Gabe continued as if he hadn't been interrupted. "We also know that the iron magician, Reggie Ferryman, was paid by the same bookmaker, as were several jockeys."

"Ah. I see what you're implying, but I want to assure you, I did not throw races for anyone." He tugged on his waistcoat hem. "Who was the bookmaker?"

"We're not interested in bringing the participants of that scheme to justice. We merely want to find out who killed Daniel Barratt, and possibly his wife and children. Finding out what happened to them is our main priority."

Mr. Goreman swallowed and nodded. The mention of Rosina and the children seemed to rattle him.

"Now that you know you won't be in any trouble, perhaps you can answer truthfully," Gabe went on.

"I have been truthful." Mr. Goreman's tone wasn't nearly as arrogant as earlier.

"We have evidence that proves you were being paid by a bookmaker to throw races when you were a jockey, and—"

"What evidence?"

"—and we know that bookmaker was Ambrose Arlington."

Mr. Goreman paled. "He's dead. He can't tell you anything."

"He's not dead."

"Where is he?"

"He's being cared for by medical professionals who specialize in patients unable to look after themselves. He can't communicate, so we're trying to piece together the facts without his help. Who else knew about Ambrose's scheme?"

Mr. Goreman pressed his lips together.

Willie huffed out a breath. "Answer the goddamned question! He already told you we don't care who was paid to throw races. You ain't going to get into trouble, unless you killed Daniel Barratt or his family."

Mr. Goreman glanced at Alex. When Alex nodded, the trainer gave in. "I don't know anything for certain, merely my own suspicions. I only suspected Cody was involved after his arrest in '16 for cocaine importing. I suspected the farrier magician was being paid by Ambrose much earlier—when he was dismissed from Epsom in early '91. It made sense that Ambrose would have an iron magician in his pocket. The farrier's dismissal was also the beginning of the whole thing unraveling."

"What do you mean?" Gabe asked.

"Ferryman's dismissal left a hole in Ambrose's operation. Although he was paying jockeys—and Cody, as it turned out—he stopped winning as much as he used to. Ferryman's magic ensured the horses that wore his spell-infused iron shoes always won. Using just jockeys and doping in his scheme was a less precise science. Fewer winnings meant we weren't getting paid as much, which annoyed those of us left. Ambrose's wrath kept me working for him, and probably others, too. I was terrified of asking to leave. I felt trapped. If I wanted to continue to work as a jockey—if I wanted to continue to have all my limbs—I had to keep doing as Ambrose asked. But Ferryman's departure without incident made me wonder if I could leave without consequences, too. It wouldn't surprise me if others also started to consider walking away."

Ferryman had been dismissed from Epsom in February, a month before Ambrose's riding accident. Daniel had written the note for Oscar in February, telling him where to find the ledgers and begging for his help. Mr. Goreman's assumption was right; he wasn't the only one who wanted to leave the scheme after seeing Mr. Ferryman depart without repercussions. Daniel did, too.

"What was Ambrose Arlington's reaction to your request to leave?" I asked.

"He was furious. His temper could be something to behold when he unleashed it. He doubled down on his threats, and I believed he'd follow through if pushed. So, I stopped pushing. It seemed Ferryman was special."

The lack of repercussions for Ferryman was probably due to his magic. The magician could rain iron down on Ambrose with the whisper of his spell. Ambrose was just as afraid of what Ferryman could do as Goreman was of Ambrose.

"Did Ambrose's family know what he was up to?" Gabe asked.

"How could they *not* know?" At Gabe's arched brows, Mr. Goreman sighed. "I can't say for certain, but you must admit it looks likely. Cody was employed at their stables and was doping their horses. Surely Ignatius was suspicious. And Syme. He was assistant trainer to Ambrose at the time. After Ambrose's accident, he was promoted. He married Ambrose's sister, ensuring his place in the family. Just as Ferryman's arrest left a hole in the cheating operation, Ambrose's accident left a hole in the family order."

It was a bold suggestion, but it had merit. It also sent my mind reeling in another direction, one that cast an even more sinister shade across our investigation. What if Ambrose's fall from his horse wasn't an accident? What if someone had purposely startled the animal? It put Mr. Syme squarely in the picture, but I couldn't rule out Mrs. Syme, either. She may have hoped her father would promote her to the position of trainer. Some siblings could be ruthless when family fortunes were at stake.

Despite the heat, a shiver prickled my skin.

"There is another candidate for the murder of that fellow, Daniel Barratt," Mr. Goreman went on, frowning. "Although I'm uncertain of the timing. He died that year, too, but I can't recall precisely when."

"Who?" Gabe asked.

"Lord Coyle. He approached me shortly after Ambrose's accident, telling me he was going to resume the illegal bookmaking operation. I don't know how he knew about it, but he knew I was involved. He threatened me, just as Ambrose had. Nasty fellow. Anyway, he died before he could make a go of it."

Coyle's name didn't come as a complete surprise. It had appeared in the hidden ledger. We were aware he knew the magician players—Daniel Barratt and Reggie Ferryman. It stood to reason that he learned the other names, too, and decided to revive the scheme. If it gave him money or power, Coyle seemed like the sort of man who would want a share.

None of us told Mr. Goreman that Coyle couldn't have killed Daniel, because he was already dead himself.

"One more thing," Gabe said. "You mentioned you suspected Arthur Cody was doping Arlington-trained horses for Ambrose's operation."

"I didn't suspect him until *after* his arrest."

"He visited Ambrose in 1916, shortly before his arrest."

Mr. Goreman's eyes widened. "He knew Ambrose was alive?"

"We find it too coincidental that he was arrested mere weeks after the visit."

"Now look here. His arrest was nothing to do with me. I'm telling the truth. I didn't know he visited Ambrose. I didn't even know Ambrose was alive until you told me! Nor did I know Cody was doping horses at that point. I've been a trainer since 1910 and hadn't worked as a jockey for several years before that. I would have been no use to a race fixer anymore. If you want to find out who told the police about Cody, look to the stables where he worked. Ignatius Arlington is as ruthless as his son was. Ask yourselves why he let the world think Ambrose was dead. What sort of father does that?"

We left Mr. Goreman scratching his balding head with one hand and gripping the top of the stall door with the other. He looked like a tired old man having a very bad day.

Willie glanced at him over her shoulder as she trudged ahead of us to the Vauxhall. "Someone ratted on Arthur Cody in '16, but I don't reckon it was him."

"Whoever it was, they may have also killed Daniel years earlier," Gabe said. "Cody got off lightly."

Gabe opened the door of the Vauxhall for me, but we both became distracted by the approach of the veterinarian, his steps brisk, purposeful. I thought he wanted to speak to us, but instead he placed his bag into the back seat of the large burgundy Daimler parked next to our vehicle.

Gabe decided he wanted a word with Mr. Wellington. "You're also the vet for Arlingtons, aren't you?" he began.

"That's right." Mr. Wellington put up a finger to make a point. "I didn't know about that cocaine-doping fiend, though. He left before I took Arlington on as a client."

"Did you know Mr. Arlington has a son named Ambrose?"

"I saw him trackside from time to time, before his accident."

"After the accident, did Ignatius Arlington ever mention him to you? Or mention him in your presence?"

Mr. Wellington blinked in surprise at the question. "No. Never."

"Did his wife, Ambrose's mother?"

"I didn't have any dealings with Mrs. Arlington. Just Ignatius, his daughter and her husband." His frown deepened. "Now that I think about it, neither of the Symes have mentioned Ambrose either. In fact, I'd forgotten all about him until now. It's as if he never existed. It is a little odd, but understandable given his death must have upset them terribly."

Gabe didn't tell him Ambrose was alive. He thanked him and climbed into the Vauxhall. We drove off ahead of Mr. Wellington.

"I reckon Goreman's right," Willie said. "The Symes and Arlington know more than they're letting on. They must have known Cody was doping the horses, and if they knew he was guilty, then it means they knew he was doing it for Ambrose."

"Especially Syme," Alex added. "He was assistant to Ambrose. You can't live and work with someone and not know they're the brains behind an illegal bookmaking operation."

I wasn't entirely convinced. I'd lived with my mother for years and not known a single thing about her life before she gave birth to me. Even so, I was suspicious of Syme, too. "Mr. Syme may have had a double reason for wanting to get rid of Ambrose —to step into the void he left as head of the race-fixing operation, *and* the void he left in the family."

Willie stabbed her finger in my direction. "He didn't leave a void in the family. Ignatius had a daughter."

"You've met Ignatius. Do you believe he valued her as equally as he valued his son?"

She crossed her arms over her chest. "Idiot."

I suspected she was referring to Ignatius Arlington, not me, considering she stopped arguing.

Alex slowed at the intersection and waited for a horse-drawn cart laden with barrels to pass. "I agree that Syme may have wanted to get rid of Ambrose in order to take over the role of trainer and male heir, but not the race-fixing operation. He may have known about it, but he didn't continue it after Ambrose's accident. The operation seems to have come to an end in '91."

Gabe glanced in the side mirror, something he did frequently to make sure we weren't being followed. "We're losing sight of the investigation's purpose. We're not looking for a motive to get rid of Ambrose. We're looking for Daniel's killer. The only relevance Ambrose has to the case is that he organized the race-fixing operation and it finished when he was no longer capable of running it. He couldn't have killed Daniel. Nor could Coyle, the only other person who knew Daniel was involved."

"That we know of," Willie pointed out.

Gabe nodded. "What happens to a man's belongings after the family are told he will never recover and never return home?"

It would be the same thing that happened to his belongings if he died. I knew that process all too well. Going through my brother James's things after we'd been told of his death had been extremely difficult. "The family will look through them," I said. "They would throw some things away and keep others."

Gabe gave a rueful smile. "If we assume the task fell to his parents, then Mr. and Mrs. Arlington would have stumbled across details about his secret bookmaking scheme. Yet Ignatius denied knowledge of it when we confronted him."

"Vehemently," Alex added.

"He *must* know more than he let on. He probably knows the names of everyone in Ambrose's operation. If he confronted Daniel Barratt and asked for the ledgers, but Daniel refused to hand them over, then perhaps Ignatius killed him to keep him quiet. For a proud man and a well-known trainer, having his son's name bandied about as a race fixer and corrupt bookmaker would have been devastating, not just to his pride, but also to the family business."

Alex suddenly stepped on the brake pedal instead of downshifting through the gears as he often did. He turned the steering wheel to the right at the intersection, but London was straight ahead.

The abrupt change of direction caused me to slide across the seat into Willie, while her hat tumbled onto her lap then the floor. She pushed me off her and swung around to look behind. "Someone following us?"

"No. Sorry." Alex shrugged his massive shoulders. "This will take us to Derby Stables Road faster."

Willie snatched up her hat from the floor. "Can you give us some warning next time? Sylvia looks like she's about to faint from the fright."

"I do not faint from fright, thank you," I snipped. "But a little warning would be nice, Alex. That and something to strap us into the seats."

We stopped at a roadside teashop called Kettle and Cake for

a light luncheon. The sign claimed they served the finest fruit buns in England, but Willie declared it to be untrue, after eating four.

We stopped once more to refuel and unfold the Vauxhall's convertible top, securing it in place so we wouldn't get wet if it rained. Clouds rolled in, although they weren't dark. If it did rain, it would be light. The cloud cover did lock in the day's heat, however, and with less air circulating around the cabin, the ride to Yew Tree Lodge became increasingly uncomfortable.

We found Mrs. Syme talking to a groom outside one of the stalls. She didn't look pleased to see us, and somewhat reluctantly told us we could find her father and husband in the tack room. She led us there herself, calling out as we approached.

The tack room was neatly arranged, with most equipment hanging on the three walls around a long, central table. Saddles were positioned over iron racks, while bridles hung from hooks above them. The room smelled of leather and horse. It made me think of the Hobsons and their leather magic. They would feel at home in here, even though their specialty was boots. The leather would soothe them. The same could be said for an iron magician. If he knew a spell to make iron move, like Mr. Ferryman did, then such a magician had many weapons nearby.

Ignatius Arlington's reception was even frostier than his daughter's. "What do you want now?"

Gabe launched into our reason for being there, not bothering with a preamble. "We called on your son at the Putney Hospital and Home for Incurables."

"What!" Mr. Arlington exploded.

I was more interested in the reaction of the Symes. Mr. Syme's worried glance flew to his wife. She pressed a hand to her throat. It shook.

"It was known as the Putney Private Asylum for Incurables when you admitted Ambrose," Gabe went on.

"We know," Mrs. Syme said, her voice a mere whisper.

The veins in Mr. Arlington's forehead protruded like welts,

and spittle foamed at the corner of his mouth as he spluttered. "How dare you invade our privacy! Who is your superior? I'll be filing a complaint."

"Address it to Detective Inspector Bailey at Scotland Yard," Gabe said mildly. "As I was saying, we visited your son. We hoped he could communicate in some way and help us with our inquiries, but unfortunately not."

"He couldn't help you even if he could speak!" Mr. Arlington snapped. "Your investigation has nothing to do with him."

"That's not true, as you're well aware, sir." Mr. Arlington continued to protest, but Gabe spoke over the top of him. "Ambrose was operating an illegal bookmaking scheme from this very property, something you discovered after his accident when you went through his belongings."

Mr. Arlington fell silent. Perhaps he was surprised by how much we knew, or perhaps he'd simply run out of steam. The veins in his forehead subsided and he looked like an elderly man on the cusp of giving up.

It was left to his son-in-law to ask Gabe what he meant. "What illegal bookmaking scheme?"

"Come now, Mr. Syme, don't pretend innocence. As Ambrose's assistant, you know precisely what I'm referring to."

Mr. Syme glanced at his wife again. She'd gone quite pale.

Gabe filled the taut silence, before one or both of them had the chance to deny their involvement. "Ambrose paid a farrier magician to place a spell on horseshoes and Arthur Cody to dope two of your own horses, Arabian Prince and My Tribune. There may have been others, but they're the ones we're aware of. The horses won when they shouldn't have. Once they gained a reputation after winning several races, Ambrose had the farrier and Cody stop. He also paid jockeys to throw races. Meanwhile, he took illegal wagers. He probably had someone place legitimate bets on his behalf to launder the money. *You* knew what Ambrose was doing, Mr. Syme."

The room suddenly felt airless. Mr. Arlington staggered. Alex caught him. He tried to lead him to a stool, but Mr. Arlington shook him off. He brought his fist down on the table. "This is nonsense. My son is innocent!"

A cry escaped from Mrs. Syme. She spun around to hide her face, but not before I saw tears fill her eyes.

Mr. Arlington pushed past us and strode out of the tack room. No one tried to stop him. He wasn't going to give us the answers we needed. He would deny Ambrose's involvement until he had no more breath left in his body. The Symes, however, might talk.

Mr. Syme needed no prompting. "Ambrose's scheme ended with his accident. I can assure you, these stables have been clean since then. Ignatius made sure of it."

"Cody continued to work here," Alex pointed out.

"Yes. As did I, even though I knew what Ambrose was up to, as you said. I can't speak for Cody, but I can tell you that I was coerced into the scheme by Ambrose. He told me to turn a blind eye to his activities or suffer the consequences."

"What consequences?" Gabe asked.

"Dismissal from my position here, at the very least. Physical harm if necessary. Call me a coward, but I was a young man without family to protect me. My position here meant everything to me." He touched his wife's shoulder, but she shook him off. His hand dropped to his side. "Ignatius understood my predicament and graciously allowed me to stay on after he found out."

"Thanks to me," Mrs. Syme muttered.

"Yes."

She sniffed but didn't turn back around.

"Did you know who else was involved in Ambrose's operation?" Gabe asked.

"Other than Cody? No. Ambrose didn't confide in me. I wasn't actively involved. I never knew the man whose death you're investigating."

"And you, Mrs. Syme? Did Ambrose confide in you?"

She turned to face us. Her eyes were dry, and the color had returned to her cheeks. It was as if she'd put on a mask, hiding her emotions. "No, he did not. We weren't close. Far from it. I despised him. He was mean with a nasty streak that our parents never saw. My brother was especially cruel to those he considered beneath him." She glanced at her husband. "I wasn't at all surprised to learn that he was doping some of our horses. He didn't care about them. He didn't care about anyone except himself. The day of his accident was the best day of my life, because it meant I was finally free of him. I know that sounds heartless, but that's how I felt."

Part of me wanted to take her hand and tell her that I didn't think she was heartless, but I suspected she wouldn't want anyone to show forgiveness or understanding. It might shatter the mask.

"Your father prefers to remember him differently?" Gabe asked.

She huffed a humorless laugh. "My parents learned what Ambrose was like only after his accident. Not only did they discover that he was a crooked bookmaker who doped our horses, but I told them a few home truths. We both did." She nodded at her husband. "I think the grooms did, too. Ambrose's accident left quite a few people breathing a sigh of relief. My mother refused to believe the worst of it." Mrs. Syme's gaze dipped before she raised it again to meet Gabe's. "She kept his memory alive with photographs around the house, and she visited him on his birthday. But after her death, my father removed all visible signs of Ambrose's existence. He's ashamed that his only son, his pride and hope, was a horrible human being, but he would never admit it. That's a step too far for him."

Mr. Syme moved closer to his wife but didn't touch her. She noticed his show of support, and some of the rigidity left her shoulders.

"Years later, Arthur Cody wanted to restart Ambrose's race-fixing scheme, didn't he?" Gabe said. "But his arrest put an end to that. His arrest came about after an anonymous tip. Did either of you inform the police that he was importing and selling cocaine?"

Mr. and Mrs. Syme shook their heads.

"Do you know who might have?"

Again, they shook their heads. "His arrest placed a stain on our reputation that we're still trying to remove," Mrs. Syme said. "It would have been better for us that his activity was never discovered. So, no, no one here informed the police."

"Ambrose's accident occurred in March 1891, and Daniel Barratt died in April, so Ambrose couldn't have killed him. It's likely that someone who knew Daniel was keeping the books for Ambrose wanted those books destroyed. Do you think Cody was capable of murder?"

"He wouldn't want anyone to know he was doping horses," Mr. Syme said. "But I don't believe he was the type to murder a man. He just wanted to make some extra money."

His wife agreed with the assessment of his character. "He wasn't a saint, but I doubt he was a murderer."

"Eliminating him narrows the list of suspects." Gabe waited to see if either of the Symes would save him from suggesting a theory they might not like. But they did not, so he continued. "Your parents discovered Ambrose's scheme when they went through his belongings. They found out who was involved in it. They knew about Daniel."

"You're accusing one of *them* of killing Daniel Barratt?" Mr. Syme asked.

Mrs. Syme gasped. "That's an outrageous accusation!"

Something behind us caught the Symes' attention. Their jaws dropped. Their eyes widened in alarm.

We swung around.

Mr. Arlington stood in the doorway, glaring at us along the barrel of a shotgun. "Get out! Get off my property! NOW!"

CHAPTER 18

*L*etting Mr. Arlington walk out of the tack room had been a grave mistake. One that I knew Gabe regretted. He tried to move in front of me, but Mr. Arlington ordered him to stand still.

"Hands where I can see them! All of you!"

"Father!" Mrs. Syme cried. "Don't!"

"I won't shoot if they leave quietly."

"Put the weapon down, sir," Gabe said as he put his hands up. "There's no need for this. We'll leave peacefully."

Mr. Arlington adjusted his grip on the shotgun. "You will not accuse my son of any wrongdoing!"

Gabe stepped slowly towards Mr. Arlington, his steps unhurried, steady. "We know he didn't kill Daniel Barratt."

Mr. Arlington's hand shook. The finger on the trigger twitched. "Do not speak about my son. Do you hear me? You will leave his name out of your investigation!"

Gabe would never agree to that demand. Ambrose may not have murdered Daniel, but the cheating scheme led to his death. If Gabe didn't reassure Mr. Arlington, however, then I had no doubt he would pull the trigger. In his mind, he had nothing to lose. He'd lost everything years ago.

Sweat trickled down my spine. I toyed with the idea of pleading with him myself. A woman's voice might break through his anger and reach the gentlemanly side of him.

But his daughter got in first. "Ambrose *is* guilty, Father. You know he almost brought this business to its knees because of his scheme. And you know what he did to me." Her voice cracked, but she didn't lower her gaze or look away. She held it steady, on her father.

Mr. Arlington's lips twisted in distaste, but he kept the shotgun focused on Gabe. Beside me, Willie held herself tense, her hands at her sides like a Wild West gunslinger ready to draw. She knew Gabe's magic would give him time to stop the bullet, but her every instinct must be screaming danger. As were mine. My insides felt like they were tied into a knot, and someone was pulling on the ends, tightening it.

Mrs. Syme stepped closer to her father. Her husband followed, as if readying himself to intervene if necessary. "Ambrose may not have killed anyone, but he destroyed lives," she went on. "He almost destroyed mine. I won't let him destroy what I have now. That includes you and the reputation of this family. Is this how you want your grandson to remember you? He looks up to you now. Don't ruin that for him. Leave him a legacy he will be proud to be a part of."

Mr. Arlington's trembling worsened.

"Put the gun down, sir," Gabe went on.

"Ambrose is gone now," Mr. Syme said gently. "But we're still here."

Mr. Arlington's face crumpled. He closed his eyes and lowered the gun. Alex grabbed it from him and removed the cartridges, pocketing them.

I released a shaky breath.

Mr. Syme accepted the shotgun from Alex. He gave Gabe a nod of understanding before going to his wife. She hadn't moved. I thought she would dismiss him and march past her father, but her mask finally shattered. She started to cry. Mr. Syme gathered her in his arms.

Alex carried the chair from the back of the tack room to Mr. Arlington and gently guided him to sit down. Mr. Arlington didn't acknowledge him. He stared into space, his face blank, his eyes devoid of understanding. He reminded me of his son.

Willie strode up to him and drew aside the flap of her jacket to reveal her gun. "You're lucky you didn't shoot."

"Willie." Alex jerked his thumb at the entrance. "We should secure the area."

She *humphed* and followed him outside.

My body started to tremble. Now that the danger was over, I imagined everything that could have gone wrong. Gabe's magic might not have worked. Or Mr. Arlington's shaking might have skewed his aim and he'd shot someone else, someone for whom Gabe's magic wouldn't be triggered.

Gabe's fingers lightly brushed my wrist. "Sylvia?" His tender voice enveloped me, comforting me. It was wonderful, although I would have preferred his arms.

Mr. Syme still held his upset wife. For all her pride and strength, she needed comforting, too, and he lovingly gave it. Watching them brought on an ache deep within me.

As if he sensed it, Gabe's hand rose to stroke my jaw. "Sylvia..."

"You two!" Willie barked from the entrance. "Stop it."

Gabe drew in a deep breath. "She's right. We shouldn't." He sounded like he no longer believed his own words.

As much as I tried to, I wasn't sure I did either. The reason for staying away from Gabe didn't seem as insurmountable anymore.

* * *

THERE WAS one other man who could give us a clearer picture of what happened after Ambrose Arlington's accident. The farrier magician may have been dismissed from his position at the race-track in February 1891, before the accident, but he was part of Ambrose's scheme, so it was conceivable that Ignatius Arlington discovered his name when clearing out his son's things.

Mr. Ferryman sat in the same armchair in the same room as our last visit. His daughter offered us tea. When we declined, she remained in the parlor, supervising our visit like a nurse watching over her patient.

Mr. Ferryman didn't get up this time. He simply lifted his claw-like hand in a greeting before telling his daughter to leave us. "The room is crowded enough, and I don't need a nursemaid."

She reluctantly left, although I could see her hovering in the corridor.

Gabe told Mr. Ferryman that we knew Ambrose was the bookmaker who'd paid him to make the horseshoes. "You don't have to fear him anymore."

"He's dead?"

"He's in a hospital, incapable of moving, speaking, or even feeding himself."

Mr. Ferryman drew in a deep breath and let it out slowly. He sank back into the armchair. "I see. I had wondered, but..."

"But you didn't want to tell us too much, in case he heard and came after you."

"I thought Ignatius Arlington sent him away, using the accident as an excuse. I thought he was alive and well and could come after me."

"Did Lord Coyle force you to work for Ambrose?"

Mr. Ferryman seemed surprised that we'd reached that conclusion. He nodded. "I used my spell on a set of shoes, then placed a bet on the horse. A friend placed it for me, actually. As a track employee, I was forbidden. The horse won, I collected my winnings, and the next thing I knew, Coyle was calling me a cheat. I don't know how he found out. He said he wouldn't tell a soul if I used my magic for Ambrose Arlington." He shrugged.

"It all went fine for a while, until magic came into the open. The artless began to speculate about who was a magician. Because I was efficient and my work was beyond compare, accusations were made. I was dismissed on the grounds that I *might* cheat."

"Ambrose never retaliated?" Alex asked. "He wasn't worried that you would tell the police about him?"

"I had no reason to involve the police. Why would I? Ambrose was angry that I'd been found out, though. He confronted me, and I'll admit I was scared of him." He tapped his temple. "He was mad, capable of following through on his threats. But I held my own. I convinced him I'd never tell a soul, and I reminded him of my iron-moving spell. That made him think twice and he left me alone." He smirked, but it quickly vanished. "I never believed he'd leave me alone forever. He was too unpredictable." His gaze met Gabe's. "I was relieved when I learned he'd been in an accident. At first, I thought he'd died. Most folk did. But then I got to thinking…why hadn't there been a funeral? That's when I thought he'd been sent away by his father and gone into hiding." His gnarled hand tapped his stomach. "The worry in here never really disappeared. Until now. Are you sure he won't get better?"

"The doctor is sure, and there's been no change in twenty-nine years," Gabe said. "Did Ignatius Arlington come to see you after his son's accident?"

A wheezing cough wracked Mr. Ferryman. We waited until it subsided, then Gabe repeated his question. "Aye. He waited in this very room for me to come home after work. He told me he was officially disbanding Ambrose's operation, and that I was never to speak about it."

"Did he threaten you?"

Mr. Ferryman nodded. "He told me he would see that I never worked in London again."

"He didn't threaten to kill you?"

"No. He wasn't as mad as his son."

"When did he visit you?"

"A few weeks after Ambrose's accident. He told me he was calling on everyone in the scheme."

"Everyone?" Alex prompted. "Did he mention names?"

Mr. Ferryman shook his head.

We thanked him and left.

Outside, twilight had not been allowed its moment of glory thanks to the blanket of clouds, and daytime had become dusk while we'd been inside. The air felt thick, oppressive. Even deep breaths didn't seem to fill my lungs.

Willie reached into the motorcar to retrieve the crank handle. "My eyeballs are sweating." She cranked the engine then returned to the vehicle. Despite the tight confines of the back seat, she managed to remove her jacket. "Start driving, Alex, so we can get some air in here."

Even though the air came in through the open sides above the doors, it was still hot. I plucked my dress away from my sticky skin while the men weren't looking.

"I reckon Ignatius Arlington murdered Daniel," Willie declared as Alex put his foot down to speed up. "I know Ferryman said he didn't threaten his life, but we saw what he was like."

"He didn't fire the gun," Gabe pointed out.

"Goreman reckoned he was guilty, too, and he knows him better than us."

I wasn't so sure. I was beginning to think Mr. Goreman had an ulterior motive for pointing the finger at Ignatius. "I don't believe a word he said. He failed to tell us that Mr. Arlington approached him about disbanding the operation after Ambrose's accident."

"We only have Ferryman's word that he called on everyone," Willie said.

"Why would he lie?"

Gabe agreed. "You're right, Sylvia. Why didn't Goreman mention that Ignatius told him the operation was disbanded?"

"They're rival trainers," I offered. "He wants Arlington to appear guilty. He's trying to cause trouble."

"Or was he trying to throw us off the scent of his own guilt? Perhaps *he* killed Daniel, so is casting blame onto someone else. Who better than the trainer who is his greatest rival?"

"Two birds, one stone," Alex muttered. "Neatly done."

* * *

I MULLED it over that evening with Daisy and Petra. We sat in Daisy's flat, taking it in turns to stand in front of the electric fan. It provided little relief from the stifling heat, however, and we all took to dabbing water on our faces and necks to cool down. It was going to be a long sleepless night for Londoners.

While they appeared to be listening to my account of the investigation so far, I could see their interest waning. Petra was at least more polite than Daisy. She nodded along at the right moments as she absentmindedly fanned her face with a magazine. Daisy, however, lay on the floor and yawned.

I changed the topic to something I knew would get Daisy's attention. "Have you kissed Huon again, Petra?"

Daisy rolled onto her stomach and propped her chin on her hand. "Do tell."

Petra's fanning became more vigorous. "I didn't kiss him. *He* kissed *me*. And no, he has not. I haven't been back to the Buttonhole."

"Has *he* been back there?"

"How would I know? Anyway, I don't care."

"Good for you. You deserve someone who believes in you."

Petra made a miffed sound. "Huon is too selfish to believe in anyone but himself."

I thought she was being a little unfair. Huon had obviously changed. He still had some way to go, but I suspected he *wanted* to mature. He was ready. And who better to soften his jagged edges than the very sensible Petra Conway? I suspected they'd make a fine couple if they ever moved past their rivalry. I thought it was petty, but they clearly didn't. They had a long and bitter history, and it would take some time for them to put it all behind them.

Daisy rolled onto her back again with a satisfied sigh. "I'm so fortunate to have found Alex. He believes in me, despite my fickleness."

"You're not fickle," I told her, somewhat sternly. She needed to hear it. No, she needed to *believe* it. "You've stuck it out here in London and not run home to your parents, where life is easier. That takes determination and character. You've also been a loyal friend to me."

"But I need to work. I *want* to work. I just can't decide what I want to do."

"You're twenty-five," Petra said gently. "You've lived with your parents all your life. Give yourself time to be an adult and discover yourself. Besides, you're artless."

"What does that mean?"

"It means you don't have an affinity for a particular craft. I want to work with graphite. Sylvia is drawn to anything with paper. Our magic has helped refine our choices. You don't have those natural restrictions. In a way, you're suffering from too many choices. But as you get to know yourself, and learn where your talents and interests lie, a path will open up. You'll see."

I joined Daisy on the floor and clasped her hand. "We'll be a sounding board to help you choose, if you like. As will Alex." I smiled. "You two sound quite serious. When are you going to introduce him to your parents?"

She smiled shyly. "Soon. Now, you've helped me, so we'll try to help you solve your case."

"You don't have to. I know it doesn't interest you."

"Nonsense. Just because I was yawning doesn't mean I'm not interested. It's this humidity making it difficult to breathe properly." She stood to take a turn in front of the fan. "So why did you believe the trainer, Goreman, when he tried to blame the other trainer, Arlington?"

"Pardon?"

She turned to face us, her arms out to cool herself down faster. "You knew he was trying to get Arlington into trouble, yet you confronted Arlington anyway based on Goreman's word. You must have had an inkling that Arlington was guilty, or you would have just dismissed Goreman as a jealous rival. So why did you believe him?"

Sometimes the most insightful comments come from the most unexpected quarter. Daisy's question was one none of us had considered, yet we should have. "I suppose because we didn't think Mr. Arlington and the Symes told us the truth the first time. We felt like they were hiding something."

"You already knew they were hiding the fact the son was still alive. But something Goreman said made you believe him. What was it?"

I thought back through the conversation but could think of nothing in particular. Yet she was right. That conversation with Goreman had left us feeling more confident that Mr. Arlington or the Symes were guilty of murder, even though we suspected he was simply trying to stir up trouble. Why?

Then I remembered. It wasn't *Goreman's* answers that made us look twice at Arlington. It was Mr. Wellington's. "The veterinarian was there for that conversation, and he pointed out how odd it was the Arlington family never mentioned Ambrose after the accident. It was as if he never existed, he told us. Considering the Arlington stable is his client, too, we assumed it was an unbiased opinion. He wouldn't want to jeopardize that working relationship unless he was truly convinced of their guilt. Where Goreman wanted to get Ignatius Arlington into trouble because he is his rival, we assumed Wellington had no such motive and therefore his negative opinion mattered. But what if he drew our attention to Ignatius Arlington purely to throw us off the scent of *his* guilt?"

The more I thought it through, the more confident I felt of my theory. I couldn't wait to tell Gabe.

Daisy didn't have a telephone in her flat, however. I could have visited, but I didn't want to wake the household for something that could wait until the morning.

* * *

MURRAY TOLD me they were still at breakfast when I arrived the following morning. I asked him to telephone the Glass Library and tell the professor I'd be in later. Upon hearing my voice, Gabe emerged from the dining room.

"You're early. Have you eaten?"

"Mrs. Parry made sure I ate before I left. Gabe, I have a theory."

The telephone rang and Murray answered it. He listened then told Gabe it was for him. Gabe suggested I join Willie and Alex while he answered the call.

Willie scowled at me over the rim of her coffee cup. "Why do you look so cheerful?"

"I have a new theory." I poured myself coffee from the pot on the sideboard. "Did you go out last night? You look like you haven't slept."

"I've been tossing and turning all night. It was hotter than Hades."

"Even with the window open," Alex added.

"I saw Daisy last night," I told him.

He instantly sat up straighter. "What did you talk about?"

"All sorts of things," I teased. "The weather. Her career choices. How she wants you to meet her parents. The case."

"Pardon?"

"The case. In fact, it's because of her insightful questions that I came to a new theory about Daniel's killer."

"No, before that. You said—" He cut himself off when Gabe returned, a deep frown creasing his forehead. He gripped the back of an empty chair with both hands and stared at the vase of flowers in the center of the table.

"What is it?" Alex prompted. "Who was on the telephone?"

"Your father. He was called out in the middle of the night to the Putney Hospital and Home for Incurables. Ambrose Arlington died."

News of his death didn't gladden me, nor was I saddened. He'd been a cruel man, once.

"Why were the police involved?" Alex asked.

"The doctor on duty noticed a puncture mark on Ambrose's arm," Gabe said. "An autopsy will be conducted to find out if he was injected with poison. Cyclops and the doctor on duty are convinced he was. The puncture mark is larger than a medical professional would make. Larger than any needle the hospital has in their storeroom."

"That doesn't make sense," Willie said. "Why would the killer use a large needle instead of a regular one?"

Oh God. I felt sick.

"Because that's what he had with him," Gabe said. "Think about it. Who uses large needles in their work?"

"Veterinarians," I muttered. "Mr. Wellington murdered Ambrose."

CHAPTER 19

G abe sat beside me and picked up the coffee cup I'd put
down. "You look pale, Sylvia. Have a sip."

I did, but it tasted bitter. "Gabe...I may have been
able to stop him. Last night, I began to suspect Wellington of
Daniel's murder. I decided to wait until today to tell you. But if
I'd telephoned you then..." I shook my head. It didn't bear
thinking about.

Gabe gently took the cup from my hands. "No, Sylvia. This is
not your fault. Wellington is to blame. Even if you had telephoned me, I would have suggested waiting until today. We
don't know where Wellington's practice is located, or where he
lives. We couldn't have done anything last night. We also had no
reason to suppose Wellington would be so hasty to kill a man
who couldn't communicate. It's only eight forty-seven now," he
said without looking at the clock on the mantelpiece. "We'll
drive immediately to Epsom and ask the manager where to find
him."

He told the others to finish their breakfast, but they didn't
need telling. Alex had already grabbed the remaining rasher of
bacon from his plate and was heading out of the dining room.

Willie drained her coffee cup and picked up her plate to take her food with her.

She stopped before exiting the dining room. "I agree with Gabe, Sylvia. You ain't to blame any more than the rest of us are." At my questioning look, she added, "Wellington must have overheard us telling Goreman that Ambrose was alive and being cared for. Arlington can afford expensive private care for his son, and there ain't too many hospitals in London that take on that kind of patient. Wellington probably telephoned them all to find him. He could have done that yesterday afternoon after we left Goreman's stables. Cyclops can make inquiries at the telephone exchange after his arrest." She picked up a piece of bacon from her plate. "Come on, Gabe."

"I want another piece of toast," he said. "Tell Murray to have Dodson bring around the Vauxhall. I'll meet you at the front door."

Willie leaned back against the doorframe and chewed on the bacon. "I'll wait for you."

Gabe sighed. Whether he truly wanted more toast, or he'd wanted a quiet word alone with me, he gave no indication. He grabbed some toast from the sideboard and followed Willie out of the dining room.

Ten minutes later, Alex and Willie ushered Gabe to the waiting motorcar after first checking the vicinity. With him safely inside, Willie cranked the engine.

I took the opportunity to ask the question that had been bothering me since I first suspected Mr. Wellington. "Why did Ambrose pay a vet to help with his illegal bookmaking scheme?"

Alex shrugged. "To overlook the doping?"

"But Wellington didn't work for the Arlington stables in those days. He wouldn't have known Arthur Cody was doping their horses."

"Maybe he found out, and Ambrose was paying him for his silence."

I didn't believe that explanation either. "Mr. Wellington loathes seeing the horses come to any harm. I don't think any amount of money would have kept him quiet if he knew about the doping."

"Perhaps he was threatened, not paid. Perhaps that's why his name isn't in the ledger."

It was true that we hadn't seen Wellington mentioned in Daniel's invisible ledgers, but I'd suspected that was because the ink magic had faded. Alex might be right, however. Perhaps Wellington wasn't in the books because there wasn't a monetary figure to record.

Gabe had gone quiet. Not even our speculations coaxed an opinion out of him.

Willie jerked open the back passenger door and threw the crank handle onto the floor near my feet. She didn't get in, however, but leaned on the door. "There's a taxi parked down the street with someone inside. I'm going to confront them."

"No!" Gabe snapped. "Get inside. Alex, drive."

Willie did as ordered but not without protest. "Running away ain't going to stop them."

Alex pulled away from the curb and drove off. "Gabe's right. This isn't the way to confront them. We need to do it on our terms when there are no bystanders. Don't worry. I'll make sure they can't follow us."

He turned the corner then sped up as much as the traffic would allow. He turned several more corners, taking a circuitous route out of Mayfair. The heavy traffic worked in our favor and stopped the taxi getting too close. Once we were out of the worst of the congestion, Alex sped up. Willie and I turned to peer out of the back.

"We lost 'em," Willie announced.

I breathed a sigh of relief, but she continued to watch all the way to the racetrack. Once there, we hurried through the gate and headed straight to the manager's office. Gabe asked for an address for Mr. Wellington, but we didn't need it. The manager informed us the vet was on-site for the midweek races due to start in a few hours. Alex asked him to telephone Cyclops at Scotland Yard while we captured the vet.

We hurried to the stable block, keen to bundle Gabe inside. Alex was convinced we hadn't been followed, but no one wanted to take a chance. Although the races hadn't yet started, Epsom Downs was gearing up for race day. At the stables, horses were being led by grooms to their allocated stalls, their trainers watching over proceedings. Clipboards in hand, officials barked directions while more grooms sweated as they carried equipment and supplies.

All that hurrying was hot work. I was sweating, too, by the time I reached the first stall. It may only be morning, but the humidity was already suffocating. Hopefully a thorough downpour would put an end to it. Thunder rumbling in the distance and the black clouds gathering overhead were promising.

We found Mr. Wellington in a stall with Mr. Goreman, discussing one of the latter's horses. They were arguing about whether the horse should race that day, with Mr. Wellington strongly advising against it. He stopped mid-sentence when Gabe pushed open the stall door.

Mr. Goreman clicked his tongue in irritation. "This is harassment. I've told you everything I can. I've helped at every step. I demand you leave me alone or I'll file a complaint."

"You can go," Gabe told him. "We're not here to speak to you."

"Then why are you here?" Realization dawned. He blinked at Mr. Wellington. "What's going on?"

"I'm innocent!" Mr. Wellington cried. "I wasn't involved in Ambrose Arlington's scheme. Why would I be?" He bent to pick up his bag, but Alex beat him to it.

Alex peered inside and removed a large syringe. "Is this what you used to kill Ambrose last night?"

Mr. Goreman gasped. "Bloody hell, Wellington. Is that true?"

Mr. Wellington backed up against the feed trough. With Willie outside keeping watch and Alex holding the bag, it was left to Gabe to capture the vet. It was easy. Mr. Wellington made only one, somewhat pathetic, attempt to shove Gabe away.

Gabe stood his ground. "Goreman, you may leave."

"But I need to monitor this horse!"

Gabe's cold glare sent the trainer on his way. Once he was gone, Gabe squared up to Mr. Wellington. He was younger, taller, stronger, and going by Mr. Wellington's nervous licking of his lips, he knew he didn't stand a chance if he tried to flee. "What did you inject into Ambrose last night?"

Mr. Wellington shook his head, refusing to answer.

Alex rummaged through the vet's bag and removed a bottle of liquid. He read the label. "Morphine?"

Mr. Wellington chewed on his lower lip.

Gabe settled his stance, feet apart, arms loosely by his side. With only a few subtle moves, he managed to exude calm yet stern authority. "You overheard us mention yesterday that Ambrose was still alive. You then made a number of calls to several private London hospitals, including the Putney Hospital and Home for Incurables, looking for Ambrose."

Mr. Wellington's lips pursed tighter. Then he suddenly gave up. He could see it was hopeless. He couldn't escape, and there was enough circumstantial evidence that we wouldn't believe his denial. "Ambrose didn't deserve to live. He was despicable. No one will miss him, anyway. He's better off dead."

"That's not for you to decide," I said as a flash of lightning lit up the stall.

Mr. Wellington seemed to see me for the first time. "I put down horses when they're in too much pain to go on, Miss Ashe. Why not a human?"

Thunder rolled in, louder and closer than the last one. "Hurry up before it rains," Willie said from outside.

"My cousin doesn't want to get wet," Gabe told Mr. Wellington. "The sooner you answer our questions, the sooner we can escort you to the manager's office and wait for the police. Did you also murder Daniel Barratt in 1891 by injecting him with morphine?"

The vet flinched. "That was a mistake. I'm too used to working with horses, you see, and they require a larger dose than a human. I injected Barratt with an amount I thought would make him easier to deal with, but it killed him instead. I am sorry about that."

"Why didn't the coroner notice the puncture mark like the doctor did last night?" I asked.

"An overdose of morphine can depress the respiratory system and cause cardiac arrest. If murder isn't suspected, a coroner might attribute death to natural causes. Medical science has come a long way in the twenty-nine years since. Nowadays, a good coroner will look for signs of foul play in a young, healthy male. Back then, he often didn't bother if he had no reason to suspect it was murder." Sweat dripped down the side of his face to his neck, dampening his collar. "Barratt shouldn't have refused to destroy the ledgers. Ambrose was gone. He no longer needed to keep them hidden. I think he really wanted to keep them so he could resurrect Ambrose's scheme and run it himself. I couldn't allow that."

"Is that why you also informed the police about Arthur Cody in '16?" Gabe asked. "Was he also going to restart Ambrose's scheme and you wanted to stop him?"

Mr. Wellington nodded. "Cody came to me in '16 and said he needed money, so he wanted me to keep the horses alive after he doped them. I didn't want to kill him. I hadn't wanted to kill Barratt either, but..." He swallowed. "I informed the police that Arthur Cody was a cocaine importer and seller, and they arrested him. It was my civic duty to see he was put behind bars. He's lucky, really. He deserved to die more than Barratt did, but I couldn't bring myself to deliberately inject him with a lethal dose of morphine." He removed a handkerchief from his pocket and dabbed it across his forehead. "I thought it all ended with Ambrose's accident and Coyle's death. But first Daniel Barratt then, years later, Arthur Cody wanted to restart the operation...I couldn't do it again. I couldn't be part of something that harmed horses."

"Then why were you part of Ambrose's original operation?" Gabe asked.

Mr. Wellington's gaze slid to me. He didn't seem to want to answer in front of me.

"Does it have something to do with Lord Coyle?" Gabe pressed. When Mr. Wellington glanced at me again, Gabe added, "Whatever you have to say you can say it in front of Miss Ashe. She's a friend to magicians of all sorts."

Friend to magicians? What did that have to do with Mr. Wellington? What sort of magician became a veterinarian? It didn't make sense. Yet it seemed to make sense to Gabe. He seemed to already know Mr. Wellington's answer but wanted to hear the vet say it.

Mr. Wellington cleared his throat. "You've guessed correctly, Glass. Given who your mother is, I shouldn't be surprised."

"What sort of magician are you?" I blurted out.

"It doesn't really have a name. I call it veterinary magic, but my father referred to it as zoological magic. In essence, I'm able to keep animals alive using a spell."

"For a period of time," Gabe noted.

"Yes, it's brief, but long enough to ensure suspicion didn't fall on the groom taking care of the horses before the race. They appeared perfectly fine after I used my spell. It was only hours or days later, when it wore off, that they suffered withdrawal from the cocaine solution. Or died," he added heavily. "I haven't used that spell in years, you understand. Not since Ambrose's scheme ceased operating when he had his accident. I don't need to. I'm very good at my job without it."

"Did Lord Coyle introduce you to Ambrose?" Gabe asked.

Mr. Wellington nodded. "I didn't want to be a part of the scheme, but Coyle forced me. He threatened to expose me as a magician if I didn't do as Ambrose ordered. I worked for Coyle in his stables at the time, you see, and he saw me speak my spell as I cared for one of his horses after he fell. That horse was dear to me. I hated seeing him in agony and I wanted to save him. I admit I also wanted to try the spell on a creature larger than the cockroaches I'd experimented on in my youth. I don't know how, considering magic wasn't public knowledge at the time, but Coyle realized I was a magician then and there. If he'd followed through on his threat to expose me, I would have been persecuted for being unnatural. It's one thing to use magic to make watches keep perfect time. It's quite another to restore an ailing horse to full health."

Centuries ago, a magician who could keep animals alive longer would have been accused of witchcraft. Thirty years ago, he wouldn't have been burned at the stake, but he would have been ostracized and feared. It was no wonder he did what Lord Coyle wanted.

Lightning momentarily lit up the stall again, then another growl of thunder accompanied the darkening of the sky even further. The horse tossed its head and stamped its hooves, frightened. Mr. Wellington rested a hand on its neck and murmured soothing words. It instantly calmed.

Alex signaled to Gabe with a jerk of his head towards the exit.

"Come with us to the manager's office," Gabe said to the vet. "We'll wait for the police there."

Another flash of lightning and rumble of thunder startled the horse. Mr. Wellington didn't attempt to soothe it this time. He put his hands together and appealed to Gabe. "You're the son of a powerful magician, Mr. Glass. You understand my predicament."

"You killed two men, Wellington."

"I had to protect myself! Imagine what would have happened to me if I hadn't complied with Ambrose's demands. Imagine if your mother had been backed into a corner like I am."

Gabe grabbed Mr. Wellington by the front of his jacket and pushed him towards the stall doors.

"Let me go, Mr. Glass. Please. We magicians must protect one another!"

The muscles in Gabe's jaw bunched with the clenching of his teeth. "I do not protect murderers." He marched Mr. Wellington out of the stall. Rather than winning Gabe over, Mr. Wellington's plea had ignited a fire under his rarely unleashed fury.

Willie quickly stepped out of the way. "About time," she muttered as she straightened her hat.

Alex suddenly put out his arm to stop Gabe's progress. "Bloody hell. What does *he* want?"

Thurlow ambled towards us. Dwarfed by his two body-guards, he sported a slick smile and a confident swagger. It was race day, and he could expect enormous profits from an operation that was as corrupt as Ambrose Arlington's had been. It was a pity our investigation hadn't affected him. He was cockier than ever.

"Out of the way, Thurlow," Gabe snarled.

Thurlow took my hand and lifted it to his mouth. I jerked it back before he could kiss it.

Gabe released Mr. Wellington and moved to stand between Thurlow and me. "I warned you once before to leave Sylvia alone."

Thurlow's brittle chuckle lacked humor. "This is a new decade, Glass." He stretched his arms wide, unconcerned by the angry man towering before him. "It's the Twenties, and Miss Ashe is a modern woman. Why does she have to choose one of us over the other? Why not have both?"

Gabe's fist slammed into Thurlow's jaw. It happened so quickly that at first I thought he'd used his magic, but he showed no sign of weakness after the punch like he usually did when he slowed time. Besides, his life hadn't been in danger. Thurlow's snide remarks had triggered Gabe's anger, not his magic.

Thurlow reeled backwards, clutching his face. The two body-guards charged forward to protect their employer.

But one of them inadvertently protected Gabe.

A deafening clap of thunder erupted. At least, that's what I thought it was. But when the bodyguard fell to the ground at our feet, bleeding, I realized there'd been no flash of lightning accompanying the thunder.

He'd been shot.

I'd barely registered what happened when another gunshot rang out. In the same moment, as if the clouds had been punctured and the pressure building up behind them released, the rain came down in a torrent.

I was thoroughly soaked in the instant between hearing the gunshot and Mr. Wellington stumbling towards me. Gabe grabbed me and pulled me aside as the vet fell into the stall doors. They opened and he landed on the floor where he bled into the straw.

He'd been at Alex's side, a mere two feet from Gabe and me.

I tried to take in what had happened, but I couldn't. Chaos erupted.

CHAPTER 20

$\mathcal{A}$ scream surged up my throat but before it could escape, the storm unleashed again with another burst of lightning and crack of thunder. My already frayed nerves shattered completely.

Around me, men scattered, diving for cover from the sniper and the rain. Everyone was shouting. Willie's voice rose above them, ordering Gabe to get back inside the horse's stall.

But the stall had become as dangerous as outside. The horse reared, punching its hooves into the air before landing mere inches from the unmoving figure of Mr. Wellington.

Without knowing the sniper's location, there was nowhere to hide.

Another flash of lightning ripped through the sky, lighting up the cowering figures of men, the puddles of water and pools of blood. Thunder followed, but it was different. Cut short. The initial crack was followed by the low rumble as it faded away.

I blinked in that moment, and when my eyes reopened, things had changed. The changes were subtle. Rain still poured from a bleak sky. Horses still paced inside their stalls. Men still fled, as terrified as the horses.

Yet I was on the ground, with Gabe's body covering me. I

tried to scream his name, but the air had left my lungs. I couldn't breathe.

His own breathing came in ragged, labored bursts. His heartbeat thundered against mine. He was alive.

A wave of relief enveloped me. Tears streamed from the corners of my eyes. I circled my arms around him, and he lifted his head. It took effort, but he managed to push himself up on his elbows to take his weight off me.

He brushed my wet hair from my face. "Sylvia," he murmured. "Did I hurt you?"

"No. Are you injured?"

He drew in two deep breaths as if trying to refill emptied lungs. "I'm fine."

Alex helped Gabe to his feet then assisted me. Gabe bent forward, hands on his knees, and sucked in more deep breaths.

Willie stood, too. She'd fallen. Many of the bystanders had. In fact, everyone who'd been trying to flee or run somewhere had fallen, as if tripping over their own feet. Those who'd taken shelter still crouched in their hiding spots. A bolt of lightning lit up confused faces, but the crash of thunder got them all moving again. Those who'd been running away, continued to flee.

Thurlow wasn't one of them. One of his bodyguards lay dead on the ground, the other had disappeared in the chaos. Thurlow was on his own, but he showed no fear. His sharp gaze focused on Gabe. Where the others looked confused, he seemed fascinated.

He'd witnessed everything—the interrupted thunderclap, the fallen men, the moment when time seemed to slice in two.

I'd witnessed Gabe's magic enough times to know how it worked, and that he needed time to recover. It took a lot out of him, perhaps more this time than the last.

"You have to hide," I urged him. "The shooter might still be out there." I grabbed his hand to guide him into the stall. I'd rather risk a startled horse than a sniper I couldn't see.

Gabe straightened. He shook his head. "It's over. He's gone."

"You mean you...?" I lowered my voice. "You stopped him?"

"No. He stopped because he got what he wanted. My reaction." His gaze searched mine. Then, as if he'd weighed up the repercussions and decided he didn't care, he drew me against his chest. His arms enveloped me.

My hair was a tangled, sopping mess, my back was muddy. But I didn't care. All that mattered was that I was with Gabe, and we were both alive.

Even Willie left us alone. She went up to Cyclops who'd come running towards us, outpacing the two younger constables with him. She reassured him everyone was safe, but his gaze quickly assessed the scene for himself. His relief at seeing us unharmed was palpable.

Alex spoke to his father, who then sent his men in the direction from which the shots had been fired. The shooter would probably be well and truly gone by now, but perhaps he'd left behind evidence that could be used to identify him.

With the danger over, bystanders came out of hiding. Cyclops ordered them to remain to give statements, but some left the scene, nevertheless. Thurlow had melted away. Whether he'd given his dead bodyguard a second thought, I didn't know.

Gabe circled my waist with his arm. "The horse is calm now. Come into the stall."

The rain had eased a little, but still came down in a steady stream. Lightning brightened the sky again, but it was further away, and the accompanying clap of thunder wasn't as startling. The horse was jittery but no longer looked as though it wanted to trample us. To my surprise, Willie was the one who'd calmed it. She stood beside it, talking quietly in her American drawl, her hand stroking its neck. I supposed she'd learned how to handle horses in her youth.

I kept my distance from the body of Mr. Wellington. A quick glance was enough to tell me he was dead.

Cyclops strode towards us. "What happened?"

Gabe told him about our confrontation with the vet, and Mr.

Wellington's admission. "We were about to walk to the pavilion, but the sniper stopped us."

"It sounded like a Lee-Enfield rifle," Alex told his father. "Trained snipers used them in the war," he added for my benefit.

"Not very well trained." Cyclops nodded at the body of Mr. Wellington. "He missed Gabe."

"He wasn't aiming for me," Gabe said. "Not with the first or second shots. I think he missed deliberately, to test me. He wanted to observe me to see how I reacted."

"How did you react?"

"I didn't move. That's why two men are dead."

Cyclops crouched beside Wellington's body to inspect the wound. "I heard three shots."

"The third bullet is lodged there." Gabe pointed to a hole in the stall wall.

Cyclops stood and inspected the hole. "Did he miss? Or would it have hit someone if you hadn't been here?"

Gabe dragged his hand through his wet hair. His hat had fallen off and still lay outside in the mud. "It would have hit Sylvia."

I clutched my throat as bile surged. That's why he'd ended up covering me on the ground. He'd pushed me out of the way. His magic had activated when I needed saving. I clutched his soaked sleeve and blinked up at him. "Thank you." It wasn't enough. Not nearly enough.

A multitude of emotions swirled in his eyes as he gave me a tentative smile.

Hands on hips, Cyclops stared down at the damp straw at his feet. He heaved a sigh, seeming to reach a conclusion he didn't like. "You've got to stay home for now, where it's safe."

"I won't."

"Gabe! The sniper could try again."

Gabe shook his head. "The sniper's work proved to whoever hired him that I'm capable of something magical to stay alive. The first stage of his or her experiment is complete. Today proved that time slowed for me only for the third bullet, not the first two. It only ever does that if I, or someone I care deeply about, is under threat. I think they'll want to take a closer look at me next and perform more tests under controlled circumstances."

"Kidnap," Willie said darkly. "We're back to that again."

"Who knew you were coming here to arrest Wellington?" Cyclops asked.

"No one," Alex said. "But we were followed when we left the house. I lost them while still in London, but it's possible they guessed we were coming here. We've been to the track previously as part of this investigation."

"We spoke to the manager when we arrived," Willie said. "He telephoned the police. What if someone at the Yard informed Jakes?"

Gabe wasn't convinced. "Thurlow," he growled. "He had no legitimate reason to be near these stables. So why was he? Was it so he could observe my reaction up close?"

"His bodyguard died," Alex pointed out.

Gabe shrugged. "Thurlow wouldn't care."

Thurlow witnessed everything; the two deadly bullets and the third one that missed. I couldn't tell from his reaction if he knew why it had missed. I wasn't convinced he'd hired the sniper, nor that he was behind the earlier kidnapping attempts. But I did know one thing for certain. He suspected Gabe had somehow saved himself from being struck by the third bullet.

If he hadn't believed before that Gabe was a magician who could manipulate time, he most likely did now.

* * *

THE STORM BROUGHT an end to the oppressive heat that had been blanketing London for days. I slept soundly in my blissfully cool room and awoke feeling refreshed.

I walked to work, skipping over small puddles and skirting

larger ones, my umbrella keeping me dry from the drizzling rain. The sky was the same shade of gray as far as the eye could see, but it wasn't as dark as it had been at Epsom Downs. I was in a buoyant mood, determined to put the previous day's horrors behind me. Dwelling on them would do no good. In fact, my positivity could be directly attributed to what had transpired at the racetrack. For one thing, we'd solved the murder of Daniel Barratt. Knowing his sisters-in-law weren't involved meant I could talk to them without worrying about affecting the case. For another, I'd come to a conclusion about Gabe. More specifically, about Gabe and me.

Life could be cut short in the blink of an eye. Yesterday proved that every day ought to be enjoyed, every moment seized, and every loved one should be, well, loved. It was a lesson I should have learned from the war that took my brother, and the influenza epidemic that killed my mother. Perhaps those events started my journey to this realization. They were certainly the catalyst for my move to London and everything that followed. But yesterday's events had brought the realization into sharper focus.

I wouldn't waste a moment of my life going forward. I would live it for all those who couldn't, whose lives had been lost in the trenches of a senseless war. I'd begin with letting Gabe know how I felt. If Melville Hendry was my father, we would contend with the issue when, or if, the time came. If Gabe's family didn't want the daughter of a mad magician near their son, that too would be dealt with when necessary. In the meantime, I wouldn't jeopardize my time with Gabe for a man who might not even be alive or may not be my father. I would love Gabe as if tomorrow might not come.

As much as I would have liked to visit Gabe, I headed to the library. Professor Nash greeted me with coffee and asked me to tell him what had happened the day before. I told him everything over two cups of coffee in the ground floor reading nook.

Gabe telephoned late morning to see how I was feeling. He

invited me to dinner that night at his house. I could tell from his voice that he was in a positive mood, too. The day suddenly seemed even brighter.

At three-thirty, the professor announced that we should pause for a cup of tea and slice of cake. Clutching the book about dung beetles and the concept of rebirth in ancient Egyptian mythology in which Daniel Barratt had written his invisible plea to Oscar, I settled on the sofa and accepted a cup of Twinings tea. At the sound of the front door opening, the professor excused himself. He returned with three women, two of whom I recognized. The third had some very familiar characteristics about her.

My pulse drummed as dramatically as yesterday's thunder.

"Rosina," I said, not waiting to be introduced.

The middle-aged woman with white streaks through her fair hair and freckles scattered across her nose approached me. We stood a foot apart, each of our gazes assessing the other. She was the same height as me, but her figure was fuller, rounder. I'd inherited my slim figure from my mother, not my father's side. The rest of me, however, came from the Hendry side.

Rosina recognized the similarities, too. The corners of her gray eyes crinkled with her sudden smile. She closed the gap between us and drew me into an embrace.

I glanced at her sisters, standing back. Naomi clasped her hands together in front of her chest, her smile matching Rosina's, her eyes filling with tears. Myrtle stood stoically beside her, her eyes dry, but a small smile touched her lips, too.

Rosina drew away from me. "Sylvia, is it?"

"Yes." My voice was thick, my throat tight. "You came home."

"Detective Bailey from Scotland Yard called on my sisters late yesterday and told them the man who killed Daniel was dead." She bit her lip and drew in a fortifying breath. "They fetched me immediately."

"She and the children have been hiding in Whitechapel all

these years," Naomi said. "We didn't tell anyone where she was, just in case Daniel's murderer came for her, too."

"We couldn't trust anyone," Myrtle added.

Not even Fred, it would seem. Considering the sisters knew he hadn't lost his hand at work, they must have known he was somehow involved. Although we'd not asked Mr. Wellington about it before he died, I suspected he was the one who'd threatened Fred then sawn off his hand when he failed to locate the ledgers. As a veterinary surgeon, he must have performed amputations before.

"You hid in Whitechapel," I said. "Near the ledgers?"

Rosina nodded. "In the same court. I saw you from my window. My sisters have been visiting me for years, bringing food when we needed it. These days, I don't need it. My children have grown up and are employed in good positions. But Naomi and Myrtle still bring food for the other residents and keep me company every Sunday afternoon."

Naomi took my hand and squeezed. "There's something we want to tell you, Sylvia. May I call you Sylvia? It's such a pretty name." Before I could answer, she continued. "We came here so that Rosina could meet you. We wanted her opinion." She bounced on her toes, grinning like a child.

Myrtle rolled her eyes. "Let the girl go, Naomi. You'll cut off the circulation in her hand if you keep squeezing like that."

Naomi released me. "I can't help it. I've been wanting to say something ever since meeting you, and Myrtle has finally given permission."

"What my sister is trying to say is that we believe you may be family. You're a paper magician and you look like a Hendry."

"You look a *lot* like a Hendry," Rosina added.

"I noticed the similarities, too." I bit my lower lip. "So…am I your niece? Am I Melville's daughter?"

Myrtle frowned. "It's very unlikely Melville had children."

"Why?"

The sisters exchanged glances. Myrtle and Naomi seemed

uncomfortable, embarrassed even. But not Rosina. "He didn't like women," she said. "He wouldn't have...done what was necessary to father children."

"Oh! I see." It was like a weight lifting off my shoulders. If these women doubted that I was Melville's daughter, then I believed them. I could be with Gabe and not attract the attention of a mad magician. Willie could finally stop worrying.

My relief didn't last long.

"That's not to say he *couldn't*." Myrtle's point seemed to be directed at her sisters as well as me. "How old are you, Sylvia?"

"Twenty-six. I was born in 1894. I knew my mother as Alice, but her real name was Marianne Folgate. She was a silver magician from Ipswich."

The sisters all stared at me. "Silver!" Naomi cried. "I thought they all disappeared years ago. My dear, you are special to have silver magic in your veins."

"I inherited paper magic, not silver," I told her. "Is my mother's name familiar to you?"

They shook their heads.

"We lost touch with Melville in '91," Myrtle said matter-of-factly. "He disappeared, taking the family journal with him." She sounded more disappointed by its loss than that of her brother. "He had no right. It belonged to all of us."

Naomi sympathized with her sister then steered the conversation back to me. "There's no reason to believe Melville couldn't have met your mother and fathered you."

"Except that he didn't like women," Rosina pointed out. She took my hands and smiled gently. "You're a Hendry, though. I'd stake my life on it. How strong is your paper magic?"

"I've been told it's quite strong, but I'm not sure yet. I'm running an experiment. Rosina, did you make that paper rose on the hall table in Myrtle's house? It's so beautiful. Will you teach me?"

She beamed. "Yes, of course, I will. I made that a few weeks ago. My magic is rather weak, I'm afraid, so it'll wilt soon. This is so exciting! I can't wait to introduce you to my children."

I'd been so focused on the sisters that I hadn't noticed Professor Nash disappear. He now returned carrying a tray with more tea things.

"Come upstairs to the larger reading nook," he said. "Sylvia can tell you all about her life, and you can tell her about the Hendry family."

The sisters enthusiastically agreed. I smiled. I couldn't help it. The identity of my father might still be a mystery, but I'd found a family. The picture of my life was becoming clearer. I was part Hendry, part Folgate.

* * *

I WASN'T the only dinner guest at number sixteen Park Street. The Bailey family were sipping cocktails in Gabe's drawing room when I arrived. I suspected the youngest, Lulu, had doctored her cordial with alcohol, going by the way she giggled as she hugged me. From Willie's smirk, I suspected I knew how she'd done it without her parents' knowledge.

"You're a bad influence," I told Willie when she handed me a martini. "Cyclops would be furious if he found out you added something to Lulu's drink."

"Lulu will be fine. I'll watch out for her."

That wasn't much of a comfort.

"Just so you know," she went on, "Cyclops ain't the scary one. It's Catherine you got to watch out for. She's smarter than she looks, and she watches the girls like a hawk."

Sensing that we were talking about her, Catherine suddenly glanced our way. Willie raised her cocktail glass in a salute.

Catherine joined us. "What are you two talking about?"

"Alex and Daisy." Willie nodded at the couple, ensconced together on the sofa, their fingers touching. Daisy was quite the regular at Bailey family dinners lately. "What are you doing here anyway, Sylv?" Willie asked me. "I thought I told you to stay away from Gabe. You being around him ain't safe."

"I'm not Melville Hendry's daughter," I said. "According to his three sisters, anyway. They believe I am a Hendry, but not their niece. Melville didn't like women and is unlikely to have been with a woman."

"Unlikely, but possible. And you mean two sisters, not three. Rosina's still missing."

"She came out of hiding."

Gabe, standing close by, overheard. "She's alive? What a relief."

Not even Cyclops knew about Rosina's return. I told them everything I'd learned from the sisters that afternoon, including repeating their belief that I wasn't Melville Hendry's daughter. "They're sure I am a Hendry, but they don't know the precise branch I'm from yet. They plan to ask distant relatives."

Gabe's warm smile lit up his face. "I can see how happy the news makes you. I'm glad for you, although your family's identity never mattered to your friends."

Willie grunted.

"Any news on the sniper?" I asked.

Cyclops shook his head. "Witnesses think they saw him leave the vicinity the shots were fired from, but no one is sure. There was a great deal of confusion at the time."

I addressed my next question to Gabe. "Had you heard of veterinary magic before yesterday?"

"I'd never given it any thought," he said.

Catherine touched my elbow to get my attention. "We have some news. Well, there are two pieces of news, actually, one good, the other not so much. The good news first. India and Matt are coming home."

"That's wonderful," I said. "I look forward to meeting them." I watched Gabe through lowered lashes to gauge his reaction.

He dipped his head, a shy motion I'd never seen him make before. "I can't wait for them to meet you, too."

It was just the response I wanted to hear.

"By the time they get home, it will be almost six months since they left," Catherine said. "It's gone so fast. Their last letter said they can't wait to see everyone. The friend they're traveling with is eager to return to his work here, too. He's a doctor," she added. "He and his wife are such dear friends. We'll have to host a dinner party to hear all about their adventures."

"They'll find some changes when they get home," Gabe said, watching me. "Nothing they don't already know from my letters, but still... Everything is different now."

"Oh yes," Catherine barreled on cheerfully. "Their plan worked."

"What plan?"

"To delay your wedding to Ivy by going on holiday."

Gabe stared at her, his lips slightly apart. "Is that true? Cyclops?"

Cyclops sipped his martini.

"Willie?"

"Don't look at me, Gabe." She narrowed her gaze at Cyclops and Catherine. "I wasn't told anything either."

"They didn't say it in so many words," Cyclops said. "But it was obvious."

"Not to me."

"Nor me," Gabe said, sounding thoughtful.

Catherine placed her hand on his arm. "They knew Ivy wasn't right for you. They would never have said so, but by leaving the country for a while, it gave you time to truly discover who Ivy was, but more importantly, who *you* were. That's all you needed, Gabe. Time."

"Ironic," Willie muttered.

Gabe studied his martini as he swirled the liquid around the glass. "Not just time."

He didn't look at me, but Catherine, Cyclops and Willie did.

I sipped in an attempt to hide my warm cheeks.

"Speaking of Ivy," Gabe went on. "That's the other piece of

news, Sylvia. She telephoned just before you arrived. Her father died."

"We knew Mr. Hobson was ill, but it seems sudden," I said.

"Apparently he was sicker than we realized."

His death meant Bertie became head of the family and the company at a time when the latter was under fierce scrutiny. I doubted he was up to either task. At least he could call on his mother and sister for help. Perhaps running the company would give them something to do and take their attention away from me.

Bristow announced dinner was served and we filed into the dining room. The array of Mrs. Ling's Chinese dishes tasted delicious and there wasn't a morsel left by the time we finished. The lack of conversation as course after course came out was a testament to how much we enjoyed the meal.

Afterwards, we returned to the drawing room for port or coffee. I was very aware of how little Gabe and I had spoken to each other throughout the evening. The frequent glances in my direction from across the dinner table promised much, but we'd not had any time alone. I began to wonder if we would. Whenever Gabe and I drew near to each other, Willie intercepted.

Our moment finally came as Cyclops struck up an argument with his eldest daughter. Ella, the almost-qualified WPC, wanted to work in the East End after her training ended, while her father preferred her to work in the Westminster Borough.

"It's safer here," he said.

"That's because nothing happens in Mayfair," she whined.

"There are burglaries."

She crossed her arms over her chest and *humphed*.

Gabe signaled for me to follow him out of the drawing room. Willie rose from the armchair to stop me, but Catherine and Cyclops both asked for her opinion on the argument.

"You agree with us, don't you, Willie?" Catherine said.

Willie shrugged. "Ella should do what she wants." Her gaze and her full attention were not on the family discussion. She looked like she would excuse herself to join Gabe before I could reach him.

Until Cyclops took the argument up a notch. With a wink for me and his wife, he cleared his throat. "Female constables shouldn't be allowed to work in the dangerous areas."

Willie rounded on him, hands on hips. "Ella is as capable as any man."

Either Ella was in on her father's scheme, or she'd guessed, because she urged me to leave the drawing room with an encouraging nod at the door through which Gabe had exited. She then invited Willie to explain the meaning of gender equality to her father.

I slipped out of the room. Before I'd taken two steps into the corridor, Gabe pulled me aside. He took my hand and led me further away into a recessed doorway.

"I finally get you to myself," he murmured. He dipped his head but did not kiss me. He seemed to be waiting for my permission.

"I thought you were worried about leading an angry mob of Hobsons to my door," I said. "Did Ivy's father's death change your mind?"

"No. I'd already decided I wouldn't let them come between us. If we let fear of retaliation keep us apart then they win." He leaned in, but I put my hand to his chest to stop him. He pouted.

"They might dig up even more unsavory information about my past. So far, they've only managed to start rumors about me being a nobody. But what if they, or someone else, discover I am Melville Hendry's daughter?"

"It won't change how I feel about you. I only care that it might prove dangerous for *you*. But I promise you, I'll do every-thing in my power to make all our problems go away so we can be together. I can't stay away anymore. I've been trying..." He pressed his forehead to mine. "It's no use. I have to be with you."

I wanted to tell him I understood, and that I wanted to be

with him, too, more than anything. But my constricted throat made speaking impossible. All I could do was nod.

No, not all. There was one other thing I could do to get my point across.

I pressed one hand to his spine, another to the back of his head, and kissed him thoroughly.

Available from 4 March 2025:
THE JOURNAL OF A THOUSAND YEARS
The 6th Glass Library book

DID you know the Glass Library series is a spin-off of the Glass and Steele series? Go back to where it all began with book 1, The Watchmaker's Daughter by C.J. Archer.

A MESSAGE FROM THE AUTHOR

I hope you enjoyed reading SECRETS OF THE LOST LEDGERS as much as I enjoyed writing it. As an independent author, getting the word out about my book is vital to its success, so if you liked this book please consider telling your friends and writing a review at the store where you purchased it. If you would like to be contacted when I release a new book, subscribe to my newsletter at http://cjarcher.com/contact-cj/newsletter/.

ALSO BY C.J. ARCHER

SERIES WITH 2 OR MORE BOOKS

The Glass Library

Cleopatra Fox Mysteries

After The Rift

Glass and Steele

The Ministry of Curiosities Series

The Emily Chambers Spirit Medium Trilogy

The 1st Freak House Trilogy

The 2nd Freak House Trilogy

The 3rd Freak House Trilogy

The Assassins Guild Series

Lord Hawkesbury's Players Series

Witch Born

SINGLE TITLES NOT IN A SERIES

Courting His Countess

Surrender

Redemption

The Mercenary's Price

ABOUT THE AUTHOR

C.J. Archer has loved history and books for as long as she can remember and feels fortunate that she found a way to combine the two. She spent her early childhood in the dramatic beauty of outback Queensland, Australia, but now lives in suburban Melbourne with her husband, two children and a mischievous black & white cat named Coco.

Subscribe to C.J.'s newsletter through her website to be notified when she releases a new book, as well as get access to exclusive content and subscriber-only giveaways. Her website also contains up to date details on all her books: http://cjarcher.com

Follow her on social media to get the latest updates on her books:

f facebook.com/CJArcherAuthorPage
X x.com/cj_archer
O instagram.com/authorcjarcher

9 781922 554925